ROLLS *and* RIVALRY

Also by Kristy Boyce

Hot British Boyfriend

Hot Dutch Daydream

Dungeons and Drama

Dating and Dragons

Rolls and Rivalry

Kristy Boyce

Delacorte Romance

Delacorte Romance
An imprint of Random House Children's Books
A division of Penguin Random House LLC
1745 Broadway, New York, NY 10019
penguinrandomhouse.com
getunderlined.com

Text copyright © 2026 by Kristy Boyce
Cover art copyright © 2026 by Liz Parkes

Penguin Random House values and supports copyright. Copyright fuels creativity, encourages diverse voices, promotes free speech, and creates a vibrant culture. Thank you for buying an authorized edition of this book and for complying with copyright laws by not reproducing, scanning, or distributing any part of it in any form without permission. You are supporting writers and allowing Penguin Random House to continue to publish books for every reader. Please note that no part of this book may be used or reproduced in any manner for the purpose of training artificial intelligence technologies or systems.

DELACORTE ROMANCE with colophon is a registered trademark of Penguin Random House LLC.

Editor: Wendy Loggia
Cover Designer: Casey Moses
Interior Designer: Megan Shortt
Production Editor: Jamie Johnson
Managing Editor: Tamar Schwartz
Production Manager: Liz Sutton

Library of Congress Cataloging-in-Publication Data is available upon request.
ISBN 978-0-593-89922-9 (trade) — ISBN 978-0-593-89923-6 (ebook)

The text of this book is set in 11.5-point ITC Galliard.

Manufactured in the United States of America
1st Printing

The authorized representative in the EU for product safety and compliance is Penguin Random House Ireland, Morrison Chambers, 32 Nassau Street, Dublin D02 YH68, Ireland, https://eu-contact.penguin.ie.

Random House Children's Books supports the First Amendment and celebrates the right to read.

To Debbi,

thank you for believing in me

since day one.

Chapter One

Coming into senior year, I thought there was nothing left at band camp that could surprise me. But one step into the band room shows me I was mistaken. Past the plastic chairs, black instrument cases, and clusters of excited students is my childhood crush, Max Coleman, chatting with my best friend, Nova.

I freeze at the sight. Mom mentioned his family was moving back, but I hardly let myself believe it. I haven't seen him in three years. Our parents played D&D together on Sundays when Max and I were in junior high, and we spent countless evenings hovering over board games, watching YouTube, and messing around with D&D ideas we never actually got around to playing. He'd been a great friend . . . who also happened to be very cute, even during that gangly, awkward middle school phase. And I was maybe, possibly, obsessed with him.

In the past, of course. Not now.

Though seeing him again after all this time is making it hard to breathe.

He points to Nova's shirt and says something that makes her smile. That, in and of itself, is enough to catch my attention because Nova does not smile easily. Once she trusts you, she'll be loyal forever, but otherwise she kind of hates everybody.

Before I can get ahold of myself and walk over to them, a very familiar voice snags my attention.

"Hazel!"

I whip around to see my mom bustling into the music room. She takes a moment to smile fondly at the space, like she does every time she walks in. She played first chair trumpet here in high school, and I doubt there's another alum alive who loves this band more than she does. But that doesn't mean I want her hanging around. It was one thing when I was a freshman, but now I'm a senior and I don't need her fussing over me.

"You hurried away from the car so fast that you forgot your lunch!" She holds up the insulated lunch box like she's holding baby Simba for the entire animal kingdom to witness. "I was almost out of the parking lot when I noticed. You'll be starving without it."

I catch Max's eye for a split second, but he turns away and looks back at Nova. I was half wondering if he'd come over to say hi to Mom and me since he's also known her for years, but I guess I can't blame him for not wanting to engage so early in the morning.

"Thanks, Mom." I take the lunch from her. "I guess I was just excited to get started."

"Of course you are! I'd be shocked if you weren't sprinting into the building. Big things are going to happen for you this year, I can just feel it." She turns in a dreamy circle to fully take in the surroundings. "Good morning, Sire!" she calls and waves to my band director, who was fondly given that nickname years ago since we're the Glen Vale Marching Knights.

He waves back warmly, but I'm not loving this. Mom (and Dad as well, honestly) is already overly invested in every aspect of band. The last thing I need is for Sire to ask her if she'd like to oversee first-day rehearsals. She has a hectic job as the project manager of a local construction company, but she'd 100 percent whip out her phone and call in sick if given the opportunity.

"Okay, well, thanks again," I say, my voice louder than before. "But I should really start getting prepped and I know you need to get to work, so . . ."

She frowns. "And you're sure you don't need anything?"

"Yep. Totally fine."

"All right, I'll get out of your hair, then." She pulls me into a tight hug, and I wither in her arms. I know she means well, but I didn't want to start band camp looking like a coddled baby who still needs her mom to bring her lunch and give her hugs.

It's only after she's walking out the door that I finally look back at Nova and Max. Except that Max is nowhere to be seen and Nova's watching me with an amused expression. I race to her side.

"Your mom loves band so much I'm surprised she doesn't try kicking Sire out of his job." She stands and pushes her short hair away from her pale face. Nova isn't *goth,* exactly, but the girl does love her black. She's been dyeing her already dark brown hair black ever since her mom gave permission when she turned fourteen, and she loves chunky silver jewelry and fitted black clothes.

"You talked to Max?"

She glances around in confusion. "The guy from a few minutes ago?"

"Yeah. He's the one I told you about before. Remember, the kid who used to come to my house all the time in junior high?"

"Wait, *that's* the same kid?" She shakes her head in surprise. "He came up and started talking to me about D&D after seeing the mind flayer on my shirt. You know I hate when strangers talk to me, but . . ." She purses her lips like she's debating. "He actually wasn't the worst."

Whoa, high praise. I need all the details of their conversation, and I need them *now,* someplace where no one else can overhear us. I'll feel more comfortable talking to him myself once I'm better prepared for what to expect. I motion Nova to the instrument closet, careful to pick my way past the large black cases on the ground. Luckily, as section leaders, we're both here early enough that the space isn't overrun with people yet.

"What did he say?" I ask her, trying and completely failing to keep the high-pitched intensity out of my voice.

Where Nova is all blasé energy and sleek dark lines, I'm high emotions and wild hair. I admire her ability to be calm and cool under any circumstances, but I've never been able to copy that. I have a hard time hiding how I feel. Or hiding in general, given that my hair is curly (and usually frizzy) enough that people need to give me extra space when walking past my desk in a classroom.

She crosses her arms and eyes me. "Calm down, we didn't talk for long. Are you still breathing? You look sick."

I give a strangled laugh and lean against the metal shelving that lines the wall. "Sorry. It's just . . . he's back. He's *here.* He could be standing on the other side of that door as we speak."

We both turn to look at the door, but thankfully it doesn't magically swing open to reveal Max's gray eyes and wavy black hair.

"Okay, what's with the freak-out? You always made him sound like some random kid you hung out with when you were young, but you're about to hyperventilate. Do we hate this dude?" She tilts her head to study me. "Or do we really like him?"

Ugh, of course she'd know exactly what's going through my mind. Although that's one of the things I love about her. We became best friends freshman year, after Max had already moved away, when we were both new to marching band and were feeling nervous and lonely. We've been inseparable ever since, even though she plays clarinet while I'm in color guard. I don't need a lot of friends when I have Nova . . . which is good since I don't have a lot.

"We . . . like him."

"*Oh,* I see. Good to know."

"I mean, in a normal way. It's just nice to have another friendly face here."

She smirks. "Right. Of course."

My cheeks warm. There was never anything romantic between Max and me. We were nerdy tweens, and neither of us was mature enough to date. But that didn't stop me from thinking about the what-ifs then or in the years since he left. I knew nothing about boys when Max and I were friends. Sure, he was funny and easy to talk to and accepting of me and my dorky interests, but I didn't realize how rare that was. I figured there had to be other guys like that, but without Max's competitive streak and propensity for cheating at board games. But after he left and I started talking to other guys, I realized there was no one else like Max.

I was too naïve before, but now I know. And we're about to spend our senior year together.

"You know he's a percussion player, right?" Nova asks.

I scowl. To be clear, I don't hate *all* percussion players as a rule. But the Glen Vale percussion and color guard sections have a long history of hating each other. Each year we compete to see who will perform best during the season, and each year the color guard loses spectacularly. Most of our "competitions" result in a handful of percussion players rubbing our suckage in our faces, and I can't stand them.

"Just because he's in percussion doesn't mean he'll be like Brody and the others. I'm sure he's better than that."

She leans against the shelving, facing me. "As usual, you're way too optimistic about the human race in general, and teenage guys in particular. But we can hope. He did give me some very helpful character advice, so he isn't dead to me yet. Maybe this is a sign to finally get our D&D game going like we always talk about?"

I snort-laugh. We've been talking about starting our own D&D game for literally years, and we never do it. I'm too intimidated about running the game as the Dungeon Master and Nova never follows through. We've tried joining a few other games over the years, but that hasn't worked out either. We're just destined to talk about playing forever.

"We could invite Max to join us," she continues. "I bet *that* would get you interested."

Time to change the subject.

Just then the door opens, taking care of that. My stomach flies into my throat, expecting Max to be standing in the doorway like I conjured him with my thoughts. Instead, it's Mr. Hicks, a.k.a. Sire. He's a middle-aged white man with thinning hair, horn-rimmed glasses like he's living in the 1950s, and the put-upon look of a high school teacher who's seen more than his share. But there's still a friendly gleam in his eyes that I don't see in many of my other teachers'. Sire *loves* marching band, and that makes it easy for all of us to love it—and him—too.

But that doesn't mean he's laid-back about band.

He narrows his eyes at us. "Is there a reason why two of my section leaders are hiding out in the instrument closet instead of helping orient our incoming freshmen? I hope you already know that I expect you both to be leaders this year."

We bob our heads. The last thing I want is to lose his respect just as band season is starting.

His expression softens. "Are you excited for the new show?"

"Extremely," I reply. Our flag choreography this year is no joke, but I can already imagine how amazing we could look . . . assuming I can get the rest of the group as invested as I am. I have such high hopes as color guard captain, but the majority of our members this year are brand-new to guard, and I'm nervous about pulling us all together.

"I'm excited too," he says with a wink. "Now, I need everyone in the band room. We have a lot of work to do."

Soon the rest of the band members arrive, and we all gather together. There's palpable energy for our first day and lots of jittery conversations.

"Good morning, everyone," Sire calls out and we quickly come to attention. Even the troublemakers shut their mouths. Next to him stand his assistant band director, Mrs. Lewis; the percussion instructor, Mr. Jenkins; and Faith, our latest color guard director. "It feels like we were just wrapping up the last school year, and already we're gathered to prep for the new marching band season. Now, I know we lost a lot of really talented seniors last year. So many that we might call this a 'rebuilding year,' but we have an amazing group of upperclassmen, and a whole crop of new freshmen, and I don't plan to take it easy.

"To that end, we have chosen a compilation of classical works by Mussorgsky this year, including selections from *Pictures at an Exhibition* and one of his more famous pieces: *Night on Bald Mountain*," he continues. "It's going to be a challenging competition show. Significantly more challenging than what many of our fellow high school competitors will be performing, but I know you all are up for it. We've proven ourselves to be one of the best marching bands in Ohio and I expect you to continue that legacy." He glances around the room, and I can almost feel his pride surging over us. "During our two weeks of band camp, we're going to learn as much of the show as we can. We'll start this morning inside to begin rehearsing the opening number, and then this afternoon we'll be outside to run through drills and start field placement. Color guard, you'll be practicing in the gymnasium during the morning."

Others start to shift around, thinking that Sire is finished with his speech, but he clears his throat to call us back to attention. "One last thing. Before we start rehearsal, I want to introduce a new member to our band who has just transferred to Glen Vale. I've had a chance to hear him play and I believe he's going to be a big asset to our group." Sire smiles and gestures to Max, who is sitting in the back of the room with the rest of the percussion section. "This is Max Coleman. He's playing quads, and I hope you'll make him feel welcome."

More than a hundred people turn to stare at Max, and my heart aches with empathy. I wait for him to give a small wave or maybe just bob his head and avert his eyes. Being awkward introverts together was one of the things that bonded us.

To my surprise, he stands up and smiles broadly at the group.

"Hey, everyone." His voice is loud, deep, and confident. I barely recognize it from the scrawny eighth grader I last knew. "Thanks for the welcome. I used to play with Oak Grove High, but I'm stoked to be here."

There are a few groans at the name. Oak Grove is about two hours away and is our biggest competitor. We always vie with them at competitions, and it's one of my great ambitions in life to finally win Best Overall Auxiliary against them this season.

He laughs good-naturedly at everyone's reaction. "Fair enough. I have to admit that I kind of hated you guys in the past too. *But,* now that I'm here, I'm happy to share their trade secrets so we can take them down."

The band explodes with hoots and cheers. A few of the percussion members clap him on the back, and even Sire seems amused by his declaration.

"Wow, he's cute," Madisyn, one of my guard members, whispers behind me.

"Super cute," her bestie, Addison, replies. "Thank god we have some new blood here."

"Band just got more interesting."

Adrenaline rolls through me. Nova catches my eye from her seat in the clarinet section and raises an eyebrow as if to say *whoa.* I agree. When did Max become the kind of person who could make impromptu speeches in front of strangers? And now he's got my color guard members thirsting for him within thirty seconds? I've been working since sixth grade to win over the band and still haven't succeeded.

I don't have more time to think about it, though, because Sire sends the color guard on our way. Faith takes us through a series of warm-ups and then she and I review the beginning phrases of our first song. It feels like some of the girls are struggling to pick up even basic moves, but I guess

I shouldn't be surprised since we didn't have a lot of people try out and had to accept everyone who did.

It's no secret that our color guard has struggled in previous years, which explains the difficulty in recruiting new members. One of our biggest issues is that we've yet to find a reliable guard director to oversee our program. Sire had to scramble to find someone again this year, and the only available person was Faith—an alum who's four years older than me, just out of college, and starting her first "adult" job in addition to working with us.

I want to help the guard in whatever way I can, but I'm not sure how to handle things yet. Some of our members aren't paying much attention, but it's their first day. I bite my lip and swallow down my worries. It's probably just nerves that will settle out soon.

It isn't until we're all walking out to the field later that I see Max again. He's laughing with a group of other percussion players. I fiddle with my hair. I know I should be happy that he's making friends quickly, but they're absolutely going to taint his view of the color guard—and me—if I don't talk to him soon.

I wave him down, feeling nauseous. Here we go.

"Hey, Max." My voice is strangled, and I'm not sure he even hears me.

The guys around him stop talking, as if they're intrigued to see how this will go down. Probably hoping he'll be as rude as they are. He's much taller than I remember him, although I guess that makes sense since he's had three years to grow. His jawline is also more defined, like he's lost the last of his chubby-cheeked kid years. But his hair is still the same wavy jet black, always long enough that it'll fall in his eyes when he reads or studies a board game. His gray eyes lock onto mine, and my heart hammers in my chest like I'm thirteen all over again. I'm not sure I realized just how much I missed him until this moment.

"Hey," he replies.

"It's been a while, huh?" I continue hesitantly. "Good to see you again."

"Yeah."

"It's crazy that we're at the same high school now."

His face doesn't light up in the way I was hoping it might. "It is crazy. At least your band's good."

"Better than Oak Grove. I would say 'no offense,' but I wouldn't really mean it."

There's a flash of amusement in his expression and I take a calming breath. Okay, this is awkward, but it's workable.

"Sorry you have to be part of our percussion section, though," I say with a lowered voice. "Are you sure you don't secretly have a talent for saxophone or flute so you can switch?"

"What are you talking about?"

"Well . . ." I pause, searching for the right words and landing on: "They suck."

His face goes blank. "If I remember correctly, Glen Vale actually beat us for best percussion at one of the competitions last year. We were all seething about it for days."

I roll my eyes. He doesn't need to remind me. The percussion players were absolutely insufferable after that win. They made T-shirts and big *Winner* pins and even a special handshake that they loved to do in front of the color guard to remind us how we've never won best in show.

"I don't mean as players . . . I mean as *people.*"

His expression darkens. "They've been cool to me."

Oh god. I realize a beat too late that I've completely stepped in it. And while I'm right about the percussion section—especially Brody, their section leader and captain of the jerks—I shouldn't have been so quick to say that. It's only Max's first day, and he'll figure it out soon enough. He doesn't need me to rub his face in it.

My brain whirs as I try to recalibrate, but before I can start over, Max speaks again. "You know, Hazel, maybe it's a *you* problem. Sorry if we can't all reach the level of perfection you're used to."

I blink at the heat in his voice, wondering if I misheard him. "Wh-what?"

"Not everything revolves around making sure your life continues just the way you want it."

"That's not what I'm saying at all." His words hit me harder than I could have anticipated. "It's just, you're new here and I wanted to warn you as a friend. Brody can be awful." I swallow. "And he hates me."

I hope that detail will matter to him. Instead, Max regards me with an indifferent expression.

"I'm not going to turn my back on my section, Hazel. Like you said, I'm the new kid, *again,* which means I have to adapt. This is me adapting. Now do me a favor and stay out of it."

He walks away and I stand there, dumbfounded.

What. Was. *That??*

I feel like an idiot. What happened to the funny, nerdy boy I used to know? I thought he might be happy to see me, that he'd even miss me like I've missed him all these years. But clearly my assumptions about Max were actually delusions. He's not the person I remember at all.

Chapter Two

The following morning, I'm determined to start fresh. Who cares about Max and the repulsive attitude he apparently acquired in the last three years? I'm at band camp to help color guard get a head start on our competition season, not to worry about boys who aren't worth my time. Nova was right about my unearned optimism.

Sire makes his usual morning announcements and then guard is released to the gymnasium.

"Hazel?" Sire calls as I'm about to leave with the rest of my group. "I think you'll be needing this."

I turn to find him holding something out to me with a smile on his face. It's a small silver key attached to a musical note key chain. I take it, squeezing the cool metal in the palm of my hand. This is the key to the guard's outdoor shed where we store all our nice show flags for the season. Usually only the band and guard directors have copies of the key, but

Sire's made an exception for me. The realization makes me both excited and nervous. It means a lot to have his trust.

"Now you're *officially* captain." He squeezes my shoulder. "It's going to be a good year. I have complete confidence in you."

"Thank you," I say and swallow down my nerves. Yesterday our new guard director, Faith, was here the entire time. Unfortunately, that's not true today. But it's all good. I can totally do this on my own.

I jog over to the gymnasium and survey the nine other guard members—eight girls and one guy—who are spread out around the gymnasium. We need to keep a lot of distance between each other right now, so no one accidentally cracks another person in the head while throwing their flag in the air. Madisyn, Addison, and Devin, in the very back, are our returning seniors. They're together so much—whispering and giggling and gossiping—that I still can't keep their last names straight despite years together. They even look similar—they're all white with brown hair and perfectly shaped eyebrows.

Rosa Sanchez is our only returning junior and I'm glad to have her even if she spends as much time messing with her long black hair as she does practicing the routines. She recruited her best friend, Yori Fujii, this year. She has potential, but I'm pretty certain she only agreed to join because her new girlfriend plays trumpet.

Callie Armstrong, Keira Webb, and Deja Williams are our new sophomores. Deja told me yesterday she hates competing, which isn't a good sign knowing our band, but I like her anyway. Callie and Keira, on the other hand, are the ones who make me the most nervous. Callie seems perpetually disgruntled, and Keira doesn't have great coordination, but beggars can't be choosers.

And then there's Li Xiang, our only freshman. She might be the most bubbly, excited, eager-to-please person I've ever met. I feel immediately protective each time I look at her.

I roll back my shoulders, and clear my throat. "Good morning!"

Callie puts a hand on her hip. "What's going on? Where's Faith?"

"Faith has a full-time job, so it's going to be a little harder for her to make all our practices, but she'll be here as much as she can," I explain. "And she'll come for all the football games and competitions, so don't worry."

I try to sound confident and chill about this fact, but this is one of the things I'm most scared about this season. The fact that she can't be here for all our practices is extremely unusual, but since she's new at her job, she's not able to miss much work. Sire told me I'm responsible enough to run our practices solo, but I'm not convinced.

"What did you say?" Keira calls. "I can't hear you. You need to talk louder."

I clear my throat again and repeat myself. Why is this already so much worse than I was expecting it to be?

"Wait." Callie glances at Keira and their other friend, Deja. "So, you're telling me we don't have any teachers overseeing us? No one micromanaging our every second?" She claps her hands in delight and her ever-present ponytail goes flying. "Let's go do something fun, then! I bet they won't notice if we take a quick break to grab coffees."

The others look to each other, and I can read the surprise and uncertainty in their expressions. Irritation fizzles through me.

"We're not going anywhere," I say. "We might not have an adult watching our every move, but I think they'd notice if the entire color guard bailed during band camp. Plus, we have a full show to learn and some of the choreography is really tricky. We need to get serious."

The girls sigh audibly as I pick up my flag and gesture for them to grab their practice flags from the pile. Everyone meanders there and back like they're walking through molasses. I swallow down a groan of frustration. If this is our level of hustle, we're not going to get through *anything*.

"So, like, what's with the percussion section?" Keira asks just as we're finally about to get started. "I could swear I'm getting a *vibe* from them."

"Totally," Deja agrees. "It was super weird."

"It's . . ." I want to say it's nothing and move on with rehearsal like we need to, but that's a blatant lie. There's way more than nothing between the color guard and percussion sections.

"We hate them," Rosa tells them matter-of-factly. "And they hate us just as much."

"Nah, they hate us more," Madisyn says.

Addison nods in agreement. "It's their life's mission to make sure they beat us every chance they get. They thrive off watching us fail."

"Which means they're always thriving," Devin adds, and the three of them glance around in confirmation.

"Are you serious?" Li asks. She adjusts her bright pink

glasses and glances around in horror at the others. Callie, Keira, and Deja look uneasy as well.

I take a deep breath and put down my flag. "Okay, here's the deal. Our band is competitive. *Really* competitive. We have a long history of winning grand champion trophies and getting straight Superior ratings at state, and that's partially because of our competitive culture. Each of the sections wants to be the best, absolutely, but percussion and color guard . . . it's gotten personal the last few years."

Madisyn snorts. "That's one way to say it. More like their section leader's a prick."

I bite my lip to keep from laughing, even though I want to. She'll get no arguments from me there.

"Brody and I have a history," I continue to the new members, since the others already know this all too well. "He doesn't respect color guard, and he never got over the fact that I won Most Valuable Member over him freshman year. Our sections have been battling it out ever since."

A flicker of anger burns in my chest at the reminder of all the snide comments that our groups have exchanged, the nasty chant they came up with for us sophomore year, how they sabotaged us during our band field day last spring when we were *this* close to first place. There's nothing I want more than to put them in their place. Just once, I want color guard to be seen as the best, instead of the section that's pulling down the band every year.

"And that's why it's more important than ever that we nail our routines this year." I glance to each member as I continue. "We're going to show them just how amazing this color guard can be. We'll take all the Superior ratings we earn and shove them down their throats so they never forget what losers they are."

Deja's eyes widen and Li takes a small step back. Only the returning members give small nods of approval. I don't need to convince them.

"Uh, no pressure, I guess?" Callie says sarcastically.

I pick up my flag and try to shake off my emotions. I need to be focused, but not scary. "Don't worry about them. All you need to worry about is learning our drills and routines and everything else will take care of itself. Okay?"

Someone laughs (sarcastically) but I'm not sure who. I'm hoping the other seniors—Madisyn, Addison, and Devin—will come to my aid, but they only watch the scene with detached expressions. I get the impression they're planning to skate through senior year with minimum effort. The others look similarly unenthusiastic or incredulous.

Awesome. Another great day here at band camp.

I'm so grateful when we can take a break for lunch. As I walk outside to a cluster of picnic tables where Nova and I always sit, located between the school and the practice field, I try to remind myself that everything is going to be okay. The first days are rough no matter what, plus half of the guard is completely new. But that's not going to stop me. This is my senior year—my last year—and I *will* be the one to finally turn our color guard program around and get us the Superior ratings I know we're capable of.

And if I win Most Valuable Member again my senior year? Well, that'll just be an added bonus.

"Do you see that?" Nova asks as I sit. She points over at the football field next to the practice field. I have to stand and squint to see what's going on, and I'm not the only one doing it.

"Is that Max running laps right now?"

"Yep. In ninety-degree heat." She shakes her head.

I sit down and pull out my lunch. Somehow Mom had time to make my favorite—chicken salad with avocado chunks and crackers—despite her usual hectic schedule. If she was in my position, she'd already have the guard whipped into shape with enough time to sew everyone costumes and coordinating flags.

"Why is he doing that? Sire didn't make him run laps as punishment or something, right?"

"No, Sire might punish him *for* running. He said he shouldn't be exerting himself in the heat when we have to march all afternoon." She shrugs like she couldn't care less. "I heard Max lost a bet with Brody."

"What kind of bet?"

"Who knows, probably something dumb. Did you already hear Max made a bet this morning with Mrs. Lewis about whether or not he could roll his feet in his boots, and she had to do a push-up when she lost?"

"But she's old!" I cry. Mrs. Lewis must be at least sixty.

"That's what I thought too, but she did it, kind of. Everyone thought it was hilarious."

She doesn't laugh, but I can tell she's holding back out of

loyalty to me. I told her about how Max acted yesterday, and she promised to ignore him out of solidarity. I want to hold her to that promise even if it's petty. I glance back over at the track and shake my head. One of the things that had bonded Max and me was that we were always both competitive to a fault. The rest of him might have changed, but it looks like that trait stayed the same.

"How'd your morning practice go?" she asks.

"It was . . ." I try to think of a nice way to phrase it and can't. "It was a pile of absolute burning garbage. I don't think I'm cut out for this."

"Stop that. You've been the best guard member our entire time in band. Your solo last year was the only reason you guys got an Excellent at state."

She glares at me, but I know she's only trying to intimidate me into saying nicer things about myself. Nevertheless, my mood sinks further. Maybe we shouldn't care, but everyone in band is obsessed with our ratings. Earning a Superior, the top rating in a band competition, is considered nonnegotiable. Our band has a decades-long history of not only making state every year but earning Superiors when they get there. And I don't even want to think about my band-obsessed parents and how much they've pinned their hopes on the guard getting Superiors this year. Usually, the color guard is lucky to get an Excellent. Judges have told us we're so bad we detract from the show instead of enhancing it, and, unlike the rest of the band, we haven't earned a Superior rating in the last eight years. I'm determined to change that.

Shouts catch my attention. Max is jogging back from the

track with a huge grin on his face. The humidity has made the curl come out in his hair, but on him it looks like soft waves he can brush off his forehead, whereas the humidity makes my curly hair look like a big puffball. Even the sweat makes him glisten. It's infuriating.

"Are you sure that was four laps?" Brody calls.

"One mile exactly," Max says. He grabs the closest water bottle and chugs the whole thing. "Are you up for another bet? I need to win back my reputation."

Brody shrugs noncommittally. I notice that everyone around us is also watching this play out, but then again, the guys aren't exactly being subtle. I'm pretty sure Max is raising his voice on purpose to make sure the rest of the band can hear.

"How about we bet on whether or not I can play the first competition song without making a mistake?" Max asks.

"With or without sheet music?"

"Without."

Brody scoffs. "No way. You said you got the sheet music yesterday morning. No one can memorize it that quickly."

Max shrugs. "Just because you can't, doesn't mean I can't."

Brody rolls his eyes. "I'm happy to watch you lose twice during lunch."

"Yeah, right. When I win, you have to . . ." Max trails off and looks around. A dangerous grin flashes across his face, one that I recognize from the times I was about to lose at a board game against him but didn't know it yet. "You have to drink from the spit valve of one of the trombones."

Brody retches at the suggestion, and Nova and I both gag.

"Oh my god, I think I might puke," Nova says under her breath. "Boys are *so* gross. I don't understand how you can want to date them."

I snort-laugh. Nova is an avowed lesbian who finds the very idea of heterosexual romance disgusting. Although, she also hates people enough in general that she basically never dates.

She might be the smartest person I know.

I nod empathetically about boys being gross, but I don't take my eyes off the scene. It's definitely a disgusting bet, but if there's anyone in the world who I'd like to see drink spit, it's Brody.

Brody's eyes flit around, probably looking for an escape, but no one comes to rescue him. Finally, he lifts one shoulder arrogantly. "Fine. You're on."

"Hold up," another percussion player says and stands up. He's Black, with a thin build and glasses. He's sitting off by himself a little, clearly not included within the "cool" percussion group, which tells me to hold off on judging him too harshly. I think his name is Felix, but he's only a sophomore so I barely know him. "Sire?" he bellows across the practice field.

As one, the entire band looks over at our band director. He's in conversation with the assistant directors.

"When did you give Max the sheet music?" Felix yells.

"I gave it to him yesterday when he arrived," he calls back. "Why? Is there a problem?" He puts a hand on his hip and surveys the group. He's worked with teenagers enough to recognize shenanigans.

"No reason, just curious!" Felix sits down, trying to look innocent.

"Whatever's going on over there, you have eight minutes until practice starts again, so make it quick."

"All right, let's hear this perfect playing," Brody says.

I pull my lip between my teeth. I can already see the resentment building up just under the surface of Brody's skin. His expression is the same as when I won the MVM award freshman year. He couldn't believe that a *color guard member* beat a "real" member of the band, to the point that he even argued the issue with Sire. Brody's hated me ever since. And if Max isn't careful, he's going to make an enemy of him too.

Max walks over to his quad drums and lifts his shoulder brace so that his four (technically five, which is weird since they're called *quads*) drums sit at hip-level. Quads are the kind of drums that allow you to *really* show off when you're good. Even I'm begrudgingly impressed by our quad players because they're playing multiple different drums at such fast rhythms and even twirling their drumsticks when they feel fancy.

Everyone goes silent as he pulls out his drumsticks and takes a deep breath.

Max is . . . insanely good. I've had a recording of the competition music for a while so I could learn the color guard choreography, and I've memorized it at this point. Max might as well be playing the percussion recording right now. He learned all this in a *day*?

An elbow nudges my side. "Wipe the drool from your mouth," Nova whispers.

I duck my head in embarrassment, but I don't pull my

eyes from Max. I don't care if the guy is on stage at a rock concert or standing in a high school marching band practice field, anyone who can play drums this well is *hot.* A quick glance shows me I'm not the only one in the band thinking the same. I'm livid with myself for reacting this way after how he treated me yesterday, but there are some things the human body just can't fight.

By the time he gets to the last few phrases, it's clear he's showing off. He twirls one of the drumsticks in his fingers before hitting the final beat and slowly bowing.

"Damn," someone whispers.

"Looks like there's new competition for the MVM award this year," another person behind me mutters.

That catches my attention. There's no way I'm letting Max waltz into my band, disrespect me, and then take the award I've been working toward for years. Clearly no one else is worried about that, though. The band breaks out into raucous applause. In the distance, Sire and the assistant directors exchange looks.

"What the . . ." Brody says. "How'd you do that?"

Max shrugs. "You can choose which trombone you want to drink from. Maybe some people spit less while they play?"

Brody shifts uncomfortably. We've been transported back into elementary school and the days of the old-school double-dog dare. You can back down, but if you do, you lose your reputation with it.

"Dude, I'll puke," Brody replies quietly.

Max stares him down for a second and I think he's actually going to make him do it. My whole body tenses in anticipation.

But then Max laughs and shoves Brody on the shoulder.

"I'm just kidding, man! What kind of psycho do you think I am? I can't believe you even agreed to that bet."

Brody blinks and then starts laughing, which makes Max laugh louder, and soon the whole percussion section joins in.

Nova glances at me. "I guess he fits right in, huh?"

I slump back, shove a cracker into my chicken salad, and push any lingering thoughts of him out of my mind. Yep, Max is fully indoctrinated into the percussion section now.

Chapter Three

The house smells delicious when I walk in through the garage door after band camp on Wednesday afternoon. I make a beeline to the kitchen, where a Crock-Pot filled with pulled pork sits. I open the lid and stir it, my stomach already churning for dinner. Like usual, I'm the first one home. Mom and Dad are both still at work and then they have to pick up my ten-year-old sister, Kelsey, from her latest summer camp.

I jump into the shower since we spent the majority of the day in the beating sun, learning our field placements while sweat bees swarmed my legs. Today wasn't a whole lot better than the first two days. The guard is picking up the first song more, but only because I ride them constantly to pay attention and stay on task.

I know the minute the rest of my family gets home because of the stomping and slamming doors. Kelsey might be in dance camps, but she hasn't learned how to walk quietly yet.

"Hazel?" Mom's voice calls up, just loud enough to be heard over the Veruca Salt song I have blasting in the bathroom.

"Just getting out of the shower. I'll be down soon."

"Okay, but hurry, I want to hear how today went!"

I dry my hair and take a deep breath. I'm not sure I'm ready for my mom's enthusiasm. She's been dreaming of my senior year the way some people dream of their kids going to Harvard or becoming astronauts.

When I get downstairs, Kelsey is sitting at the island with Mom, working on a gem suncatcher craft. Kelsey loves anything sparkly or girly.

"There's our color guard captain!" Mom calls, as if I was named captain this morning instead of the beginning of summer. She's changed into one of her 5K shirts and her dark curly hair looks pristine as always. I inherited the curls from her, as did Kelsey, though Mom is smart to keep her hair shoulder length since it's easier to take care of. She claps her hands together, looking me up and down. "How was it today? Did you all make good progress? Are you leading your group to victory?"

I have to tap down the immediate irritation that rises at her excitement. She had such a perfect band experience in high school that she can't imagine it going any differently for me.

"Mom, we're not going to war, we're just swinging flags around."

Kelsey laughs and I grab silverware to set the table just so I have something to distract myself.

" 'Swinging flags around'?" Mom repeats. "Hazel, I hope

you don't say things like that in front of your group. It's up to you to motivate them and help them understand how important they are to the band. You never want to diminish their value or make them feel less than the other band members."

I should have taken a second shower so I could avoid hearing more of her advice and preaching. The thing is, Mom isn't *just* a band alum. She was first chair trumpet, section leader, and chosen as Most Valuable Member both her sophomore and senior years. Each winner is chosen based on a weighted combination of votes from the band directors and all the band members, and it's a really big deal at Glen Vale to win it—kind of like the Oscars of our marching band. Mom was beside herself when I won freshman year since I was "carrying on the tradition."

Her plaques are still some of her most prized possessions. She has them hanging on the living room wall next to a photo of Dad dotting the *i* when he was a tuba player with The Best Damn Band in the Land at The Ohio State University. Dad may have "won" in college, but high school band was all Mom. They always dreamed that I'd follow in their footsteps and be first chair in my chosen (brass) instrument, but when I picked color guard instead, Mom quickly recalibrated.

"Of course I'm not making my guard feel bad," I argue. "We're going to be the best color guard our high school has seen in a decade."

She points to me. "Yes! That's exactly the energy I love to hear. You all are going to kill it. Is everything starting to fall into place with your choreography?"

"Mm-hmm," I mumble.

"It's going to be amazing. You've got this year's MVM in the bag."

Luckily, I don't have to respond because Kelsey interrupts. "This is jazz week in dance camp and we're learning a performance to a Whitney Houston song. You should come and teach us how to do flags too, Hazel."

"Would you listen to my instructions if I did?"

"If you were nice. And brought me a milkshake."

I shake my head. "No such luck, then."

Mom asks Kelsey about her camp, and I have a few minutes to myself until Dad comes home, and I get the same questions all over again.

Dad opens the Crock-Pot and grabs a bite of pulled pork before Mom can yell at him. He's a sucker for her cooking, which is a good thing because she likes making big meals. He's still in his polo shirt and jeans from work, where he manages an IT help desk for a local community college.

"So, did Max end up joining the band?" he asks. "You haven't said a thing about it."

"Yeah, he joined."

Mom and Dad glance at each other. They know how well we used to get along, and I bet they had secret conversations planning (or dreaming) about how happy I was going to be now that Max was back in town.

"Well . . . that's good to hear," Dad says a second later. "Do you think he's transitioning pretty well?"

Images of Max running laps and laughing with his percussion buddies and giving me the cold shoulder rise up in my mind. I roll my eyes. "I wouldn't know."

"Are all teenagers this sulky?" Kelsey asks without looking up from her craft.

"Only teenagers who have little sisters that ask dumb questions. So you'll be fine."

"What's going on? I thought you and Max would be fast friends again," Mom says.

"Yeah, well, people change."

"Give him time," Dad replies. "He's going through a lot of change, but I'm sure he'll come around eventually."

I don't care if Max had to move senior year, it's no excuse for being so rude for no reason.

Mom stands and pulls plates from the cabinet. "Actually, I'm going to reach out to Melanie again about coming to D&D this Sunday."

"Great idea," Dad says. "Max could come and that'd give you two some time to catch up."

My parents have been hosting their D&D game for as long as I can remember. Every Sunday night, their friends come over with snacks and they all head down to the basement. I always wanted to be down there with them when I was a kid, but Dad said it was a no-kid zone because they didn't want to accidentally teach us a whole new vocabulary of curse words. Once Max started coming over with his parents, I wasn't so disappointed. Kelsey always went to our aunt's house on Sundays, so Max and I got to eat all the snacks and watch all the TV we wanted.

"Max wants nothing to do with me."

"You like him, don't you?" Kelsey asks with a grin. "Your cheeks are pink."

"I do *not* like Max!" I say louder, and Kelsey bursts out

into laughter. "I'm going to practice the routines in the backyard." I stalk over to the back door.

"Dinner will be ready in fifteen minutes. And don't worry, I'll talk to Melanie, and we'll work this whole thing out," Mom says.

I swivel back to her, eyes wide. "No, don't say anything to his mom about this."

"Why not? She's so understanding, I'm sure she can help."

"But I don't *want* help. I don't want you calling his mom and telling her Max was being mean to me like we're still in third grade or something. I can handle myself and I can handle Max."

Dad gives me a reproachful look. He hates when I say anything to Mom that isn't the most respectful because, in his words, *Your mom is a superhero. Nothing works around here without her.* But sometimes Mom is too eager to swoop in and use her superhero abilities to save everything. The meddling might have worked when I was still Kelsey's age, but I don't need it anymore.

She puts up her hands in defense. "I'm just saying, communication is never a bad thing. If you don't want me to help, then fine, but that means you need to be the one to reach out."

I can't think of a thing to say that won't get me in trouble, so I march out to the backyard. It's easy to tell me to reach out, but they didn't see Max's expression when I tried to make simple conversation with him. It was like I was an owlbear trying to eat his face off.

In a different world, I'd love to be friends with him again. I haven't forgotten all the evenings we spent around the dining room table, playing Uno and Monopoly and eating way too many nachos, while our parents were downstairs. No one ever made me laugh the way I laughed with Max. But no one ever irritated me as much either. Unfortunately for me, he seems to have retained only one of those talents.

Chapter Four

"Can we have a break?" Rosa complains on Friday during morning practice. "We've been doing this forever, and I'm so sweaty my hair's getting ruined."

Rosa *does* have enviable shiny long hair, but I can attest that it won't last long in color guard.

"Actually we just had a break twenty minutes ago," I say.

Yori sighs and leans her head on Rosa's shoulder. "But I'm tired."

A few of the others nod, looking slumped and exhausted. I can't blame them. People think color guard is easy, but it isn't. We're constantly in motion, and our timing and synchronization have to be perfect. But the thing is, it's not going to get easier by not practicing. In fact, it's likely to get a lot worse, because when the weather changes during the fall, we're almost assured to have at least a few stormy or windy football games and competitions. This is nothing compared to swinging around a massive, waterlogged flag flinging mud in your face.

"How about this?" I say and try for a cheery tone. "Let's run through the field commands one time, then run through our first competition song once, and *then* we'll get a break. Yeah?"

I think it's a decent compromise, but no one is thrilled.

"Hiya!" a voice calls and we all spin to see Faith. She looks stunning as always, her long blond hair perfectly straight and parted in the middle, in a stylish dress and flats. In comparison, I'm wearing my band shirt from freshman year and my hair is more frizz than curl. She squeals at the sight of us. "Look at all of you! This brings back so many memories. I brought iced coffee and doughnuts!"

Everyone screams in delight and runs to huddle around her. She sets down a huge jug and brown paper bag and works her way through the group, giving hugs to each of the members.

"Faith!"

"Omigod, your timing is perfect!"

"You're the best!"

I stand apart from the group, agitation growing in me even as I try to push it away. Of course everyone's happy to see her—she's bringing them free food and a break from practicing. But it would've been helpful to know she was coming today, and that she planned on bringing all this. I could have pitched in or at least planned our rehearsal accordingly. Now I look like even more of a jerk.

"I had a dream of bringing you all real iced coffees, but

your girl's too broke for that!" She laughs and they join in, utterly charmed by her. Only Li looks back to check on me. I wave her on to get a doughnut. "I tried my hand at making iced coffee at home and grabbed some doughnuts. Hopefully, this'll be enough."

"It's more than enough!" Keira says. "We haven't gotten any fun things at camp. I heard the percussion section is having pizza delivered today for lunch, and the flutes are going out for ice cream after."

I squeeze my eyes shut. Welp, that would explain why the group seems on edge today. Now that I think of it, Nova mentioned that the woodwinds have a sectional dinner planned for tonight. And the trumpets all dressed up like superheroes today. Ugh, I'm the worst color guard captain ever.

"What's on the schedule for this afternoon?" Faith asks.

"Drill down," Devin says.

"Oh my god, it's drill down day?" Faith's eyes flash with excitement. "I used to love drill down."

"What's drill down?" Callie asks.

"A competition to see who knows the field commands the best," Madisyn replies in a bored voice.

"I hope you all represent out there," Faith continues. "And whatever you do, don't let the percussion players beat you. You can't start the season like that."

I nod emphatically. At least she's a recent alum, so she gets it.

"Thanks for bringing stuff for everybody," I tell her quietly as the others happily eat their snacks. "I totally dropped the ball."

"Happy to take an early lunch and swing by." She looks down at her phone. "Actually, I can't stay much longer. Do you want to show me what you have so far?"

Not particularly, I think, but I don't say that. She calls everyone together, and to my surprise, they don't complain when she does it.

"Okay, I want to see what you've been working on before I have to go! I know you're going to kill it!"

The others don't look confident, but I smile and give them a thumbs-up. "You've got this."

I play the music, and we run through the first song. Faith watches the whole thing with a smile on her face, cheering them on no matter how many dropped flags and missed marks there are. They all congregate around her after, and I swallow down my nerves. She and I both know how atrocious that was.

Her gaze sweeps over their faces. "All I have to say is . . . awesome job!"

I swing around to stare at her.

"The choreography is hard, and you've only been working on it for a few days, so don't get down on yourselves. If you just keep up the energy and confidence, then I know you're going to get it! And don't forget to smile—the judges love that!"

I wait for her to shift into the critical part of her comments. You know, the compliment sandwich and all that. But instead, she picks up the empty box of doughnuts and gives them one more smile.

"I'm sorry I can't stay for drill down this afternoon, but I'll be back to check on you all as soon as I can, and I'm definitely taking time off to see the performance at the end of band camp next week. I expect big things!"

She heads toward the car, and I do a double take and jog after her. "That's *it*?" I whisper as I follow her out to the parking lot. "But it was so bad."

"I mean, yeah, it wasn't great, but this is the end of week one."

"You and I learned it from the choreographer in one day."

"And that's why we were both color guard captains."

"But, it just feels like, if maybe you told it to them straight, it would scare them a little bit and make them work harder."

"I don't think your first reaction as captain should be to scare your guard." She puts her hand on my shoulder like she's some aged adviser rather than a twentysomething just out of college. "I know you're putting a lot of pressure on yourself this season, Hazel, but you can't let that bleed into the way you act around the group. Relax. Life doesn't end after high school marching band."

That same frustration from before fizzles up in me, but the last thing I need is to get into a fight with my director during the first week of camp. "Right. Well, thanks for coming with the treats. That really boosted morale."

"No problem. I'll see you next week." The corner of her mouth lifts in a smile. "And blow the rest of the band out of the water this afternoon."

"All right, it's the moment you've been waiting for! It's drill down time!" Sire's voice projects through his megaphone across the football field and I swallow down my excitement and nerves. "Clarinets, I want you on the fifty-yard line. Color guard, head to the forty-five. Percussion, take the forty-yard line." He continues calling out directions, but I stop listening. Of course we're going to be right next to percussion.

I bounce on the balls of my feet and take a deep breath. Nova strides by and lifts her hand for a high five, which I easily return.

"I'm coming for you, Buchanan," she says with a smile.

"You better watch out, Walsh," I call behind her and laugh. We aren't usually competitive with each other, but all bets are off during sectional competitions.

A shadow falls over me and I turn to find Max in my personal space. My skin flushes at his nearness. I still haven't gotten used to how tall he's grown.

"The forty-yard line is over there," I say and point behind him. "But if you don't know that, I don't think you'll last long in what's coming next."

"I don't appreciate you tattling on me to your mom." His voice is low and rough.

"What? I didn't *tattle* on you."

"Then why did my mom tell me off about how I haven't been welcoming?"

"I don't know." I cross my arms, hoping it'll make me appear indifferent so I can hide how his closeness has flustered me. "Maybe because it's the truth."

"See, exactly, I knew you were talking about me. And then your mom had to get in my family's business like always."

My stomach flip-flops. "What do you mean, *like always*? My family hasn't seen yours in years."

Brody steps up beside Max. "I know you're new, man, but we don't talk to losers here. Particularly losers who aren't even in band."

Max turns to Brody in confusion.

"She's in color guard," Brody continues. "There's a big difference. You'll figure it out as soon as drill down starts."

"Shut it, Brody," I snap. "This doesn't concern you." Brody's lucky I don't take one of his drumsticks and shove it someplace that'll make it *very* hard for him to march later.

He shakes his head and lets out a whistle. "Don't take it out on us just because you can't keep up. In fact, maybe you should go sit down on the sidelines now since you'll be there in another few seconds. You can save yourself the embarrassment."

"More like I'll outlast both of you." I glare at Brody before turning my anger on Max. "In fact, I'll bet you that I'm the last one standing."

"A bet?" Max asks. Interest flashes in his eyes and it makes my pulse leap. "What do we get when you lose?"

"She has to bring dessert for the percussion next week," Brody says immediately. "Popsicles. It's supposed to be ninety degrees out."

"And when *I* win, you're bringing the color guard Popsicles. One per member," I add because I know how sneaky Brody is.

"Fine. But bring the blue ones. That's the only good flavor." Brody heads for his yard line.

I expect Max to follow him, but instead he steps closer to me. He leans in, as if he's about to tell me a secret, and I can't help holding my breath.

"You shouldn't make bets you can't win," he whispers.

I jolt upright. My skin is hot and tight from the feel of his breath in my ear, but his words are what send fire licking up my spine and through my limbs. How dare he lecture me. He doesn't know who he's messing with.

"Why don't you take your own advice because I'm about to *bury you.*"

Our eyes lock in a wordless battle. I'm practically crackling with energy, waiting for his next move. The corner of his mouth twitches, like he's fighting a smile, and then he spins on his heel and strides to his yard line. For a moment I'm frozen, but I shake out my limbs and take a deep breath to clear my head. I'd almost forgotten how competitive Max and I get with each other.

"Are you okay, Hazel?" Li asks in a small voice from behind me.

I'm not sure how much she overheard but it was probably too much. I roll back my shoulders and give her a big grin. "I'm absolutely fantastic, Li."

The field commanders step onto the grass and my attention goes to them. I push away thoughts of Max and Brody and get into the zone. I'm going to prove them all wrong.

"Okay, you know the drill . . ." Sire trails off. "See what I did there? Drill?" He chuckles and then continues. "Our field commanders are going to be calling out commands. They'll start simple—if you've been paying attention—but it gets fast and confusing very quickly, so *listen up.* If you miss a command, you're eliminated and you're to walk to the sidelines and sit down. Whoever's left standing wins." There's silence on the field for a few moments. "Marjorie and Greg, you may begin."

"De-tail, to the ready!" Marjorie calls and we all stand with our feet shoulder width apart, hands together in front of our bodies.

"De-tail, atten-hut!" she calls, and I bring my left foot in and move my hands to the sides.

"De-tail, right face!"

I turn sharply to the right.

"De-tail, left face!"

I turn back to the front.

"De-tail, parade rest!"

I take a wide stance, my right hand in front of my stomach and my left hand on my lower back.

And on and on we go.

In my peripheral vision, I'm vaguely aware that people are dropping like flies as our field commanders call out command after command. We have a lot of talented band members, but it's so easy to lose focus for a second and make a silly mistake or turn in one direction when you meant to turn to the other. Eventually we turn enough times that I'm facing the back, and I can see that most of my guard have already dropped out. Only Li, Rosa, and I are left. I take a moment to glance toward the percussion. My eyes find Max immediately, his back to me, and my stomach somersaults at the memory of him whispering in my ear.

"De-tail, mark time!"

I falter and almost miss the command. More people drop out around me, and I kick myself for thinking about Max when I should be paying attention. My heart races and sweat drips down my back.

"De-tail, right face!"

"De-tail, left face!"

"De-tail, about face!"

There are groans and moans and flocks of people jogging to the sidelines. Someone to my left cusses and I allow myself the tiniest of smiles. Brody is out. He's always been too cocky for his own good. After a few more commands, only a handful of us are left. Although I can't look left or right without breaking protocol, I know Max is still on the field with me. I can sense him, and my craving to beat him grows with each passing command. I don't care about winning anymore. I only care about winning over *him*.

Marjorie and Greg take us through a ridiculous set of commands that I can barely keep up with. It's always this way when we get to the very end. Sire gets antsy for a winner and the field commanders get desperate and start throwing everything they have at us. I do another left face to find that only Max remains on this side of me. His posture is ramrod straight, his positioning perfect, and I glare hard enough that I hope he feels my anger burrowing into his skull.

There's another right face, about face, parade rest, and to the ready. I almost lose it on the last command but manage to hit the position.

"Dammit."

A tall figure with dark hair moves in my peripheral vision and I almost jump in happiness.

Max is out . . . which means I *did* it! I beat the entire percussion section. I swallow a scream of joy. I'm tempted to run after him so I can throw my win in his face, but that would mean forfeiting, and there's no way I'm doing that.

"De-tail, atten-hut!"

I come to attention.

Who else is left? We do an about-face next and I see that it's only me and Nova. A laugh bubbles up in me.

"De-tail, mark time!"

"All right, I'm calling it, or we'll be here all night knowing these two," Sire calls out through the bullhorn. "Nova, Hazel, you two are the official drill down winners for this season. Well done!"

At that, we break from our positions and run screaming to each other. I wrap my arms around her and pull her into a huge hug. "Omigod, Nova!"

"We are awesome!"

The rest of her clarinets run up to congratulate her, and the color guard follows suit with Li leading the charge. I make eye contact with Max over their heads.

"You heard Sire. Official. Winner." I wiggle my fingers in his direction like I'm waving him away. "Thanks for the Popsicles, old friend!"

Chapter Five

"Kelsey, I need your cat ears and tail from last Halloween," I say as I walk downstairs late Sunday afternoon.

I'm still buzzing from beating Max at drill down on Friday. It felt amazing and I smile every time I think of it, but my win isn't going to help the color guard with our season. I need them to fully invest so that we can become a cohesive team.

Which means, naturally, that we're dressing up as cats.

Kelsey puts a bookmark in the latest dragon book she's reading and then eyes me with suspicion. "Why do you need my costume?"

"For color guard."

"You dress up as *cats* in band?"

"You're doing group costumes?" Mom calls from the dining room. "I always loved that."

Of course she did.

"I don't want you getting my costume sweaty," Kelsey says and goes back to reading.

Can't anything be easy? I walk over to the doorway that separates the living room and dining room. The table is almost completely covered in D&D manuals and notebooks as Mom preps for her game this evening.

"A lot of the sections have already dressed up, and I figured it would be fun for everyone. Like a bonding exercise." I survey the table. "What are you working on?"

"Last-minute details." She leans back in her chair and stretches. "I have a big encounter planned, and I want to make sure to get it right."

I'm sure she will, as she always does. Mom takes her role as Dungeon Master *very* seriously. It's like an extra part-time job. Everything she does is "homebrew"—meaning her campaigns and non-player characters are created from scratch—and she meticulously studies each of the characters in her campaign to decide how the storyline should progress. Dad says the NPCs are more three-dimensional than his own character.

It's incredibly impressive, and I'm sure that's why she's been playing with the same group for the last six years. But it's also intimidating. Nova's been bugging me to DM a game for at least a year, but every time I think about it, I freeze up and abandon the idea. I don't want to run a half-baked game. Like Mom, if I'm going to do something, I need to do it full-out or not at all.

"Have you decided on your sectional dinner yet?" Mom asks and flips to the back of the *Monster Manual*. "If you're doing it at a restaurant then you'll need reservations given the group size."

I nod along as if I'd already considered this, but inside, my anxiety cranks up another notch. Right . . . I need to plan a section dinner too. I should already have that in the works, but I haven't even begun to think about it.

"Would you want them to come here?" Mom asks in a softer voice. I must not be hiding my panic well. "I don't want to take over," she adds quickly, "but I'm happy to help if you'd like."

"Actually . . . that would be great. I've been spending so much time thinking about our routines . . ."

"I get it, you have lots on your mind. My work schedule is light on Wednesday. Why don't you tell everyone to come over after camp for dinner—it'll be a good way for you all to relax midweek. Oh, and Kelsey's costume is stuffed into the top of the hall closet. She won't even notice if you take it."

"Thanks, Mom. You're a lifesaver."

I'm grateful, but a sinking sadness hits me all the same. I wish I didn't need her to come to my rescue. I wanted this to be the year when I could handle everything on my own, but so far it's been the opposite.

I arrive at camp Monday morning feeling a little silly. I did my best with Kelsey's meager costume: securing the cat ears with bobby pins, attaching the tail to my gray shorts, and using some eyeliner to add whiskers to my cheeks. I won't be winning any awards, but it gets the point across.

Li went full-out. Not only does she have ears and a tail, she's wearing a leopard print shirt and leopard face paint.

"You look adorable!" I cry.

She beams and does a spin as she walks in the band room door. "I rummaged through my mom's closet and came up with this. You look great too!"

To my surprise, the sophomores—Callie, Deja, and Keira—have great costumes as well. Actually, the entire guard really brought it today.

"I love a reason to dress up," Callie says when I pull the group together for morning rehearsals.

"This is so much fun," Deja agrees. "I wish we could do this every day instead of worrying about rehearsals and performances."

It's hard to hear her over the raucous laughter that fills the air. A half dozen percussion players, including Max and Brody, are circled up together in the back of the room, bent over at their waists laughing. One of the guys is trying to do a handstand and keeps falling.

"It's kinda too bad the percussion section hates us," Keira says longingly. "They seem fun."

"And cute," Deja adds.

"Keep a wide berth," I say and shoot a quick glare at the guys.

Unfortunately, Max looks over at that moment and catches my eye. My pulse leaps and I spin away. The last thing I need is for him to think I'm talking about him.

"Like you did on Friday at drill down? I saw you talking to Max and Brody—what was going on with that?" Madisyn asks.

The whole group encircles me. I get the impression they've been hoping for some gossip.

"They thought they were going to beat me at drill down, so I had to put them in their place. I can't stand their egos."

"You certainly seem to bring it out in Max. He looked pissed," Addison replies.

"We used to know each other, and our parents are friends, so everything is . . . weird," I explain. "I can't believe what a jerk he's turned into."

Devin glances back at him. "But he's so hot."

I'm tempted to look over at Max again but fight the urge. "Just because he's hot doesn't mean he's nice."

"If you say so," Callie says.

Just then the percussion section breaks out into their stupid chant: *"Good luck? All day! We suck? No way!"*

I roll my eyes and turn my back fully on them. I hate that chant with my whole being. It barely makes sense, it's not creative, and I've heard them scream it at the top of their lungs more times than I can count.

"The only time I want to interact with them is when they're delivering our Popsicles. Otherwise, we should be focusing on ourselves," I remind the guard. "Speaking of which, I'd love to do a color guard sectional dinner. How about this Wednesday? I was thinking we could meet at my place to hang out and eat a bunch of food?"

Everyone's quiet, and it occurs to me that they might refuse. How mortifying would it be if I can't get them to eat a free dinner with me? I could never tell Mom. Maybe I have enough in savings to bribe them into coming if necessary.

"Uh . . ." Madisyn glances at her friends. "I have a date at eight, but I can come for dinner beforehand."

Addison and Devin nod in agreement.

"I'd love to come!" Li says eagerly.

"I can probably be free," Rosa adds.

The others agree and I'm able to breathe again. "Awesome. Okay, then let's go work our tails off!" I shake my fluffy tail at them.

"Nooooooo," Callie groans, while a few others boo at me . . . but they're smiling. Right now, I'll take what I can get.

Our afternoon practice on the field is scorching. August in Ohio can be absolutely miserable with the high heat and humidity, and Sire keeps giving us extra breaks to gulp down water and apply extra sunscreen (not that most people take advantage of that). The guys in particular seem to compete for worst sunburn by the time band camp is over.

"I should have brought my own Popsicles for the guard," I say to Nova during our latest break. She hauled in a cooler filled with ice and rainbow Popsicles for all the clarinets. She might hate people in general, but there's no denying she's a great section leader. I take a gulp of my sad lukewarm water. "Why did I think the percussion would actually fulfill their side of the bet?"

"I wish I had enough for both our sections."

"No, it's my fault. Once again, I wasn't cynical enough. I need to learn your ways."

I'm seriously debating asking if I can have some of the melting ice from her cooler when Max jogs up to us. "Those Popsicles are probably sounding pretty good right now, huh? I'll go grab them for you. And *no,* I didn't forget. I never go back on the bets I make."

And then he smiles at me. I feel it all the way down to my toes.

I only have enough time to blink before he's jogging back into the high school.

I turn to Nova. "Did he just *smile* at me?"

"I saw his teeth, so I'm pretty sure that's an affirmative."

"Well, now I'm officially scared." I glower at his back and take another swig of water.

"Maybe he's coming around to you again?" She takes a bite of her Popsicle. "Or he was impressed by your drill down skills?"

"Maybe . . ."

"Well, whatever it is, I hope it sticks. Max seemed genuinely interested in D&D and it got my hopes up that we might get a game together after all this time."

The rest of the color guard circles around Nova and me when Max comes back, and the percussion also meanders over. He holds out the box to me. I recognize it as one of those generic brands of Popsicles where it's really just colored water frozen in narrow plastic pouches. It's not my favorite kind of Popsicle, but with this heat I'm willing to take anything.

"You won fair and square, so here's your box," he says. "From the percussion to the color guard."

This doesn't feel right. He's still smiling, but now I notice that the rest of the percussion is too. That can't bode well.

As soon as I take the box, I realize what they're smiling about.

"These aren't frozen!"

The whole color guard groans in dismay. Callie takes the box from me as if she doesn't believe me. "Are you serious right now?"

Max looks from her to me. "You said that if you won, we had to bring you Popsicles. You never said they had to be frozen."

"I shouldn't have to specify—they're *Popsicles.* Of course they're going to be frozen!"

Anger burns through me from my head to my fingertips. I can't believe I thought Max might act like a decent human being today. Who does something like this?

"Welp, there goes my D&D game," Nova mutters under her breath.

All around him, the other percussion members are laughing at their hilarious joke and watching him like he's some god. "Was this your idea?" I ask him.

"That box is a twenty-count—that's double the amount we agreed on. You should be thanking me."

"You are the most arrogant, irritating joke of a person I've ever met, and that's really saying something." I squeeze my hands into fists and step closer to him, tilting my chin up to meet his gaze with contempt. "You lost our bet and now you need to pay up."

"I already brought you Popsicles." The corner of his mouth

quirks up in a smile and his eyes flash. "What else would you like from me?"

"I want . . . I mean, you should—" I cut off when I realize how close we're standing. Close enough that I can see his individual eyelashes and smell the scent of peppermint on his breath.

Sire's whistle sounds, indicating the end of our rest period. I suck in a breath and break off eye contact. I can't let him get to me like that anymore. It only makes me look more ridiculous.

"Gotta go!" He gives a little wave. "Enjoy the Popsicles, though!"

I stand in shock as he jogs away, then glare at the box by my feet. I want to pull out the individual Popsicles and throw them at the back of his head.

"I'll put them in our deep freezer when I get home," I tell the guard as we walk back to the field. "And I'll bring them back tomorrow if they freeze in time."

"I'm starting to understand why we hate the percussion section," Deja says.

As if on cue, they shout their stupid chant again.

"More like *they* suck all day," Li says quietly.

An idea pops into my head. "Actually, I think you may have just given us a new motivational chant, Li."

I gather the whole guard around me and whisper my hurried thoughts to them before Sire gets frustrated that we aren't on the field yet. Our rhymes aren't great, and the chant is still corny, but it'll annoy percussion and that's all I want right now.

"As loud as you can," I whisper and we all turn to the

percussion section. "Hey, we wrote you something!" Then we chant in unison: *"Good luck? No way! They suck? All day! Big yuck, don't play!"*

We burst into laughter and a flurry of high fives. To my surprise, Max looks unbothered by our new and improved chant. In fact, his mouth twitches like he's trying not to laugh. Granted, he's only been a Glen Vale percussion member for six days. The rest of the percussion is livid, though. Brody's face goes bright red, and I know that's not from a sunburn. They've passed their chant down for years. To them, it's sacred.

Whoops. I guess that'll teach them for trying to humiliate us.

Chapter Six

When the guard pulls up to our house on Wednesday evening for our section dinner, I'm not surprised to see that Mom has outdone herself yet again. The front yard is filled with massive letters that spell out *Welcome Knights!*

"Come on in, it's great to have you here," Dad says as he beckons everyone inside and toward the kitchen. Kelsey waves from her spot in the living room but is surprisingly quiet. Though it's hard to be louder than ten teenagers who are eager to dissect the day's rehearsals.

"I hope you all like tacos!" Mom calls as they walk in. "We have hard and soft shell tortillas, rice, a Crock-Pot of shredded chicken, and a skillet of peppers and onions for any vegetarians in the mix, plus all the toppings. Please help yourself!"

The guard stands around in awe for a second before jumping into line.

"Thanks, Mom," I say quietly. "I think everyone's impressed."

"I'm glad. This evening is important, so I wanted to help you get it right. I remember how close our entire trumpet section was—we were inseparable. It's one of the biggest reasons why we were so successful."

Her words make my stomach churn. I'm grateful everyone agreed to come to dinner tonight, but we're a long way from being *inseparable.* Already, I can see a few people checking the time on their phones since they have plans for later.

"Are you doing any fun bonding exercises with them after you eat?" Mom asks.

Bonding exercises? I glance at her in alarm. Isn't it enough to just eat some food together? I didn't realize I needed to plan a series of trust fall activities like we're at a corporate retreat in order to be a good leader.

"Never mind," she says. "I'm sure you'll figure it out." She pushes me toward the group. "Now stop talking to me and go connect with them."

To Mom's credit, the taco bar is a huge hit. The dining room has been decorated with green and white balloons, streamers, napkins, and plates. Everyone happily crowds around the table, laughing and talking about the beginning of school next Monday. I sit down next to Li. I was hoping some of the other members would take her under their wings, but so far she seems like a bit of an outsider.

"Are you excited to start freshman year?"

She smiles and then frowns. "I am, but I'm also scared. The high school is so big compared to the junior high, and

I'm not sure how much I'll see my friends. That's why I'm so happy to be in color guard and get to have all of you."

My heart squeezes, remembering that scary transition. I really need to look out for her and make sure she's okay. I can't control the rest of high school, but marching band needs to be a safe spot for her.

As soon as the food is gone, the conversation dwindles too. I think back to what Mom said earlier . . . maybe I should have planned something else to do together. I hate for them to leave so soon. I glance around quickly and then see a stack of D&D books on a corner bookshelf. A thought comes to me. It's something Nova and I do sometimes when we're bored, and even Max and I used to do this back in the day.

"Hey, I have a wild idea," I say loudly.

All the heads at the table swivel in my direction.

"What if we all tried making a D&D character tonight?"

Callie and Deja look disgusted, while the seniors give me bewildered expressions.

"Um . . . why?" Devin asks.

"My *brother* plays that," Rosa complains.

I'm already regretting this suggestion, but maybe it'll be fun if people can get over their prejudices. "I'm not saying we start a campaign together," I reply. "We have way too many people for that anyway. But it's fun making characters, and you can be whoever you want." I grab a few of Mom's manuals and start passing them around. "Think of it like a personality test so we can get to know each other better. You can choose your name, what species and class you'd like to be, all your personality traits. How about everyone takes fifteen minutes and then we'll go around and introduce the characters to each other. Just for fun?"

They look back-and-forth to each other hesitantly, but no one refuses.

"Um, how do we do it?" Deja asks.

Whew, they aren't revolting yet. I start explaining, then quickly realize that going through the entire character development process is going to be too intensive, so I narrow it down to the basic elements. Soon they're flipping pages and squealing over ideas.

"Wait, I can be a dragon?" Callie asks.

"You can be dragonborn if you want to be."

"Oh, I'm totally being a dragon!" She claps with delight, surprising me with her enthusiasm. "My name is going to be Puff and I want to make swords. Do I get to choose the color of my scales?"

"Absolutely."

"Ooh, that's hard. Maybe purple?"

"No," Keira says. "You should do green like our school colors."

I laugh and turn to Li. "What are you thinking?"

"This is so cool." Her expression is bright with joy. "I've read a few D&D novels, and I always thought it would be fun to play, but I didn't think I'd get a chance. I mean, not that we're actually playing, but even making a character is fun."

It quickly becomes apparent that Li is a natural. It takes her no time at all to decide on an elf druid named Ellywich, so I point her to the section on possible backgrounds so she can add more detail. A few of the girls need a little help making decisions, and we get a ton of bards, which probably isn't surprising since many of us are in color guard because we like to perform. I pull up a name generator on my phone for a few who can't easily come up with their names.

When the fifteen minutes is up, not only does everyone have a basic character, but they look eager to share. Callie starts with her dragonborn character, which she chose so she can burn anyone she doesn't like. Madisyn, Addison, and Devin go next. Of course they all chose the same species and class—human fighters.

"Because we're the Knights!" they exclaim with grins.

Yori leans forward, her black hair slipping over her shoulder. "I'm an orc barbarian named Oof."

"An orc? Aren't they . . . super creepy?" Rosa asks her BFF.

"Yeah, but this way I can destroy anyone who annoys me."

"Like Brody, Max, and the percussion bros!"

"Can Puff get in on that action?" Callie asks.

The group laughs and Li lifts a hand to high-five me.

"What kind of weapon does your orc use?" Li asks Yori.

"Um . . . I don't know. Something that can flatten people?"

Deja holds up a book. "Use a maul."

"Perfect," Li says and starts sketching something on a napkin.

I lean over her shoulder. With the crappy ballpoint pen I gave her to write down her character notes, she's drawing a sketch that looks shockingly like the orc in the D&D manual. "Whoa, you're an artist?"

She slides down in her chair. "I'm not an artist. I just like to draw fan art." She works for a few more seconds and then sits up. Sure, it's rough, but her sketch of Oof the orc is way better than anything I could even conceive in my head, let alone draw.

I lift up the napkin so the whole table can see. "Um, I think you're an artist."

Everyone gasps in delight. "Me! Do me!" Keira calls.

"And us too," the seniors call.

"I want one!"

"Me too!"

"I'll get you some better paper," I say.

Another twenty minutes and we've met everyone's alter ego characters *and* have seen a cool sketch of each one.

"What about you, Hazel? What's your character?" Rosa asks.

"Oh, I don't need a character. I just wanted to do this for you all."

A chorus of *nooooo*s rings out.

"We all have characters. You have to make one too!" Yori commands.

"I think she should be a wizard," Li says. "They're wise, which you are, they're old, which you totally are"—the group laughs—"and they make magic. And I know you're going to help us make magic this season."

The others laugh, probably sarcastically given their optimism about guard, but I pull Li into a hug so no one can see the fact that her last sentence has me emotional.

Chapter Seven

The following day is Water Balloon Day. Each section wears a different color of shirt, the "band booster" parents provide the water balloons, and we get to end practice early so we can throw as many balloons at each other as possible. Percussion is certain to come after us mercilessly today, but I've got it covered. I spent extra money this year buying supplemental water balloons to make sure we can return the favor.

Unfortunately, all this excitement for the end of the day means the guard isn't focusing well. We've been practicing our routine for the fight song—a song we'll be performing endlessly this year—and it's looking rough.

"Keira, you need to have your flag straight up on count four so that you're able to sweep behind your back on six."

I pick up our "Glen Vale Knights" flag from the practice field sidelines to demonstrate. We use a lot of different flags in our competition show, but our standard one for football games is a simple flag with two crossed swords to represent that we're the Marching Knights. I demonstrate the combination for her once again.

"But I was doing it on four."

"No, you need to count in your head." I try my best to keep my voice light and airy. "You aren't getting there until five, which means you're behind for the whole rest of the combination."

"Um, okay." She looks confused, like she either doesn't know what I'm talking about or doesn't believe me.

"I can't believe band camp is almost done," Madisyn complains. "I bet this whole year is going to go like that. Before we know it, we're going to be graduating."

Addison and Devin nod sadly, and my own heart squeezes at the idea. There's so much I want to accomplish this year. But concentrating on that is a foolproof way to get distracted and not perform at my best.

"Okay, let's take the fight song from the top," Sire calls into his megaphone. "Flutes, I need to hear you more during the refrain. And color guard, it's still looking pretty messy. Let's try to clean that up before the first football game, yeah?"

I bob my head. Ugh, I hate getting called out in front of the whole band.

Sire releases us for a break before the water balloon fight, and I beckon the guard out to the parking lot with me.

"I drove here today so I could bring these." I open the trunk to show them a big plastic tote overflowing with water balloons.

"Whoa!" Li exclaims.

"Going a little overboard this year?" Devin asks with a laugh. "How many water balloons do you have?"

"Probably a hundred and fifty," I reply sheepishly. "But they're the kind that are easy to fill, so it really wasn't that bad."

That's . . . not entirely true. I spent at least an hour after they left last night filling all of these—and then having to fight Kelsey to get them back when she discovered what I was doing and wanted to have a water balloon fight with her neighbor friends in the backyard. But it's going to be so worth it when the percussion runs out of balloons and we get to pelt them nonstop.

"I need help carrying the tote over to the field, though," I explain. "I can't lift this, so my dad had to get it into the car for me. I think he almost threw out his back this morning."

It ends up taking four of us to get the tote to the field, and I'm sweaty enough that I'm actually looking forward to being hit by a few balloons.

Sire comes back out to the field, but this time he's switched out his horn-rimmed glasses for a pair of swimming goggles. It's a smart choice. While we all love going after each other, Sire gets hit by more water balloons than anyone else in the band.

"All right, the moment you've all been waiting for! Remember, you can only hit people if they're standing on the practice field, don't aim for their face or their crotch, and no stealing water balloons from the other sections' arsenals. This is just for fun, so there's no official winner, but we know there's always a loser." He points to himself with a smile and the whole band laughs.

"You're going down, old man," Socks yells. That's not his

real name, but all the tuba players call him that and it stuck. I'm not even sure what his real name is now.

Sire picks up a water balloon from behind him and aims it toward Socks. "Don't worry about me. I didn't come unarmed." He glances around the band. "Three, two, one . . . let the water balloon fight commence!"

We all scream and sprint to our various parts of the field where each section is keeping their supply of water balloons. We were given seventy-five balloons per section, but everyone always brings extra. I grab two balloons, run into the center of the field, and mass chaos ensues.

Within seconds I'm hit twice. I shriek as the ice-cold water bursts on my skin. There are so many people running that there's no time to look at who I'm throwing at. I chuck one of the balloons haphazardly at a trombone player, then see an orange shirt in my peripheral view. Percussion is wearing orange today. I manage to hit a bass drum player in the ankle, dousing his shoes. I laugh in triumph and run back for more supplies, getting hit twice more on the way. I can't help screeching and laughing every time.

Sire is taking the brunt of the balloons, but the whole band is dousing each other with abandon. I see Nova and get her in the stomach.

"Ahh!" she cries. She gets me on the shoulder and it's my turn to squeal.

The balloons keep flying, and I'm absolutely drenched, but I'm surprised that the percussion doesn't seem to be targeting me, or anyone in color guard. It's odd. Last year I was trailed by two or three percussion players the entire game, to the point that I could barely take a step without being hit.

Eventually, the sections who didn't bring many extra balloons slow down. Luckily, color guard still has a ton left.

"This is our time," I yell to the guard members I can see around me. "Let's take them down!"

They whoop in response, and we gather as many balloons as we can hold. I even lift the bottom of my shirt to make a little pouch where I can keep extras.

Max is easy to pick out on the field now that it's a little calmer. It could be the bright orange shirt he's wearing or how he's slightly taller than everyone else on the field. Or maybe it's the way his clothes are absolutely glued to him and distracting other girls as they sprint past. It's like he wore the tightest shirt possible so he could sabotage the rest of us into slowing down and staring. And it's working too, because someone hits me right between the shoulder blades when my steps falter.

I grit my teeth and pull my eyes from his chest. After that stupid Popsicle stunt he pulled, there's no time for anything but revenge. I won't be happy until he's balled up on the ground, begging us to stop dousing him with balloons. I grab mine and start throwing. I might as well be Buddy the Elf when he's throwing snowballs in Central Park.

Max spins in my direction. His eyes sparkle with amusement, but then his expression turns serious. "You've got a good arm, Hazel, but you shouldn't have messed with me."

"You messed with me first."

He yells over his shoulder. "It's time!"

Time? Time for what?

I look to the thirty-yard sideline where percussion is keeping their water balloons and see they have a second tote. They came prepared like us, but I'm not intimidated.

"Bring it on!" I throw another balloon at him, but he dodges away. I hit Felix in the hip and Niko, a cymbal player, in the back.

The percussion players come running from different parts of the field. They all grab balloons from the same tote and make a beeline for us. I restock, ready to hit as many as possible. Brody lands the first balloon, right in my stomach.

He cackles with laughter and doesn't stop even when I hit him in the chest.

"What the—" Callie yells out.

Devin throws up his hands. "Absolutely not. I'm out."

A second later, Rosa yells as well. A percussion player hits me on my side and a foul smell rises up all around me. I take a second to sniff my shirt, but slowing down was a bad idea. Three more water balloons hit me in quick succession, then I get another to the back of my head.

"What is that smell?" Yori cries.

What *is* that smell? I sniff again. It takes me a second to recognize it.

"Vinegar?!" I yell and spin to face Max. "You filled your balloons with *vinegar*?"

The whole percussion section bursts into laughter, but it doesn't stop them from throwing even more balloons at us. Devin's already jogging off the field, and the others scatter at the realization that they aren't being hit by regular water balloons anymore. Percussion members take off after them, and now the chaos is at a different level. The girls' screams are turning hysterical and any joy I felt is replaced with fury. I can't believe they're ruining one of the most fun parts of band camp.

I spot Max racing after Addison while Brody takes off in the opposite direction. I bean Brody in the lower back and manage to hit Max in the back of the head. I laugh in triumph.

Max twists around as a balloon from Niko bursts at my collarbones, sending vinegar splashing down my shirt and up onto my face. I scream and swipe at my mouth. Max stills, his eyes trailing down my body, and I'm reminded that I'm completely drenched. My purple T-shirt is clinging to me, and heat rises in my cheeks as I imagine how I must look.

Max puts out a cautious hand in my direction. "If you stop targeting me, then I'll stop going after you."

I scowl and hurl another balloon at him. He doesn't flinch or dodge away. He just stands there and lets me hit him, soaking him all over again. I don't allow myself to enjoy how the orange fabric perfectly defines each angle of him. My past crush is nothing compared to this present moment.

" 'Stop targeting' says the guy who filled his balloons with vinegar. I can't believe you, Max."

Another balloon smacks into my back and I jump. Brody cackles from behind me and then comes to stand next to Max. "I'm loving this guy. He has the best ideas."

"It was your idea?"

At least Max has the decency to look mildly shamed. "It's a mixture of vinegar and water. Mom uses it to clean all the time."

"See, we're doing you a favor—it's a way to keep your guard from stinking," Brody says and slings his arm over Max's shoulder. Around me, the shrieking and running is dying down. Percussion must be almost out of balloons. "Of course, it won't keep you from sucking on the field this season, but we can only do so much."

"Did you not hear our new color guard chant? I'm pretty sure it's *you* guys who suck. All. Day."

That sets off Brody just like I knew it would. He takes his arm from Max and points a finger at me. "Do *not* mess with our chant, Hazel. That's our good luck charm."

"*Good luck? No way!*" I mimic and give him a bright grin. I know I'm pushing my luck with Brody, but I can't stop myself.

Li comes up beside me. "Are you okay?"

Brody sneers at us both. "You wish guard had one ounce of our talent. You're perpetual losers. Color guard is always bringing down the band, and from what I've seen, this season will be no different."

Li falls back a step, her eyes wide. The fire inside me burns brighter until all I see is red. She's just a baby freshman, still full of excitement and optimism, and I will *not* let Brody and Max taint the guard for her.

"Color guard is going to blow your percussion section out of the water this year," I retort. "You're going to choke on all the Superior ratings we receive. In fact, I bet we'll be the first to win a best in show award this season."

"You didn't get a single Superior rating last year!" Brody cries. "That vinegar must be messing with your brain."

A few people laugh, which does nothing to dampen my anger. He isn't wrong . . . but there's nothing like pure spite to inspire a person.

Madisyn, Addison, and Devin, my fellow senior guard members, come up on my other side. I see more of the guard behind them. "Hazel, calm down," Madisyn says. "What are you doin—"

I wave her away. All our reputations are on the line and I'm not going to take one more insult from anyone in percussion.

"You should listen to your friends," Brody tells me with a smirk. "There's no way you can back up that bet. Percussion will easily get a best in show trophy before you do."

"If you're so sure, then why don't you take my bet?"

"What are the stakes? More Popsicles?"

I bite the inside of my cheek and try to decide. They all think they're so much better than us, but they have no idea how difficult color guard actually is. I want to make them eat their words. I want to embarrass them with the whole band watching, just like they're trying to do to us right now.

And then an idea comes to me.

"When *we* win, the entire percussion section has to learn our competition show—every piece of it—and perform it in front of the whole band. We'll see how cocky you are when you smack yourself in the face with a five-foot-long flag pole."

Brody scoffs, and I stand taller. I can already imagine them making total fools of themselves. The idea makes me giddy.

"I wouldn't smile just yet," Brody replies, his eyes glinting maliciously. "This year, Sire assigned the percussion section to clean the men's stadium restrooms at the end of the season. We had to do it last year too, and it was nasty. Have you seen a urinal trough before, Hazel? Or had to change out a urinal cake? Because you're going to." He looks to his section members and crosses his arms over his chest. "When we win, the color guard will be taking over that cleaning for us. And you will *hate* it."

A few percussion guys and Devin all nod adamantly. Behind me, other guard members are groaning and making fake retching sounds. Everyone hates the end of season cleaning, which is Sire's idea of community service, but the guard has never done anything like that before. Usually we just help clean the concession stand.

My resolve wavers. For once Brody is right—I *really* don't want to clean urinals. But it's too late now for second-guessing or backing down. The only solution is for us to win.

I put my hands on my hips. "Since we won't be losing, I'm not concerned. I can't wait to watch you fall all over yourselves on the practice field at the end of the season. I'll be bringing popcorn for the show."

Brody sneers. "You're on. It's your funeral." He glances around. "We're out of balloons already? Good, I'm sick of this game." He turns his back on me and walks to the sideline. Against my better judgment, I look to Max, but he's already turned away.

I blink and take a few steps back. My heart is beating so fast I feel dizzy. Did I actually just come up with that bet?

"Nice going," Madisyn snaps. "You always have to poke the bear. Now we're covered in vinegar *and* we're going to have to clean disgusting restrooms when we lose." She and her friends give me annoyed looks and stalk away to the parking lot. Other guard members are glaring as well.

Li comes to my side. Her black bob frames her round

face, and her eyes are large behind her bright pink glasses. "Don't listen to them," she whispers. "Thanks for standing up for the guard. You're the best captain ever."

My heart twinges. "Thanks for the moral support." I give her a quick, squelching hug. "We've got this, right?"

She nods happily. "Totally. We'll show them."

Chapter Eight

The color guard is standoffish the next day, which is our last day of camp. I know they're mad at me, but it's hard to feel guilty. Only Li and I were there to hear everything Brody said, and I wouldn't be a good captain if I let that kind of disrespect stand. The bigger issue is that the others seem convinced that we're destined to be the losers Brody expects us to be. We're never going to be successful if that's what they believe. But I'm not sure how to convince them otherwise.

It doesn't help that we're all nervous about our performance this afternoon. It's a long-standing tradition that on the last day of band camp, we wrap up by performing our competition show for our family and friends, followed by a chance for a family member to come march on the field with us. It's one thing to suck during rehearsal, but it's another thing to look bad in front of our parents. My parents, especially. I don't want to start the season by disappointing them.

When the time comes, we watch from the sidelines as our families file into the bleachers. Even though it's a Friday at three in the afternoon, a surprising number of parents have gotten off work to come. Mine are front and center, wearing green shirts and holding *Glen Vale Knights Color Guard* signs.

"Is this how every band competition feels?" Li asks me. Her eyes are wide and worried behind her glasses.

"Some are worse than others. The good thing is that this crowd is going to cheer no matter how we look."

Li laughs, but it sounds more painful than happy.

"Ahh! I'm here, I made it!"

Faith jogs up to us, still wearing her dress clothes. She runs around, giving each of us a hug, and then claps her hands together.

"I'm so sorry I wasn't able to get here more this week, but I've been checking in with Sire and he says you all have been coming along really well, thanks to Hazel's diligent work. I can't wait to see the show." She beams at us and flicks her long blond hair over a shoulder. "I'll keep a list of things to work on, but for now don't worry about that, okay? Just have fun!"

She hurries off to stand with the other assistant band directors, and the guard members turn to me, as if waiting for whatever pep talk I've prepared. I decide to match Faith's energy for once.

"We've got this," I tell them confidently. "You all have made so much progress over the last two weeks and we're not stopping now. So keep your head high, keep marching, and keep a smile on your face. This is just the beginning. Now circle up and hands in the center!"

We all cram together. The guard doesn't have a special chant, and I'm tempted to repeat the altered percussion chant, but we don't need any more drama. So instead I say, "On three. One . . . two . . . three . . . *Glen Vale Knights*!"

The performance is a blur. I'm so busy thinking about what I'm supposed to be doing that I have no time to reflect on how it's actually going, although I can tell it's far from perfect. Multiple times the members forget their formations and have to run to their next spot. Most of the squad drops their flag throws and we aren't close to being synchronized. But the same could be said for the band. Mom and Dad scream my name a few times, and as we hit our final positions, I look up into the stands and see them jumping up and down while Kelsey does an elaborate pom-pom dance at their side.

The guard keeps a cool demeanor as we march off the field, but as soon as we hit the sidelines, we breathe sighs of relief and share some high fives.

"You did a great job!" I say.

"I dropped my flag three times," Keira says.

"That's better than me. I ran headfirst into the guy who plays the bari saxophone," Deja replies. "How does he even march with that thing?"

"It's okay," I reassure them. "We made it through our first real performance, and it'll only go up from here."

"Band members, friends, and family, it's now time for one of our longest-held and most special traditions: the

Family March," Sire announces using the loudspeaker. We all go quiet to listen. "I would like to invite one family member to come down onto the field and find your marcher. We're going to play a recording of the first competition song and you're going to get a chance to march alongside our students. Please stay as close as possible to your marcher and watch out for others on the field because it's going to get very . . . we'll say *busy*. Marching band can look pretty easy from the stands, but now is your chance to try for yourself!"

My eyes go back to my family. Each year my parents take turns on who will march beside me, and this year is Dad's turn. However, I'm not entirely surprised to see Mom making her way to the field. In fact, it looks like Mom, Dad, and Kelsey are all coming down. I shake my head in confusion.

"We're only supposed to have one family member," I argue.

Mom puts a hand on her hip. "It's your senior year and Sire won't care. Your dad and I don't want to miss the chance to march one more time with you."

"And I don't want to be left in the stands by myself," Kelsey adds.

"Well . . ." I chuckle. "You better stay real close then, or you're going to be plowed over by the trumpets in a few measures."

"It's too bad I didn't bring my tuba," Dad says. "Then they'd have to make way for us."

No one is marching with instruments or flags, though. It's chaotic enough without trombones or flag poles smacking you across the back of the head. I glance around the guard and am happy to see that everyone has someone standing next to them. I vaguely recognize the parents of the returning members, and it looks like the new members either have a parent, sibling, or friend next to them.

I survey the rest of the band and my gaze snags on the percussion. Like everyone else, the players also have parents and even a few grandparents on the field or standing in the pit by the sidelines. That's where the percussion players stay if they play an instrument that can't be marched through the field, like the enormous gongs, chimes, or xylophones. Their families are lucky that they get to stay out of the chaos that's about to ensue.

And then I see Max.

Or rather, I meet Max's gaze because he's already looking at me. The heat in his expression sends my pulse leaping.

I do a double take, glancing into the stands and around the field, then back to him. He's alone.

It's been a long time since I've seen either of his parents, but I'm pretty sure I'd recognize them if I saw them again, and they're nowhere to be seen. He's an only child, so he doesn't have siblings he could pull onto the field, and probably his only friends in the area are already standing out here. I can't stop my heart from squeezing in sympathy. He looks so lonely. He reminds me of the younger version of himself I knew years ago.

I should look away, but I can't seem to pull my eyes from him. I wish I could cut every ounce of empathy I have out of my system. A small—and very stupid—part of me even wants to stand beside him so he doesn't have to march alone. Or what if Mom or Dad marched with him instead? But then I remember Max's comment about my mom getting into his family's business. I have no idea what he meant by that, but I'm not eager to be told off by him again.

"Oh my goodness, is that Max?" Mom exclaims much too loudly. She uses both arms to wave at him, like she's landing a plane.

"Is he all alone?" Dad asks Mom quietly, his voice edged with concern. "Where's Melanie?"

"I don't know," Mom whispers. "One of us should go over there."

"*That's* Max?" Kelsey asks and stands on her tiptoes. "I'll go over there. I can see why you like him, Hazel."

"I don't—" I begin to say just as Mom takes a step in his direction. At her movement, Max's posture changes. He rolls his shoulders back and lifts his head high like we're about to perform for judges. Any trace of sadness on his face is replaced by deep dislike. Mom hesitates, and I pull her back to me.

"He doesn't need us. He's clearly fine on his own."

"But—"

Sire's whistle calls the band to attention. Mom and Dad are both still marching band nerds to the core, so they turn their attention to our director. I spare one more glance at Max, but he's all focus now. Good. I don't want any reason to have compassion for him. It makes it easier to loathe him this way.

Chapter Nine

"Hazel, you should come downstairs," Dad calls from the hallway on Sunday afternoon.

I turn off my Fiona Apple playlist and lift my head from the notebook where I'm jotting down ideas on possible villains for the (nonexistent) campaign Nova keeps asking me to run. Okay, fine, maybe I'm doing less "brainstorming" and more writing the word *wraith* with my cool calligraphy pens, but it still counts. It might be a dorky pastime, but I love writing up notes in calligraphy. Everything looks more beautiful, even my boring D&D ideas.

"Can it wait?" I call.

"No, I don't think it can." I hear footsteps outside my door, then there's a quick knock and Dad pokes his head in. "Max and Melanie are downstairs. She came out of the blue for our D&D game."

A rush of adrenaline flies through me. "Seriously?"

I look at the time on my phone and realize it's already six

in the evening—the usual time their Sunday game starts. I'd heard the front door opening and closing several times, my clue that their other members had arrived, but I hadn't really been paying attention.

"It's a surprise for us too," Dad says. "Aunt Mary already picked up Kelsey for the evening, but you should come down to say hi to Melanie before we head to the basement for the game."

"What about Max? What's he going to do?"

Dad gives me a confused expression. "Well, I was assuming he'd hang out with you until we finish our session tonight, just like before."

"You're expecting me to babysit him?"

"I wouldn't call it babysitting when he's taller than me now. What's the big deal? You guys used to do this all the time."

"Yeah and that was before he started hating me."

Dad snorts. "I'm sure Max doesn't hate you. Come on, I don't want to keep everyone waiting."

"Fine, I'll be down in a second."

I wait until the door closes to rub my hands roughly down my face. *Max* is here? Melanie must have dragged him by the ear or threatened him with bodily harm. This is going to be so awkward. I look down at myself. I'm wearing a T-shirt and overall jean shorts. Not exactly my most exciting outfit, but at least I'm having a good hair day today. I took the time to use a diffuser this morning so that it's lying in soft curls down my back. Not that I care what he thinks, but it is gratifying given that he's only seen me exhausted and sweaty at band camp.

When I walk down the stairs, I find them both standing with my parents by the front door. I can't help it when my attention locks onto Max. While he might be slightly taller than Dad, it's hard to tell since his shoulders are slumped forward from staring so intently at his feet. His hands are shoved in the pockets of his black jeans and he's wearing an AC/DC shirt today—the kind that's trying to look vintage but you know came from Target.

After watching him act larger than life at band camp for the last two weeks, it's clear that Max is totally and completely miserable here. I should be insulted, but for some reason I find the sight absurdly humorous. This tall, cocky guy reduced to a withered figure just from the idea of being in my presence. What a joke.

I snort-laugh before I can stop myself. My laugh has always been louder than I'd like, and even this small snort makes the entire group turn my way. I put a hand over my mouth, but Max scowls and I know that he knows I'm laughing at him. I can't drum up any guilt about it.

"Hazel!" Melanie calls and steps toward me.

I haven't seen Max's mom in years, but she's instantly recognizable, even if the time away has taken a toll on her. She's curvy and a little shorter than me with wavy dark hair and dimples. She and Max look a bit alike if I squint. He got his height from his dad, but he has his mom's hair and face. Not that I've seen the dimples since he doesn't smile around me.

Her expression is joyful, and she pulls me into a hug as soon as I'm down the steps. "You look terrific!" she exclaims into my hair. She pulls back and takes a look up and down. "It's like someone's stretched you—you're so tall!"

"Well, not exactly. I'm only five four."

She laughs. "Yes, I know I'm short. It's so good to see you."

"It's good to see you too. I didn't realize you were joining my parents' game again."

She shuffles her feet. "I've been . . . caught up with things since moving back, but your mom has been such a support, and I knew coming over would be good for me." She glances back at Max. "For both of us."

It takes everything in me not to snort-laugh in her face again. Melanie is very sweet, but I'm positive her son has very different feelings.

"So, Max, how are you liking Glen Vale?" Dad asks. "Is it a big change from your last band?"

"Not really. We were really serious at Oak Grove and it's pretty similar here too. Though we didn't have fun breaks during band camp there."

"No water balloons?" I ask.

His eyes cut from me to both of our moms, like he's waiting to be chewed out about dousing me in vinegar. I thought about telling my parents when I got home that day, but instead I threw my clothes in the washer and left it at that. It wasn't worth the hassle. That would only lead to my mom calling Melanie, then more drama and more fighting.

"I'm so glad you're both in band together," Melanie says and turns to me. "Do you also play D&D like your parents?"

"Uh—"

"Actually, Hazel and her friend have been talking about starting a campaign for forever now," Mom jumps in. "I keep pushing her to, but so far no luck."

"I've been busy. And I can't run a game with just me and Nova."

"You're looking for members?" Melanie asks eagerly and takes Max by the arm. "Max would love to join. He's been looking for a group."

He cringes. "I'm not looking. It's fine, Mom." He wiggles away from her.

There's a beat of uncomfortable silence and then Dad slaps both his thighs. "Welp, it's about time for us to get our game started. I'm sure Dale and Connie are already getting restless down there, and Glenn should be here soon. You two will be okay?" Dad looks between me and Max. His expression is unsure, and I'm tempted to cling to him like a toddler and refuse to be left behind.

"Why don't you show Max around?" Mom suggests. "It's been so long."

I swallow hard. "Okay. Sounds good."

The adults shuffle off downstairs and I'm left standing in a tight hallway with a guy who clearly wants to be anywhere but here.

"Couldn't talk her out of it, huh?" I ask.

A shadow of a smile lightens his expression for a brief second. "She was insistent."

"Well, I'm not. You're welcome to watch TV in the living room. I'll be in my room." I turn back to the stairs.

"Who's that on your shirt?"

I pause and look down. Today I'm wearing my *Boys for Pele* shirt from one of my favorite albums.

I glance back at him. "It's Tori Amos."

"Who?"

I roll my eyes. "Only one of the best female singer-songwriters to come out of the nineties. She writes brilliant haunting songs and never gets the credit she deserves."

"I didn't know you were into nineties music."

"And I didn't know you were an entitled jerk, but people change. A lot, in some cases."

I make it one step before his hand is on my elbow. It's only a whisper of a touch, but it's enough to send a wave of electricity down my arm. A years-long crush is harder to shake than I imagined.

"Do you always have to make things so hard?"

His voice is low and edged with annoyance, but there's a familiarity to it that brings old memories flooding back. How many times had he stood at the foot of these stairs, waiting impatiently for me to come down so we could play board games or watch movies together? How often had he growled under his breath when I beat him at a game or pointed out a rule he'd forgotten? It's so surreal to be standing here with him now, hating him, after all our history.

I take a deep breath and twist to face him fully. "Do you always have to make things so irritating?"

We glare at each other. It's a battle of wills and I won't be the one to blink or back down. Except we're standing much too close for this. It's hard to keep my hatred at the forefront of my mind when I'm reminded of how beautiful his eyes are. Finally, he drops his gaze to the floor and takes a step back.

"Just . . . show me around, okay? I don't want to disappoint Mom."

The reminder of Melanie makes me reconsider. She's always

been such a sweet soul and so kind to me. I don't want to disappoint her either.

"Fine." I roll back my shoulders. "For your mom."

He trails after me as I walk from room to room, saying very little. Honestly, the house hasn't changed much since he moved away, so there isn't much to show.

"Your parents' altar to marching band has gotten an update," he says when we walk through the living room.

I frown and turn to see him looking at my Most Valuable Member plaque.

"It's not an altar."

He lifts an eyebrow. "I haven't been around for a while, but I remember your parents. If there's one thing they worship, it's marching band."

I bite my lip to keep from smiling. "I won it freshman year," I say, pointing to the plaque. "To say my parents were excited would be an understatement."

"I can imagine." He studies it. "Are you hoping for a repeat win?"

"Doesn't everybody want to win everything?"

I know it's selfish to want to win again my senior year since I've already been awarded it once. There are other people who are deserving, but I care so much about band, and it would be such an amazing way to end my time with the Marching Knights. Plus my parents would be ecstatic if I could pull it off the same way Mom did when she was a Glen Vale member.

Max turns away from the award. "I don't think *everyone* cares as much about winning as we do. We always had that particular flaw in common."

I'm not sure what to say to that, so I keep walking into the kitchen at the back of the house. "And there's the backyard. Tour done."

Max peers out the sliding glass door. "Whoa, you still have the trampoline."

"Kelsey uses it now. Did you . . . want to see it?"

"Why not?" Max opens the door and makes a beeline for the trampoline.

Another wave of memories rushes over me as I reluctantly follow him. We used to love jumping together. I'm half expecting him to start jumping right now, or even do front flips like we used to. Maybe I can leave him out here like an overactive ten-year-old and barricade myself in my room for the rest of the night. But he just sits down in the center and tips his chin up toward the sky.

I hesitate, then follow him up onto the trampoline.

"So," I say quietly.

"So."

I take a deep breath to brace myself. "I don't get it, Max. Why are you friends with Brody?"

"Why do you hate Brody?"

"As if that isn't completely obvious." I huff and start to stand. "Have fun."

"I'm new, Hazel. I know our lives have turned out differently and you don't know what it's like to have to move schools, but I do. The last thing I want is to come charging into a new school and a new band and immediately make enemies with my section leader."

I bite the inside of my cheek and sit back down. I wasn't expecting a real answer. And his answer *does* make sense, except that Brody is such an exceptional jerk that I can't respect anyone who likes him.

"Why do you hate him?" Max repeats quietly.

"He's a sore loser. And a sore winner, actually."

"A sore loser? Heh, I've never met one of those before." His voice is almost teasing.

"Me neither. And definitely not over something as silly as a board game."

His gaze snaps to mine. "I hope you aren't dredging up that Settlers of Catan game."

"You mean the three-week-long game I won?"

"You didn't win, you cheated with your house rules! Plus, you kept hoarding all the resources! No one can build anything without wood."

I laugh triumphantly. "That's because my settlements were near the forests. I didn't want to trade resources with you—that's the same as letting you win."

"If I remember correctly, *no one* won because our moms made us pack it away and apologize to each other."

"Well, I choose to remember it differently."

I lift my chin defiantly and am shocked when he laughs. I glance at him incredulously and he laughs even louder.

"Wow, I almost forgot that expression. You look just the same as when you were twelve."

"I do not! Take it back." God, I hope that isn't true. Between the beginning of acne, horrid makeup choices, and out-of-control hair, I don't want to look anything like my preteen days.

"Fine." He sobers and studies me. "Maybe you look a little different now."

Flutters fill my stomach at the intensity of his gaze. It's like he's dissecting me with his eyes. I blurt out a question to distract him.

"Why didn't your parents come to the band camp performance on Friday? Did they have to work?"

He squints at me for a moment, then he shakes his head. "You know what, on second thought, you were right. This was a bad idea. I'm going inside."

"Are you completely incapable of having a conversation?" I shake my head. "Actually, never mind, I know exactly how to get you to talk."

"Hazel . . ." he warns.

I stand. "I'll make you a bet. If you can do a front flip on this trampoline, then you don't have to answer any of my questions. But if you fall, you have to tell me something real about your life. Something you don't want to tell me."

"And why would I ever take that bet?"

"Because you hate to lose. And the only thing you hate more than losing is backing down from a challenge."

"You don't know me the way you used to."

The soft sadness in his voice makes me pause. What is going on with him? He never acted this way when we were younger. I wish we could have a normal conversation instead of making everything into a fight, but I don't know how else to pull the answers from him. If he's going to be difficult, then I'll be difficult right alongside him.

"I'm very aware that I don't know you anymore." I put out my hands as if to say *duh*. "Which is why I'm reduced to making stupid bets with you."

He studies me and then squints up at the sky. "Fine. I'll take your bet."

"See, I still know you pretty well. Wait!" I point at him. "Did you have a trampoline at your last house?"

"No."

"Did you join gymnastics or tumbling there?"

"No."

"When's the last time you did a front flip?"

He smirks. "Here. I landed wrong and almost broke my neck, so you took pity on me and made me a big plate of nachos and put on *The Two Towers*."

"Oh. Right."

I'd forgotten about that part of the night. It happened right after I found out his family was moving. I was heartbroken and secretly hoped that if we spent the evening curled up on the couch next to each other, he'd finally realize how much I meant to him and kiss me. Instead, he spent the whole time telling me trivia about Viggo Mortensen and how many of the Rohan riders in the Lord of the Rings were actually women in beards and makeup.

"Well, I didn't forget." He stands and starts jumping cautiously. "Those were good nachos."

"I see your eating habits haven't changed. All right, let's see this amazing front flip."

Max starts jumping higher, and I move to the edge of the trampoline so he doesn't accidentally land on me. Tension coils through me as I watch him, hoping he's as bad at front flips as he used to be, although I swear I don't care whether I learn more about him or not. I just want to win the bet.

Max has some real height to his jumps now. I hold my breath as he flips forward . . . and lands spectacularly on his back. I slap my hand over my mouth before I can yell in triumph.

He groans and rolls over on his side. “I should never have taken that bet.”

“And yet I knew you would.” I do a jumpy victory dance. “You’re not dead, right?”

He squeezes his eyes shut and slowly sits up. “Go ahead and gloat.”

“No gloating.” I consider for a moment and then do a twirl. “Actually, lots of gloating.”

He eyes me skeptically. “What do you want to know?”

What happened after you moved away?

Why are you so different now?

When did you stop liking me?

I want to know everything.

I swallow, trying to decide how much I can ask without making him stalk away in annoyance.

“Um . . . I guess I want to know what’s going on with you.”

“That’s a really broad question for a single failed flip,” he says in aggravation. “I’m just . . . I don’t know. Adjusting, like I said before. To the new apartment and new family arrangement and trying to help out Mom and be supportive when she isn’t at her best. It’s a lot.”

“New family arrangement?”

He stares at me like he can’t decide if I’m ignorant or rude. “My parents’ *separation*?”

I lean back in surprise. Mom and Dad had insinuated Max was struggling, but I figured he was just angry about having to move.

"Oh . . . I didn't know," I whisper. My animosity falls away at his defeated expression. "I'm sorry, Max. Really."

"Your mom didn't tell you all the details? You two are so close." The openness in his expression vanishes as soon as he mentions my mom.

Pain pricks the back of my mind. The last time he was around us, Mom and I *were* super close. We hung out all the time, talked about everything. I even raided her closet so I could wear whatever fit me. That's probably why I still prefer vintage clothes from the nineties. But a lot has changed since then. All her enthusiasm about my future feels smothering now. I don't want to admit that, though.

"She never said a word."

"I—" He stares at me like he can't believe what I'm saying. "I figured . . . well . . . huh."

"Your mom isn't doing well?"

"She's the one who wanted the separation, but it's hard. Money is tight and the apartment is small and . . . you know, she's sad."

"Ah," I whisper. "And I guess that explains why you didn't have anyone at the band performance."

He shrugs and messes with his shoelaces. There's so much more I want to ask him, but I'm scared to ruin this very tentative peace between us. We're no closer to becoming friends, but maybe we've shifted a few millimeters away from being enemies. I'll take it.

"I don't have any nachos to offer, but I can put on *The Fellowship of the Ring* until our parents are finished?"

He's silent for a second and then shrugs again. "Yeah, okay. Did you know that scene where Ian McKellen hits his head in Bilbo's hobbit-hole wasn't scripted?"

I sigh deeply and walk to the house. "Yeah, I think you told me that a time or two."

Chapter Ten

My first day of senior year is surprisingly anticlimactic. Same building, same people in my classes, same basic schedule. If nothing else, I'd anticipated it feeling somewhat different because of Max. I wasn't looking forward to sparring with him in my classes or when we passed in the hallway, but as the day goes by without a single sighting of him, I almost feel annoyed. How was he avoiding me so completely? He wasn't in any of my classes or lunch period, not in the parking lot at the beginning of the day or in the halls between classes. Our high school isn't that big. What if he somehow got ahold of my schedule ahead of time so that he could be sure to avoid me all day? That seems overboard even for him.

"It's weird, right?" I say to Nova under my breath as we walk to the band room for the last period of the day.

"Maybe he's sick?"

"Maybe." Though he hadn't seemed sick last night.

"I'm surprised you aren't jumping for joy. It sounds like you had a horrible time together."

I'd texted Nova when Max left to tell her how my Sunday had taken a turn. Watching LOTR for the rest of the evening hadn't been *horrible*, exactly. It gave us a way to be in each other's presence without fighting, and I do love those movies, but it wasn't relaxing either. I was on edge the whole evening, wondering how long I had until our truce vanished and he snapped at me for breathing too loudly or made another rude comment about my mom or color guard.

"I'm not sad he's not around." I shove my hands into the pockets of my rolled-up jean shorts. "More like . . . suspicious."

"Girls! Come take a look!"

Nova and I walk into the band room to find my mom standing next to a folding table covered in bags of chips, cookies, and bottles of juice. Kicking off the school year with special snacks is a band tradition she started my freshman year when she and Dad got involved with the band boosters. She and the other parents try to do things throughout the season to make it special—like providing the water balloons for band camp, or snacks on our first day, or our special celebratory Balloon Day right before we perform at state.

Of course, it's not a guarantee that we'll make it to state. The band needs to earn a Superior rating at one of the local high school contests in order for us to qualify. We have three competitions scheduled for this season, which means three opportunities to qualify, but we shouldn't need more than one. We've qualified every year for the last eighteen years, so it's a given at this point. My focus is on having the color guard earn our Superior rating and get our best in show award so we can finally put the percussion section in their place.

"This looks great, Mrs. Buchanan," Nova says and grabs a bottle of apple juice.

"Good, I'm glad. I hope everyone enjoys it."

More people gather around the free food like moths to a flame, and I'm grateful when Mom announces she's heading out. As I walk with her to the parking lot, another car comes speeding past us. Max climbs out a second later and strides toward the building with no acknowledgment.

"He's just now getting to school?" I mutter. Who does that, especially on the first day?

"I hope he's doing okay," Mom replies. "It was good to see Melanie last night. It's been too long."

"Did you know that Max's parents are getting a divorce?"

She furrows her brow. "Yes. I know it's hard on her. And Max, I'm sure."

I swallow down a wave of irritation. "If you and Dad knew, then why didn't you tell me? That's a pretty important piece of information to keep to yourselves."

"Melanie told me in confidence. It's still very new." She shrugs. "And I figured Max would want to tell you himself in his own time. You two have always been so close. It was cute seeing you watching LOTR again like in the old days."

"Mom, *no*. Max and I aren't friends like that anymore."

"What about starting your D&D game now that he's back? It'd be a great way to spend your Sunday evenings together."

Alarm bells ring in my mind. "What do you mean, evenings?"

"Well, Melanie is joining the game again, so she'll be

coming over every Sunday now. And she mentioned that Max will be coming too so—"

"Why is Max coming?" I interrupt. "It was different when he was younger, but he's practically an adult now."

"Let's not get ahead of ourselves. I wouldn't exactly call either of you adults yet. And don't look at me like that, it wasn't my idea. *But* I think it's a good thing." She bounces eagerly on her toes. "This can finally be the push you need to start your game. I know you'll have fun if you try. Look at the color guard dinner! You all had a great time building characters."

I squeeze my eyes shut. Max is going to be coming over *every* Sunday? I don't want to run my first game with him around. But there are only so many LOTR movies we can watch in tense silence, no matter how many extended cuts and BTS footage we add on.

Mom kisses my head. "You should get back inside or there won't be any snacks left for you. Enjoy the first day of your winning season!"

I wait for her to get into the car before walking back. I expected Max to be inside by now, but he's still loitering by the door to the band room, looking at his phone. Part of me wants to stride right past him like he did in the parking lot, but my curiosity gets the better of me.

"Did you blow off the first day of school? Or did you forget to set an alarm?"

He gives me an incredulous look. "It's two in the afternoon. I like to sleep in, but that's extreme even for me."

"So why weren't you at school today?"

"Because I'm not taking classes at Glen Vale."

"What?"

"I'm taking college classes at the local campus in Newark. We figured it was a good way for me to get free college credits this year."

I step back in surprise. I was aware of the concept of going to college during senior year, and had even debated it myself until I learned it would mean missing so much of senior year with Nova, but I hadn't imagined Max would ever do that. He wasn't very studious when he was younger.

"Why was your mom here?" he asks. "Is she at school a lot, bringing you snacks and checking on you?"

I wince, knowing that Mom was literally here to bring me snacks. But that doesn't mean he's allowed to make fun of me over it. "Mom was setting up a first day surprise for the band. She brought in food and drinks for *everyone*. It's something my parents started years ago."

Rather than look shamed, his face screws up even more. "You really do have a perfect life, don't you?"

I huff in annoyance. "Not in the least. Although it sounds like *you* have the great life, getting to skip all the worst parts of school and only coming in for band."

"My schedule does have some big benefits. Like giving me extra time to rehearse." He smiles, but it has an edge to it. "I'm going to need the daily practice to win the MVM award this year."

My eyes bulge. "You're trying for senior MVM?"

"Of course. I'm a senior and I like to win—you already know that about me. I intend to make that award mine, Hazel."

Resentment rises up in me. Is this because he saw my freshman award at the house last night and knows I'm trying to repeat? Or is it just his intense competitiveness coming out? It's impossible to know with Max.

"Well, get in line," I snap back as heat rushes to my cheeks. I hate that he can affect me like this so easily. "I've been working toward that award for the last two years."

"It's not about who wants it the most, it's about who's earned it. And you better believe I'm going to put the work in."

His eyes linger on my face for a moment. Then he tips a nonexistent hat to me and walks away.

Chapter Eleven

Tonight is our first football game, and already I'm losing it. Or, more specifically, losing my keys.

"Sire?"

Mr. Hicks swirls around, looking harried. The band room is a loud, chaotic mess with everyone getting on their uniforms and yelling about ill-fitting gloves and misplaced Dinkles shoes.

"Yes? Is everything okay with the guard?"

"Um, with the guard, yes. Everything's good. It's just that . . ." I swallow. I can't believe I have to admit this. "I've lost the key to our equipment shed."

My cheeks burn with embarrassment. I can't believe I did this when I know how important that key is. Our shed holds everything we need for our competition shows, plus flags from past competitions, parades, and various props. It's even possible that Sire broke the rules by giving me access to school property like this, but he did it because he trusted me and knew Faith wouldn't be around all the time.

And now I have to stand here and watch his expression slacken when he hears that I let him down.

"You *lost* the key? And you're just now telling me? Hazel, we need to be on the field in thirty minutes."

I drop my eyes to the ground. "I know, I'm so sorry. I could have *sworn* I had it—I even saw it with my things when I put them down this afternoon—but I can't find it anywhere. I don't know what happened."

"I should have the master key somewhere . . ." He glances around distractedly, and at least three other people call out to him in distress.

"There's other things I need to take care of first, but Faith should be here soon and she'll have her copy." He frowns. "But I have to say, I'm really disappointed in you. I thought I could trust you to be responsible, and now this happens for our very first show?" He shakes his head. "This better be the last time, okay?"

I nod decidedly. The threat of tears burns my eyes, but as soon as he turns away, I scrub at my face until the feeling is gone. It's bad enough that I can't keep hold of a simple key. I don't need to look like a crybaby when I'm supposed to be helping the rest of my guard.

For once, I'm ecstatic to see Faith arrive. She's more surprised than upset with me about the lost key, and luckily she has her copy so we get our flags just before we're supposed to march onto the field for the national anthem and fight song.

She squeezes my shoulder and whispers, "Everything's

just fine. Now, be strong for your group." Then she gathers us all together and exclaims, "You look spectacular!"

"Everyone's here tonight," Callie whispers. "They're all going to be watching us."

Deja and Keira glance over at the stadium, which is quickly filling with people. Attendance depends on the weather and how well the football team is playing in a given year, but I'm always surprised by the number of people willing to spend their Friday evenings sitting on cold metal bleachers.

"I think I saw Henry and Sam walking in," Rosa whispers.

"Don't worry about it," Devin says. "No one cares about us. Everyone leaves to get concessions when we're playing."

"My mom won't," Li whispers.

"Don't overthink it," Faith says. "This is what you've been preparing for."

Luckily we're stopped from more pep talks because Sire calls us to attention, and we head into the stadium for the start of the game. The sun is low in the sky and the bright stadium lights are on. Cheerleaders line up in front of the bleachers, and the stands are filled with a mix of students and families. Many of the adults are bundled in green-and-white sweatshirts, while the teenagers are happy in their T-shirts. And, of course, there's the group of guys sporting only body paint on their upper halves.

Football is definitely popular in Ohio, but our school doesn't have the money or enrollment to build a really good team. The end zones aren't painted with fancy designs, and there are no balloon arches for the players to run through as they enter the field. But we have a good cheerleading squad, and a very big band, and we manage to get the crowd fired up nonetheless. Of course, it helps that band parents make up a strong contingent of the attendance. As soon as our shoes hit the turf, screams and cheers fill the air.

I scan the crowd and easily find my parents and Kelsey. It's impossible not to see them when they're holding enormous *GO HAZEL!* signs over their heads. I swallow down my nerves. Hopefully Sire and Faith keep the key mishap to themselves. For three years, my parents have watched the color guard struggle. For once, I want to impress them.

The beginning of the game isn't too scary because all the guard needs to do is stand at attention while the band plays the national anthem, then do our simple combos of windmills, figure eights, and carves for the fight song. Then we head to the end zone, where special bleachers have been set up for only the band. Percussion sits near the bottom because many of their instruments are too large to haul up into the stands. And the color guard is expected to sit along the bleacher edges to frame the band. Luckily, Nova and I are well versed in this, so she makes sure to sit at the end of a row so I can sit next to her.

The first half of the game goes fast. I'm used to the usual schedule: cheer and play from the stands during the first half, then a short halftime show, followed by free time during third quarter. We only perform our first competition song, so there's not a lot to mess up, but even those few minutes aren't clean. I see several guard members dropping catches or being out of place and I have to fight to keep a smile on my face. I pray Brody and Max are too busy marching to notice.

I walk with Li over to the concessions when we're released during the third quarter. "Hey, can I talk to you for a second?"

"Is it about that last catch? I know it wasn't as smooth as it could have been, but I promise I'll get better before our competition," Li says, a worried expression on her face. "I'm going to keep practicing every day."

"Oh no, that's not it at all," I reassure her. "I didn't even notice the catch. You're doing awesome."

Li's quickly becoming one of our best members. I can tell how much she's been practicing away from school because every time she comes to rehearsal, things are cleaner than they were the day before. I've even had her help some of the other members, although I don't know how much they appreciated that since she's the only freshman.

"I actually wanted to talk to you about something else entirely," I continue. "Nothing is certain yet, but I've been debating about starting a D&D group, and I wanted to see if you'd be interested in that? Just hypothetically. And, fair warning, I've never run a game before, so I don't want to promise anything."

Since Mom and I talked on Monday, I've kept returning to the idea of running a game. There are a ton of reasons not to do it. The time commitment alone is scary once I factor in the actual game time plus the additional time I'll need to plan out our campaign details. And then there's Max. I'd be a lot more excited about this if he wasn't involved. But I know how much it would mean to Nova for her to finally get to play her ranger after thinking about it for so long. Plus, as the Dungeon Master, I'll be the one in power and I can shut Max down whenever I need to.

I figured it was a good idea to put out some feelers before investing any more thought into the idea. One look at Li tells me that she didn't pay attention to my warning or the idea that this is hypothetical. Her whole face transforms with joy and she starts jumping up and down.

"Are you serious? Like *seriously* serious? You want me to join your group?" She jumps even higher.

I laugh, feeling a bit jumpy myself. "If it actually happens, then absolutely! I've never done this before, but having someone so excited feels like a good start. But again, it's not set in stone yet."

She gives a little shriek, and her glasses almost fly off in her excitement. A few other band members watch us, probably wondering what in the world could be making her this happy. "Omigod, I'd love to! Ooh, can I use the character I made at your house?"

"I don't see why not."

Her excitement is so infectious that I can't help grinning myself. Even my guilt about the lost key and worries about Max feel lighter right now.

"Thank you so much! This is like the coolest thing ever. I promise I'll be a good player!" She claps her hands together. "Who else is playing with us?"

"I'm still working on that, but Nova for sure. She's been bugging me for years about this, so she's all in." I rock back on my heels. "And . . . well, possibly Max."

That stops her short. She freezes mid-jump and her expression falls. "*Percussion* Max?!"

Her voice is loud, much louder than I've ever heard her before. I glance around. There's enough commotion happening around us that most people aren't paying attention, but Max is close by. He's laughing with a few percussion kids, though thankfully not Brody. He narrows his eyes suspiciously at us.

I take her elbow and pull her away a few steps. "I'm not sure about it either," I say in a quieter voice. "That's why I said I didn't want to make any promises. We might only make it one game before we have to kick him out. But our parents are old friends, and they want me to include him."

She glances over my shoulder—where I'm sure Max is glowering at me—and slowly nods. "Okay. I can't imagine it going well, but I don't want to be left out either. Unless he starts being a jerk to me, and then I'm out."

"If he says anything to you—to *any* of us—I'm kicking him out. It's my campaign and my house, so he has to do what I say."

She giggles. "I like the sound of that. Now I kind of hope he does say something just so I can watch that."

"Let's not hope *too* much for that. But you're in?"

"Totally." She pulls me into a quick hug. "I'm going to grab a slice of pizza, do you want to come?"

"You go ahead, I need to find Nova first."

She practically skips away and my heart wobbles. She's so sweet. I hope I haven't just signed her up for a nightmare D&D experience.

I glance around for Nova, eager to tell her the news, but instead Max stalks up to me.

"Were you two just excitedly planning my murder?"

The question is so unexpected that I laugh before I can think better of it. "Yep. I needed an accomplice and Li is *very* excited to lend a hand. You should expect us in three to four business days."

His mouth quirks up into the tiniest of smiles and I feel weirdly triumphant that I can still get that reaction out of him.

"Seriously," he continues, "why was one of your color guard members screaming my name like that? It was disturbing."

I hesitate. I'm still not sure, but I guess I'm going to have to talk to him about it at some point.

"Do you know if your mom is planning to have you come to my house every Sunday from now on?"

Any hint of laughter drops from his expression, and his mouth presses into a straight line. "We're still discussing it."

"So, that's a yes. My mom already said as much."

"I'm sure she did."

I shake my head in annoyance. "What's with you and your vendetta against me and my mom?"

"What's with you and your mom talking about me all the time?"

We both glare at each other for a moment and then I sigh. "You know what, never mind. This was never going to work."

"I have no idea what you're talking about."

"I'd been debating starting a D&D game on Sunday nights. Nova's been asking me to do it, and I thought it might be something you could do with us on Sundays if your mom is forcing you to come. Li was freaking out because I'd just asked her to join as well." I put my hands on my hips. "But it's obviously a horrible idea. I don't want to run a game where one of my players is going to question everything I say, or have constant snide comments, or just be insulting. It's not worth it. You can watch TV downstairs, I'll stay in my room, and our parents will have to deal."

I walk away, shocked by the disappointment welling up inside me. Not because of Max, but because I won't be able to spend this time with Nova and Li. Maybe I can still hold the game some other time when Max isn't around. Fridays and Saturdays are hard right now because of football games and competitions, but once marching band season is over it'll be different. Nova and Li will be sad, but they'll understand that we need to wait.

Max jogs up so that he's standing in front of me, and I'm forced to stop.

"You wanted me to join your D&D game?"

"*Wanted* is the wrong way to phrase that."

"Okay, but you were willing?"

"I was."

His jaw works back and forth, and his eyes study my face. "We always talked about starting a game together."

His words fill me with unexpected emotion. We *had* always talked about it. We spent hours and hours reading the D&D manuals and brainstorming stupid characters and thinking about campaign ideas. I had loved that time together—honestly, I'd loved all our evenings—but the way Max acts now makes it seem like none of that ever happened. It's as if he doesn't even remember it. To hear him acknowledge it now is a gut punch.

"It won't work, Max. We can't get along for more than two seconds."

He looks back at his percussion group as if he's debating something and opens his mouth. Then he closes it and takes a breath instead. "One." Another breath. "Two. There, that was two seconds. Probably even three."

"I . . ." I blink in surprise. "Are you saying you want to be part of the group?"

"I don't know. Maybe. I've never played a tabletop role-playing game before. Although, what are the chances I could get you to run The One Ring instead?"

I throw my hands in the air. Three seconds into this conversation and he's already trying to convince me to change the game I'm running. "No, we're not switching to a Lord of the Rings–themed game just because you might be joining."

"Fine, fine. I like the sound of your game too."

"Good . . . well . . ." Honestly, I don't know what else to say.

Someone calls Max's name, and he looks back over his shoulder.

"I'll give you an answer on Sunday, okay?" he says.

I guess that means he's coming over again.

"Yeah. Okay."

He heads back to his friends, but I stay there, still trying to wrap my head around what just happened.

Chapter Twelve

I wish I could say I'm totally nonchalant over the weekend, listening to my nineties singer-songwriters, playing with my calligraphy pens, and living my best life. But, in truth, I can't relax knowing Max will be here at the house. I keep going over it in my head, and I can't figure out a way for our possible D&D game to be successful. In D&D, the players need to feel free to be silly and vulnerable and to make mistakes without being scared that they'll be laughed at. *I* need to have that flexibility. I was already psyching myself out about DMing even before we threw Max into the mix. So, I've decided the game is off the table (somewhat literally) unless he can convince me that I can trust him. And he's not up to that challenge.

I take my time coming downstairs after hearing Melanie and Max arrive. His mom's high-pitched voice is very recognizable, but I'm not going to rush around my own house for him. It's a good five minutes before I finally saunter down.

Max is standing in our living room, looking at the "marching band altar" he'd noticed last Sunday. He's wearing tight black jeans and a black Nirvana shirt that hangs on him perfectly. His hair is wet and curling into waves that fall over his forehead and into his eyes. Everything about him screams "drummer," and unfortunately the whole look *really* works on me.

He glances at me. "I see you've decided to grace me with your presence. I'm honored."

I open my mouth, then immediately change my mind. Nope. Not today. I don't care how good this boy looks, I'm not dealing with his attitude. I turn back around and head for my room.

"Wait, hold on," he calls. "You can't go, we have stuff to talk about."

"No, we don't," I retort. "The idea of us sitting around a table for hours every week, talking and joking and throwing out ideas is laughable. You can't stand me, and I don't want to open myself up to any more insults *or* put Nova and Li in the extremely awkward position of being our mediators. The discussion's over."

His jaw drops open. "You can't just decide that."

"I'm the DM and it's decided."

"Just because things aren't working out perfectly for you doesn't mean—"

"When do things work out perfectly for me?"

He gestures around the house. "Uh, always?"

"Max, don't pretend like you know me or my life *at all*." I take a step closer and jab him in the chest with my index finger. "You waltz back into town and into my house as if you know everything, and I'm over it. How could you ever expect me to include you in this game when you can't even talk to me like I'm a human being?"

He wraps his hand around my finger and tugs slightly so it's pressing harder into his chest. "Then let's talk," he whispers. "What do you want to know?"

My pulse leaps. "Everything."

"You want to know everything?" His chest rises and falls. "Then why don't you start by asking me something specific?"

This is a game. It has to be. Some sort of competition I don't understand, because why else would he be watching me so intently now? Why else would he be touching me? I want to wrench away from him and call him names and leave him standing here alone, but somehow I think that would mean I'd lost.

And I don't ever plan on losing to Max again.

I step closer, so that only a few inches separate us, and lift my chin defiantly. "When did we go from being best friends to *this,* Max? Why don't you start with that. Because I was heartbroken when you moved away, and it seems like you're heartbroken to be back."

That does the trick. He jerks away from me and breaks eye contact. His jaw works back and forth, and for a second I think I've finally shut him up.

"I am," he says quietly. "But not in the way you think."

"Then enlighten me."

His gaze shifts around the house suspiciously. "How soundproof is your basement?"

He makes a fair point. I'd hope that our parents are too engrossed in their game to eavesdrop on us, but I can't guarantee it.

"Maybe we should go back outside."

We walk in silence to the trampoline. He sits down in the middle, but I stay on the far edge so I can jump down as soon as he says something rude. He rubs the heels of his hands over his eyes and sighs deeply.

"You want to know everything, huh? Fine. What do you know about my parents?"

I shake my head. "That they're separated. And that they played D&D with my parents until you had to move because of your dad's new job."

"That was a lie. We moved because my parents were fighting all the time. I guess Dad thought moving closer to his family might help, and he did get a job he really liked there. Once we moved, things got a little better. Mom and Dad both loved the new house, and everything was . . . stable. Or maybe I just wanted to believe that." He blows out a breath, still keeping his gaze away from me. "And then, all of a sudden last month, Mom announced she was separating from Dad, and I had to choose who I was going to live with. I had no idea it was coming—it felt like someone had punched me in the throat when she told me. I've never seen Dad that angry either. It was horrible."

I look down at my Lilith Fair concert shirt rather than make eye contact. The weight of his words are heavy enough that I feel like I'm being pressed deeper into this dusty trampoline.

"Once we got here," he continues, "I finally got up the

courage to ask Mom what happened. Like, how had they gone from being okayish to being separated so quickly? And that's when she told me that she'd gotten back in touch with your mom, and their conversations were what convinced her to leave."

I lean back in shock. "I . . . My mom . . . *What?*"

My mind spins at the idea. Granted, I don't know what was going on with his parents, and Mom does tend to get into everyone's business, but this seems extreme even for her.

"Ever since, I can't stop thinking about you and your mom and how happy your family has always been. Just the same as you were years ago with your big Sunday game nights and parents who can drop everything to bring you a lunch or volunteer for the school or bend over backward to make sure you never need a thing. I wish I had a life that was even a fraction like that." He shakes his head. "I know how close you are to your mom, Hazel. And the idea that she might have mentioned something—that you might have known my parents were separating before I knew—it's haunted me." He sucks in a deep breath. "Tell me the truth. Did she say anything at all to you?"

I sit back in shock. Part of me wants to scream at him for all his baseless assumptions about my life and family. But the expression on his face . . . he looks utterly broken. He had his anger before, and now I can see that was his armor. Without it, there's nothing left behind but misery.

"Max." I lean forward and say the next words cautiously. "I didn't know anything about your parents. I swear it."

He squeezes his eyes shut and then nods, very slowly.

"My mom and I . . . we aren't the way we used to be. And my life is far from perfect."

"It seems pretty perfect to me," he whispers, but there's no heat or accusation to his words now.

"That's only because you're looking at my life from the outside."

He tilts his head up to the sky, and his Adam's apple bobs. "Maybe I don't want to be on the outside anymore."

I stare at him for a second, my heart racing from his confession, then lie back on the trampoline. It's dirty and hot from baking in the summer sun, but it's still easier to look up at the clouds than at his expression. After a moment, he follows my lead and lies down next to me.

"I'm not saying I have a bad life," I say quietly. "I don't. I have a really good life, I know that, and I'm grateful for it. But my parents—Mom especially—they just have such big hopes for me. And whatever happens, there's always something more I should be working toward. I've never been able to live up to their expectations. So this year is it. It's my last chance. I need the guard to be the strongest it's ever been, and I need to win the MVM award."

"*You* need to or *they* need you to?"

"I need to . . . or, I don't know, maybe it's both. But if you think Kelsey and I sit around with our parents every night singing songs and telling each other all our secrets and dreams, you're sorely mistaken. Mostly I spend my time in my bedroom to get away from the pressure."

I bite the inside of my cheek and wait for him to say something snarky. But he doesn't. We just lie there in silence and watch the clouds pass by.

“This isn’t going to stop me from competing with you in band,” he says finally.

“I wouldn’t expect you to.”

“And the bet is still on. I have no interest in embarrassing myself trying to learn your choreography.”

“And I’m not cleaning the men’s restroom.”

There’s another beat of silence, and then Max clears his throat.

“But . . . I’m sorry. I was jealous and angry, and I took it out on you.” I can feel the moment he turns his face toward mine. “Does that count as telling you everything?”

I shouldn’t turn to meet his gaze. Our faces will be too close, and it’ll be awkward and weird.

But I do it anyway.

His dark hair is falling across his eyes, and his expression is contrite in a way I’ve never seen before. Heat floods through me at his nearness. I know I can’t trust him—not after everything we’ve said and done to each other in the past few weeks. But, at least in this moment, I can’t find it in myself to hate him either. Not when I can *almost* see the boy I used to be half in love with. My skin flushes and I sit up quickly.

“You’re really gunning for this D&D game, huh?”

He chuckles and sits up next to me. “You know I’ve always wanted to play. I could never find anyone at my last school. Although I do have some stipulations.”

“I haven’t agreed to let you play yet. Don’t get ahead of yourself.”

“Listen, let’s be real. You need me. You clearly don’t have a huge list of people lining up to join D&D, or you and Nova would already have a game going on. As it is, you only have Nova and Li, and that's not enough for a very fun campaign."

I screw up my face in defiance. Max may have a point, but I'm not going to let him know that.

"And if you think about it, this whole thing isn't actually fair to me." He stands and starts bouncing on the balls of his feet. I stand as well so I can easily scramble off this trampoline if needed. "Right now the party will consist of your best friend, who I'm sure you've turned against me, and one of your color guard members, who clearly already hates me if her horror-filled screech on Friday is to be believed."

He starts jumping higher and I follow suit, not wanting to be left behind. "And could you blame Li? She had to wash her clothes three times to get the vinegar scent out."

He has the audacity to laugh. "I mean, come on. That was a *little* funny, right? I chuckled the entire time I was filling those balloons."

"It was not funny, and you are not helping your cause."

"All I'm saying is that there needs to be some equality to the party. Some balance."

"If you're about to suggest Brody as a possible player, I will push you off this trampoline and ban you from the house."

"I'd like to see you try." He smiles in a cocky way, and I'm so tempted, but then he puts out his hands in defense. "No, not Brody. He doesn't care about gaming. I was thinking about Felix Jackson."

I hesitate and bring his face to mind. He's the younger snare player I've seen hanging out with Max on a few occasions. He's percussion, so that's a big hit against him, but I don't remember him being overtly aggressive or rude, unlike some of the other players.

"Isn't he pretty quiet?"

Max nods. "Definitely. He's a cool kid, no matter what you might assume, and I think he'd be interested in learning to play. Plus he's struggling to find his place in band."

My thoughts go to Li. I'd almost respect Max for looking out for the younger members of his section, but I'm still too nervous about this arrangement he's proposing.

"So, you're saying the group would be split—you and Felix and then Nova and Li."

"I don't think it's a good sign if the DM is already envisioning the party being split down the middle. Haven't you watched the livestream of *Don't Split the Party*? If not, you need to remedy that."

"Actually, I have. I'm sorry, it's just hard to imagine everyone suddenly getting along."

"But we aren't ourselves when we're at the table. We're playing characters, right? So it shouldn't be a problem."

I take a deep breath and try to consider this from a neutral mindset. If the roles were reversed, I'd want a friend at the game table with me too. And if everyone is willing to lay down their weapons when they come to the table (and pick up fictional ones instead), then this could possibly work.

"When we're playing, there won't be any band politics or sarcastic comments or infighting," I say, pointing at him. "We all have to make a commitment to the group and be loyal to the rest of the players. Are you going to be able to do that?"

He stops jumping suddenly, which makes his knees buckle.

"I'm looking forward to it." His voice sounds sincere. I still don't know if I can trust him, but I guess we could give it one try and see how it goes.

"*One* session," I say and hold up a single finger for emphasis. "And I reserve the right to cancel if it doesn't go well."

His face breaks into a huge goofy grin, and my chest tightens at the sight. I know that grin. I used to love that grin.

"Finally something we can agree on."

Chapter Thirteen

Next Saturday morning, the band loads onto school buses headed to the next town over, where the local high school is running an invitational competition. This is the first of our three local contests, and I'm crossing my fingers that the band can squeak out a Superior rating today so that we know we've already made state and can relax. Really though, as long as percussion doesn't win best in show today, I'll be happy.

Band members are allowed to sit on whichever bus we want, so Nova and I make sure to avoid the percussion section. We head toward the back with the other seniors and settle into a seat together like always. It's weird, but riding the bus with Nova might be one of my favorite parts of band. It certainly keeps us entertained. Some people might think band kids are total dorks, but our buses are no joke. There are more people making out, making up, or breaking up on a band bus than almost anyplace else. The key is to sit far away from the chaperone and keep your eyes to yourself. No one wants to see what goes on under the lap blankets on the bus, especially when we're driving back in the dark.

Nova and I spend the next thirty minutes trying to predict how this D&D game tomorrow is likely to go.

"I'm not sure I've ever spoken to Felix," she says.

"Me either. Though I don't get the impression he speaks much at all."

She sighs. "I know I was the one begging you to start this game, but now I'm nervous. This could fall apart really quick."

"Agreed. But I love having an excuse for you to come over every Sunday. That alone makes it worth it."

"Hopefully. I wonder—"

She cuts off at the first sound of musical notes. Behind us, a few trumpets have started singing their parts of our opening song. Nova gives me a grin and twists around toward them. Then a trombone sings his bass notes, and two junior flute players lend their voices as well. A tuba player tries her best to hit her low notes and there must be a percussion player or two hidden on this bus because someone is hitting the seats like they're drums. I glance around, wondering if Max snuck on here somehow, but I don't see him. It's almost too bad since I bet he'd nail the drum solo. I push thoughts of him from my mind. The less focus on Max today, the better.

Instead, I climb onto my knees so I can see over the seats to the other band members. Soon, the entire band bus is singing their parts of the show songs at the top of their lungs. A mixture of excitement and nostalgia fills me. It's an informal tradition for Glen Vale to sing our performance show on the way to a competition. There isn't much I can do to help out, but I do mark our choreography from my seat and eagerly nod along with the music.

As they get to the end of *Night on Bald Mountain*, people start to lose the rhythm a bit. Nova shoots up in the middle of the aisle. "*One,* two, three, four," she calls and starts conducting them as if she's a field commander rather than section leader of the clarinets. Our actual field commanders must be on the other bus since no one jumps in to help, but Nova gets them back on track quickly. Honestly, she could have been an amazing drum major if she'd wanted it, but when I asked she said she'd rather play her clarinet than conduct the entire band. And now she has a gorgeous solo in our show, so it was probably a smart call.

We're still humming and laughing when we file off the bus. We get our instruments and flags, and Sire finds a place for us to rehearse in the grass next to the high school. At least five other high school bands, including some from our competition class, have staked out space close by, and it's intimidating to see everyone decked out in their uniforms, standing in circles with their plumed hats by their feet, as they run through their music a few more times.

Faith is with us for the entire day, but rather than feeling calm knowing that she's here to oversee everything, I'm aggravated. Whenever she's with us, she has us doing different warm-ups or rehearsing in a way we aren't used to, and it confuses everyone. But since she's our guard director and technically a real grown-up, I can't exactly tell her she's doing it wrong. I take her direction, but I'm sweating—literally and metaphorically. It doesn't help that it's almost ninety degrees, and it's clear that our guard isn't ready for this competition.

"—right, Hazel?"

I snap my attention to Faith. I'd been studying Oak Grove High School, Max's old band, across the field from us. They're massive, with tons of funding and support from their community, and their guard is stellar every year. Even in practice, their flags are perfectly synchronized.

"Right," I repeat back to Faith. "Uh, what was that again?"

She gives me a sharp look. "I was saying that the most important thing is to keep your eyes on your own paper, go out there with your chin high, and try your best. This is only the first competition. We have more to come, and you don't want to stress yourself out before the performance."

I frown. Maybe we *need* to be stressing a little more rather than being so chill about everything. How are we going to get better if no one cares about the results?

"Yes, we definitely want to try our best," I say and take a step toward the rest of the guard. "But that means we need to be *clean* out there. Everyone has things they can be more aware of. Keira, I noticed you tend to get off count when you're in the back field during the push. Really pay attention to that today. And Yori, you tend to lag—"

"Actually, you know what," Faith interrupts, "we really should start warm-ups. Everyone, head over there under that tree and start stretching. I need Hazel's help with the flags. We'll be right back."

She jerks her head toward the buses and I follow uncertainly.

When we're far enough away that they can't see us anymore, she stops and puts a hand on her hip.

"They won't know what to do." I look back over my shoulder. "I always lead the warm-ups."

"It's *stretching,* Hazel. I'm sure they can figure it out." I start to argue, but she holds up a hand. "You've got to cool it. I know it's important to you that the group does well, but did you even see their faces? They're scared. For some of them, this is their first time ever performing in a competition. Calling out their mistakes by name is not going to help them."

"But pretending like all they need to do is 'try their best' isn't helping either. I'm not sure if you've realized this yet, but their best isn't good enough."

Faith pinches the bridge of her nose and takes a breath. "No one is at their best yet. It's the first competition."

Just then, Max's voice booms in the distance. "Good luck?!"

"All day!" the rest of the percussion calls back.

I stifle a groan at their stupid cheer, as well as the fact that when they start playing a moment later, they sound stellar. I swallow down my rising anxiety. What if percussion actually manages to get best percussion today and win our bet? Not only will we be cleaning the men's toilets at the end of the season (I have to squeeze my eyes shut so I don't gag), we'll have an entire season of them rubbing it in our faces too. We have to get better ASAP. I need to find a way to help them.

"I want you to take a deep breath." Faith puts a hand on my arm. "What the group needs right now is to have a captain who is cool, calm, and collected. Be a role model for them, okay?"

I bite my lip and nod. "Yeah, okay."

I swear, I really try. I act calm, I smile, I do everything right . . . but it doesn't matter. Within the first minute, I can tell we won't be winning any trophies today. The beginning measures of our show start spooky and a bit chaotic, as the band mimics the sounds of storm winds blowing through the football field and the color guard erratically waves our huge lightning bolt–shaped flags. We're trying to set the mood for *Night on Bald Mountain* and also show a sharp contrast between the frenzied "storm" in our first minute followed by us snapping to attention a minute later. When the band hits their first few notes with full power and volume, it's essential that every member of the guard hit our choreography with matching synchronization. Unfortunately, we do the opposite.

The guard isn't listening to the music well enough, and they get off count—though it doesn't help that the band gets off count a few times as well. My adrenaline spikes and I call out the counts to whoever can hear me, hoping that will be enough to get them back on track. I can't call out the moves to everyone, though. Our show requires us to move constantly throughout the field, often separated by large sections of the band.

Then, to my horror, I see that Keira accidentally grabbed the wrong flag from behind our prop screen on the field.

We've practiced this exchange so much already, but somehow Keira is performing the second song with a gold-and-red flag, while everyone else has purple. I'm screaming internally, but I keep a smile on my face like it was totally planned that way.

I see urinal cakes in my future, though.

The next forty-five minutes in the stands are misery. The whole band waits for the results to be announced at the end of the competition. I have no hope for color guard, but I'm praying that percussion had a bad day as well. Max catches my eye as he climbs the bleachers with the rest of his percussion friends. Neither of us says anything, but we don't glare or throw barbs at each other, so I'll take it.

The announcer eventually begins to list the awards. Nova's shoulder presses against my own as we wait. There are only four Class AA bands—a category for large schools—in this competition, so surely we'll at least get a trophy. But as the announcer continues through the awards, we realize we're in fourth place. Out of *four* bands? Murmurs and cries from others rise up around me. Maybe the color guard has a history of struggling in competition, but the band is always good.

"And the award for Best Overall Auxiliary goes to . . . Oak Grove High School!"

Nova groans next to me, but I only feel a tinge of disappointment. If we can't manage to get matching flags on the field, it's pretty obvious we aren't winning best in show awards today. Plus, Oak Grove has won almost every competition I've ever been a part of. It's no surprise they'd win again today.

"Our next award for Best Overall Percussion goes to . . . Oak Grove High School again!"

To our left, Oak Grove shrieks in excitement, and for once I'm tempted to stand up and join them. Thank *god,* at least we haven't lost our bet to Max and Brody yet. I hesitate, then glance behind me to where Max is sitting. His shoulders are slumped, and he looks totally dejected. I almost feel bad for him . . . until I remind myself of how much I don't want to clean bathrooms. Max lifts his head to find me staring. He presses his lips into a thin line and nods slowly. I return the gesture. We don't speak, but I know what he's trying to say. *Next time.*

The announcer continues until finally it's time for him to list all the bands who have qualified for state today by earning a Superior rating at the competition. While I know the guard won't be getting a Superior rating for our specific performance, we will still be set for state as long as the overall band gets a Superior.

"The bands who have qualified for state at this competition are River View High School, Laurelburg High School, Twin Valley High School, and Oak Grove High School! Congratulations on your impressive work today, and a huge thank-you to all the schools for coming out and performing. Thank you for attending and please drive safely!"

Wait . . . seriously? We didn't qualify?

Around us, chatter begins as the crowd stands and moves toward the exits, but Glen Vale doesn't move. After a moment, Sire gestures for us to follow him. Mom, Dad, and Kelsey call to me from the crowd and I give a half-hearted wave in return. I hate seeing the strained expressions on their faces, as if they want to cringe but are smiling for my benefit. It was a waste of time for them to even come here today.

“We knew this was a rebuilding year,” Sire calls once everyone is huddled together by the band buses. The others are buzzing around me with a combination of angry and depressed whispers. “It seems that some of the judges were not as impressed with our musicality as I was hoping, which is why they gave us an Excellent today. But all this means is that we have to keep working harder than ever during rehearsals to make sure we qualify for state. We have two more competitions, including one a week from today. We’ll make it happen.”

Keep working harder.

Sure. But how far will that get us? I have no doubt the band will earn a Superior next time. They’ve done it a billion times before and they’ll figure it out this time too. But for the guard? I don’t know how to fix us in time.

Chapter Fourteen

Despite my color guard worries, I'm able to knock out my homework early on Sunday so I can spend the rest of the day obsessing about the D&D game tonight. Originally, I thought about using a pre-made campaign, which would make things much easier, but if I'm going to finally be a Dungeon Master then I really want to *do* it. Mom never uses pre-made campaigns. She says she likes doing something unique and using her creativity.

It's intimidating, though. Not only do I need to know what the storyline is and have my non-player characters figured out so I can role-play them myself, I also need to know the rules for how the others will play. What if someone plays a sorcerer and I have to know all their possible spells and how they could affect encounters with the monsters I have them fight? Or what if someone misunderstands what their character is capable of and I don't catch it? And, of course, that fear has ratcheted up knowing that Max and Felix are joining the game. The very last thing I want is to screw up in front of them or have one of them point out my mistakes.

I'm knee-deep in research when Mom pokes her head into the dining room. I've stolen her usual D&D prep space so we have a table for our game, but she and Dad are too thrilled about me DMing to complain.

"Still working away?" She looks over my shoulder at my open *Monster Manual.* "You're going to be a great DM just like you're a great guard captain."

I wince. I'd rather not be reminded of band right now. In fact, if I'm being honest, that's one of the reasons I've thrown myself into prepping today. If I'm thinking about D&D, then it's easier to forget how my other big commitment is failing.

"Everything takes time," Mom continues. "Yesterday was the first competition. You learn from it, and you grow. The same thing with this game—today will be your first time and everything won't go perfectly and that's okay."

I nod and keep my eyes glued to my manual. I know she's right, it's a process and I'm sure I'll mess up today. But all I can hear is her saying: *You're not good enough yet. Maybe, if you keep working, and try really hard, you'll suck a little less. But not yet.*

There's a knock on the door and then Melanie calls hello in her high-pitched voice. Moments later both she and Max are visible at the edge of the dining room.

"Hope you don't mind that we let ourselves in," she says.

"Not at all! You're always welcome," Mom replies and gestures to Max. "What's all this?"

Melanie glances fondly at him. He's looking a bit helpless

while holding two bulging grocery bags. "Oh, we brought some food for dinner. I figured it was only fair since you're going to have a whole group of teenagers in the house. And Max insisted on supplies for nachos."

I frown. He insisted on nachos?

"Do you need help getting it all ready?" Melanie asks him.

Max shakes his head. "Thanks, but we got it. Don't worry." His voice is so warm with his mom that I barely recognize it.

She kisses him on the cheek and gestures for my mom to come to her side. "Sounds like we have some time to get caught up, then." They both laugh and wave before heading to the basement.

I expect Max to have a snarky comment about our moms sharing more secrets, but he doesn't. He's being weirdly silent and it's freaking me out. After a moment, I scramble up and wave him toward the kitchen. He drops the bags onto the counter and pulls a family-sized bag of tortilla chips, a package of ground beef, and two kinds of shredded cheese from the first bag.

I lean against the counter and survey him. "Okay, what's your deal?"

"I don't have a deal. I'm just . . . on my best behavior."

"Your best behavior is absolute silence?" I laugh. "Actually, I can work with that."

He rolls his eyes and takes out more supplies, including salsa, sour cream, and an avocado. "I'm trying tonight."

"And I appreciate it, but you're so serious and quiet. Why don't you try . . ." I pause to think. "Try channeling that thirteen-year-old version of yourself that used to eat half the shredded cheese out of the bag every time we'd make nachos here."

His mouth drops in horror. "That Max was a total dork."

"I'm not arguing." I smile and dump the ground beef into a skillet. "But he was also fun and goofy, and that's the goal. Although, if we can get through tonight without a full-blown fight, I'll still take it as a success."

"Is that a challenge?"

His eyes are glimmering with excitement, and it sends a jolt of heat shooting down my spine. I don't know what to do with Max when he looks at me like this, with his arms crossed over his Radiohead shirt and the corner of this mouth twitching with amusement. It reminds me too much of the past and my old feelings for him.

"Everything is a challenge with us, but fine." I put out my right hand to shake on it. "Whoever is the first to say something rude tonight loses."

"You're on." His hand wraps around my own and flutters dance through my belly. "The loser has to bring food for the next game."

There's a knock at the door and I run over to find Li on the porch, shifting her weight and chewing on her hair.

"Hey, come in! And you don't need to wait in the future, feel free to just walk into the house." I usher her into the kitchen where Max is adding the taco seasoning to the beef. "So, obviously you two know each other, in a manner of speaking, but I don't think you've ever been formally introduced. Li, this is Max. And Max, this is my friend and fellow color guard member, Li."

Max smiles and waves. "Nice to officially meet you. And sorry about the vinegar."

Her eyes dart to me and back to him. "Uh, hi."

Just then the front door opens again. Nova walks into the kitchen, Felix trailing behind her. "We ran into each other as we were walking in." She surveys the room. "So, the gang's all here?"

"Yep."

We stand in an awkward circle, glancing around at each other like we're in a standoff and someone's about to pull a weapon. I try smiling at Felix, but it probably looks like I'm grimacing in pain. Which is the truth because inside I'm wound up so tightly that my body is one big cramp. This is exactly what I was afraid of. Tonight is destined for disaster.

Nova catches my eye and lifts her eyebrows meaningfully. *Right.* I'm the Dungeon Master, so I guess it's my duty to get us on course.

I clear my throat and step forward. "Clearly there's some tension right now. And that's understandable, but everyone should know that Max and I talked, and we've agreed on a full truce during D&D nights. No fighting, no competitions, no betting—"

"Except for our bet about no fighting—"

"That's not—" I shake my head. "Anyway, when we're here, we aren't representing color guard or percussion or clarinets. We're not band members at all." I glance around at them. "We're just five people who are going to role-play some characters, fight some monsters, and hopefully have a good time."

"And eat nachos," Max adds and gestures to the stove.

"The ground beef should be almost ready, so grab a plate and make what you'd like."

If my speech didn't dissolve the tension in the air, the mention of food does the trick. Felix makes a beeline for it and soon everyone is crunching on big plates of nachos.

Felix adjusts his glasses. "Thanks for accepting me into the group, Hazel."

"Yeah, thank you," Li says with a head bob. "Although I haven't played before, so don't be too hard on me."

"None of us have played before," I say. "Which either makes this group a great choice or a total nightmare. But we won't know until we try. So . . . shall we?"

They exchange nervous looks before following me into the dining room.

Chapter Fifteen

Everyone finds a seat at the table, Max and Felix sitting on my right side, Li and Nova on my left, and me at the head. They turn to me expectantly and I swallow tightly from behind the DM screen, a trifold plastic barrier sitting in front of me on the table. The reality of being a Dungeon Master—and possibly making a huge fool of myself—looms larger than ever in my mind.

"Okay, well . . . welcome. Thanks for coming. Nova and Li, I know you both have characters already created. Maybe we should start by having you introduce them to us?"

Li slides deeper into her chair like she can disappear, but Nova leans forward eagerly. "I'd *love* to. You don't know how long I've been waiting for this or how long I've harassed Hazel to get us here. Thank you all for agreeing to play." She puts her palms on the table. "Okay, I'm playing a gnome ranger named Stump. She's a total introvert and hates most people and crowds. She'd much rather be tromping through the wilderness than having a conversation, but she'll make exceptions for a few people."

"She sounds like someone I know," I interrupt with a wink at her.

"Yes, she and I *might* share a few characteristics. But she does have a love in her life, and that's the animal companion she can have as a ranger. Zelda is a very large dog, and Stump travels by riding on his back since she's so small."

"Zelda?" Felix asks with raised eyebrows.

"It was my choice for our family dog's name, but my parents overruled me. I was very into the game."

"I didn't realize rangers could have animal companions," Li says, her eyes bright with excitement. "That sounds so cool."

"Do you want to explain why you've loved this character build for so long?" I ask.

Nova grins. "Because Zelda is based on my real-life dog, Zoinks. Don't judge that name either—my parents are big Scooby-Doo fans." She pulls out her cell phone and passes it around so the others can see a photo of Zoinks. Nova loves her dog more than any human, including her parents, and I can't blame her. Zoinks may very well be the cutest dog in the history of dogs.

Li squeals so loud when she sees the picture that my ears ring. "Your dog is so fluffy!"

"He's an Old English sheepdog, which means my family spends half our lives brushing him, but it's worth it." Nova's expression softens like it only does for Zoinks.

"Can you bring him to our games?" Li looks between

Nova and me like we're her parents and she's asking for extra birthday presents.

"I . . . um . . ." Nova glances at me for help.

"Well, I guess I'll need to double-check with my parents, but they've always loved Zoinks, so I can't imagine they'll mind. Do you think he'd be okay here?"

She chuckles. "He'd be beside himself with happiness. And beside all of you because he'd need constant petting—he loves new people. And smells."

"I love dogs," Felix says.

"It's decided, then," Max says with a nod. "Our campaign is already better than everyone else's since we have a dog companion. And a real one at that."

Everything's a competition with him, but I have to agree. Having Zoinks here for future games will be so fun. Plus, no one can be angry or fighting with him here. He'll be like our D&D therapy dog.

"I guess I can go next, then?" Li asks tentatively.

She pivots between anxiety and excitement so quickly. I hope she can gain more confidence before this year is out.

When we nod encouragingly, she shifts in her seat and pulls out a notebook. "So, when I was here for the section dinner with Hazel, we all made D&D characters, and I made an elf druid named Ellywich."

"You did that together?" Felix says. "That actually sounds fun."

Of course he'd be shocked that the color guard does anything enjoyable. I swallow down my annoyance, but then Max elbows him and Felix sits up straighter.

"I didn't know you did that with the guard," Max says. "That's a really cool idea."

I blink, but once again there's no sarcastic follow-up. It's weird . . . and nice.

"I've been thinking about her ever since," Li continues, "and I think she's a gardener and farmer. She loves growing food for her family and having others over so she can cook for them. She gets up early and stays outside as long as she can every day, and the only reason she comes back in is to cook what she's grown. But, uh, if that doesn't work for this game then I can change it and do something else."

Nova and I shake our heads immediately. "No, don't change it. That's great," I say.

Her cheeks get pink. "And, um, she looks like this." Li pushes a paper into the middle of the table, and everyone leans over to see a gorgeous purple-haired elf wearing orange overalls and holding a huge basket of produce.

"Whoa," Nova says.

"Did you draw that yourself?" Felix asks.

"Yeah. I drew all the guard characters too. I'm happy to draw yours as well. I mean, if that's something you think you'd want."

"Um yes," Nova says immediately. "Although mostly I want a picture of Zelda."

"That's awesome, Li. Thank you," I say. "Felix, how about you? Did you get a chance to think about a character?"

"Uh . . ." He looks down at his phone and then back up. "I took some notes, but I should redo it. Or I could skip this session if it takes too much time."

"But you said before you were pumped for your character," Max argues.

Felix rubs the back of his neck. "It's just . . . this is totally weird, but I actually created an elf druid as well." He glances up at Li and there's a moment of recognition between them. Like they hadn't quite seen each other until right now. "But we can't have two of the same character when there are only four of us, and Li came up with hers earlier—"

"No, it's fine," I say at the same time that Li says, "I can make a new character if you need me to."

"No one needs to make a new character," I interrupt. "It's a little unusual, maybe, but druids are a versatile class. The party will need magic users and healers. I think it can work. In fact, I bet it could add a fun new dimension to the party. Maybe . . ." I hesitate, knowing what a huge ask this is. "Only if you want, but maybe you two could chat sometime about your character backstories? Or text each other if that's easier?"

"That would make sense," Nova says. "Maybe your characters could share some early experiences or even know each other?"

Li and Felix lock eyes across the table and I hold my breath. I know how nervous Li has been. But Felix nods and she gives him a tentative smile.

"Yeah, we could probably do that," she says.

Whew. Okay, so far so good. I glance at Max and try to swallow down my anxiety. "Well, last but not least, what do you have, Max?"

"I'm playing Axolotl."

My stomach flips and I turn more fully toward him. "From . . . the characters we created in junior high?"

"I didn't know you knew each other before," Felix says.

"We hung out when we were younger before he moved away," I explain quickly before turning back to Max. "How do you still remember that?"

He looks incredulous. "The same way you do. You had Axolittle and I had Axolotl. They're some of my favorite things I've ever created. There's no way I'm playing some random character when I can play Axolotl, the dragonborn fighter who wields his two—" He points to me.

"Axes," I say to the rest of the group.

The others chuckle at the silly gimmick name, but I'm shaken that he's held on to that for so long. I never would have guessed that he cared that much. Granted, Max had fallen off the couch laughing when we thought up the characters, but he'd been a dorky thirteen-year-old, so the bar for making him laugh like that was low.

"Okay, well it sounds like we have our party, so . . . I guess we should get started." More anxiety rolls through me. They're all looking at me eagerly, and it hits me how this whole thing rests on my shoulders. Sure, they have to do their own role-playing, but ultimately the game can't continue unless I can hold my own. I'm grateful that the DM screen is there to hide my jittery hands.

We spend a little time making sure that everyone has complete character sheets and stats and then move into the actual campaign.

"All right, we start in a wide-open field outside the city

of Darkthorn. You are all part of an enormous crowd that's formed around a large wooden stage. Each of you is here to attend the Darkthorn music festival, one of the most well-known festivals in the land."

"You have us at a concert?" Max asks. "Are all of the performers women?"

I blush. "Actually, yes."

When I created this opening, I figured I should choose something that would be in my repertoire. I haven't been to many concerts or music festivals, but I've always thought how cool it would be to have gone to Lilith Fair, an all-female concert tour in the nineties. So, I took that as the inspiration.

The others ask questions about the details of what everything looks like, and what types of people are around, but I anticipated this and am able to answer everything.

"The final act comes onto the stage, and the crowd surges forward," I say, adding urgency to my voice. "Just then, there's a rustle in the surrounding forest, and an enormous opossum comes barreling toward the crowd. It's as tall as a person and has glowing red eyes and vicious, long teeth."

Everyone sits back in surprise, and I smile to myself. I'd seen giant badgers listed as monsters, so I figured I'd use that as a template.

"People begin to scream and run away in any direction they can."

"Not me," Max says confidently. "I'm dragonborn. An *opossum* isn't going to scare me."

I knew he'd react that way. "The opossum swipes at another concertgoer who gets too close, and they go flying into the air. Do the rest of you stay where you are or run?"

“We’re staying,” Nova says.

“I figured. Then it’s time for our first initiative roll to see who goes first for this battle.” We each roll a d20—our first time doing this together—which makes everyone grin.

“All right, time to finally do some damage with these axes,” Max announces once we determine that he’s going first. He gets a 19 on his attack roll, which means he definitely hits, and gets a high roll for damage as well.

I do some calculations behind my screen while Max and Felix high-five.

“That damage is enough that the opossum falls to the ground dead,” I announce.

“That’s how it’s done!” he shouts. “One blow from me is all it takes. Wait, don’t opossums have pouches? Do you think it could be storing anything of value in there? I want to loot the body.”

“You can certainly try.”

Nova eyes me suspiciously. “Are we sure this thing is actually dead?”

Aw man, she knows my expressions too well. “Actually, all of a sudden it pops back up and turns its red eyes on you again, Max.”

“But you said it was dead!”

“It was only *playing* dead,” Felix says with a laugh.

“An extra fun reason to use it as a monster.” I turn to Max. “I believe the deranged opossum is coming for you.”

The party spends the rest of the game fighting off the giant opossum and then a giant raccoon that appears, although that one gets away and runs back into the forest. They also question a few non-player characters about whether this is the first time a creature like this has been sighted and any reasons why it might be attacking. To my utter delight and relief, there's no hint of tension or animosity as we get deeper into the session. The group is completely absorbed, especially when the raccoon gets away, and that helps me fall into my role instead of analyzing every word out of my mouth. I'm particularly proud of having the raccoon escape so that they'll want to follow its trail into the forest to get to our first dungeon crawl—a quintessential D&D adventure.

I can tell they'd like to continue, but we won't have time to get far before my parents finish their game and kick everyone out. So, we call it there and pack up.

Li pulls me into a hug by the front door on her way out. "Hazel, that was the most fun I've had in forever."

"Yeah, thanks," Felix agrees. "I'm glad to be included." He's more subdued than Li, but he seems to mean it.

Nova hugs me next. "You did an awesome job. I'm so glad we finally did this." She drops her voice and whispers in my ear, "And you managed to make it the whole night without fighting. Well done."

"No one's more surprised than me."

I wave goodbye to the others as Max comes up beside me.

"This was a new experience. I think we both managed to lose our bet today."

I'm surprised by the warmth in his expression. If I didn't know better, I'd almost think he was looking at me as if I was a friend.

"Or maybe we both won?"

"I like that explanation better. Although now we don't know who's bringing food for next Sunday." He shoves his hands into his pockets. "Assuming there's still going to be another session?"

"The group needs to figure out what happened to the raccoon. I wouldn't deny you that."

"Cool." His smile does something to my brain chemistry that I don't want to analyze.

After this past month, I didn't think it was possible, but there's no point denying it: I just spent a fun evening with Max. I guess D&D is even more powerful than I realized.

Chapter Sixteen

It's the Thursday before our next band competition, and the pressure continues to mount for our performance this Saturday. Everyone's been so focused that there hasn't even been time to clash with percussion. A small part of me wonders if Max and Felix could be talking down the others after our Sunday game, but I'm not going to get my hopes up yet.

"Before we end for today," Sire calls to us on the field from the sidelines, "I thought we'd do something fun to lighten the mood. It's a game we've played before during band camp—Glare."

The older members of the band cheer at the announcement. Glare is a kind of weird game that somehow has become a tradition at Glen Vale. Members of a section play against each other by standing in circles of five. We all stare at the ground and when the field commanders scream *Glare!*, we have to look up at someone in the group. But there's a strategy to it because you need to choose someone who likely won't choose to look at you. If you guess wrong, and the person *is* looking back at you, you're both out.

I explain the rules quickly to the new members of guard and then lead us to the twenty-yard line where we break into two circles.

"This is confusing. How are we supposed to know who to look at?" Callie asks, her hand on her hip. She always seems to have something to complain about.

"You don't, that's why it's a game," Addison replies.

"It's about knowing the personalities of your group members and being able to predict their actions," I explain. "And also it's just for fun. Don't worry about it."

"At least we get a break from practice," Rosa mutters to Yori.

"Forced fun is better than having no fun like usual," she whispers back.

My shoulders droop, but I pretend like I don't hear them. I know I've been on edge more than usual this week, but after our poor showing at the first competition, our rehearsals are more important than ever. It probably doesn't help that everyone is still annoyed about the bet I made with percussion.

"Are we ready, Knights?" Sire asks into his megaphone. I glance around at the circles spread all through the field. Happily, I can barely see the percussion at the far other end.

"Eyes down!" Marjorie commands. It's almost like being back in drill down. Just like then, I'm determined to win.

"Glare!" our other drum major, Greg, calls.

I look up at Rosa. Sure enough, she isn't looking at me. I figured she wouldn't be after what she just said. Addison and Madisyn are out first round, leaving Devin behind, much to his chagrin. We look back at the ground.

"Rosa, look at me next time," Devin whispers.

"You know that's cheating," I say.

"Yeah, but then we can go sit on the bleachers."

I shake my head. Devin never saw a task he didn't try to get out of. I'm surprised he stuck with color guard all four years.

"Glare!" Marjorie calls.

Sure enough, Devin and Rosa look at each other and I'm the de facto winner for our circle. It doesn't feel like much of a victory when my competitors were actively trying to lose, though. Deja's the winner from the other group of guard members.

"Great job so far, everyone," Sire says once each group has gotten down to their last person. "Let's keep this fun going! Circle up with the others and we'll keep playing until we get down to one."

I win the next round as well. There are only a small number of people left on the field now, and I'm not surprised to see that Nova is one of us. And so is Max.

I swallow hard and slowly make my way to the fifty-yard line to join them and the four other remaining people.

"Back together again," Nova says and knocks my shoulder with her own. "Just like drill down."

I manage a small laugh, but my mouth is dry. I can see Max in my peripheral vision, but I avoid eye contact with him, even though the game hasn't started yet. I really don't want to play anymore. With the others, it's just a dumb game. But playing with Max feels . . . intimate.

I purposely turn toward Nova and away from where Max is standing. Nonetheless, a prickle of awareness creeps across my skin.

"Is Max looking at me right now?" I whisper to Nova.

Her eyes flick in his direction and back to me. "Uh . . . yep he is—wait, he was. He just looked away."

"Why was he looking at me?"

"Don't ask me, there's nothing I understand less than guys. What's going on? Why aren't you in each other's faces, throwing out insults like usual? Do you have an official truce?"

I shake my head. I don't know what's going on with us. We aren't friends. We haven't spoken a word to each other since the game Sunday. But there's a weird tension between us now, and I don't like it.

Marjorie walks in a slow circle around us, trying to be intimidating. "Eyes down!"

I drop my gaze to my toes, and my pulse speeds. What's my best tactic here? I could look at Nova since she's probably unlikely to look at me this first round, but who knows. I don't want to take chances. My safest bet should be Max. There's no way he'd be looking at me . . . except that he just was a second ago. Had he wanted to say something? Whisper an insult or threat? Now it's too late to know.

"Glare!"

At the last second, I turn to my direct right and look

at Eileen, a trumpet player. Luckily, her gaze is elsewhere. Whew, one round down.

I make it through the next two rounds by looking at a freshman trombone player. But there's an itching in the back of my brain each time I glare at the freshman's cropped haircut. The telltale feeling of eyes on me. It makes sense that *someone* would be looking at me given the game, but this gaze feels heavy, as if I'm being touched instead of watched. I shake off the tension inching up my spine.

Greg circles behind me. "Eyes down!"

"Don't look at Max unless you want to lose," Nova whispers. She's so quiet I can barely hear her.

"What?" I whisper back.

"He's choosing you every round. Must be sabotage or something."

"Glare!"

I jerk my eyes to Nova without thinking, but luckily she's looking straight ahead. At Max, if I'm remembering where he's standing. My heart races like we're running laps rather than standing stock-still. Two more people step out of the circle, leaving just Max, Nova, and me, but I don't even bother to notice who they were.

The next round is a draw. I look at Nova, Nova looks at Max, and Max looks at me, presumably. The next round is the same.

"We're getting bored, Final Three," Sire says into the microphone. "I'm not surprised to see some of our usual suspects at the end, but let's finish this up. May the best player win."

His words remind me of the Most Valuable Member award and set my thoughts spinning in a different direction. Even though that award is partially determined by band member votes, another weighted component is the votes from Sire and the assistant band director. I'm pretty sure I lost a lot of his respect when I lost that equipment shed key, but could this be a way to win it back? Would these games play a role in who they ultimately choose? Suddenly, it feels more important than ever to win this. I try to think through the others' strategies, but my mind is garbled and the drum major is right behind me. I stare at my shoes and squeeze my hands into fists. Surely Max won't keep choosing me every round, especially with Sire commanding us to switch it up?

"Glare!"

I swallow and lift my gaze to Max. His gray eyes are staring right back at me, wide and unblinking. My chest tightens and expands at the same moment, and I can't breathe. Something in his expression shifts and I'm suddenly desperate to know what he's thinking. Is he angry I finally chose to look at him, or is it something else? Nova screams in triumph next to me and the moment breaks.

"Congratulations, Nova! You're on quite the roll," Sire announces into the megaphone.

"Ahhh!" She jumps up and down excitedly. "I can't believe I beat you both!"

Max winces and steps closer to me. "I didn't realize she was as competitive as us." He rubs a hand over his mouth.

"We're best friends for a reason. She's just better at hiding it." I reach out to give her a hug, though I'm kicking myself for giving her the win. *Why* did I look at Max when I knew I could lose?

I guess I just couldn't believe he'd be looking back.

My parents drop me off at the high school early Saturday morning for our second competition. The band buses are lined up, waiting for us to file on. There are also the huge band trailers filled with the pit instruments, color guard equipment, and everything else we'll need for today. A few percussion players are pushing xylophones up a ramp into the trailer. Just seeing them reminds me of the bet once again, and I swallow tightly.

"Feeling good about today?" Dad asks me from the passenger side.

"I guess."

"You better be, because I used my whole bottle of green glitter on the sign I made for you," Kelsey interjects from my side.

"Aww, thanks," I reply. I'd rather avoid the additional glitter-induced pressure, but there's nothing more precious to Kelsey than her glitter collection.

"The weather isn't in your favor," Mom says and glances out the window. It's gray and windy today and already spitting rain. "But I believe in you."

"We'll be screaming for you in the stands," Dad says as I climb out onto the sidewalk. "Look for us!"

I don't know how I could miss them. They already have Glen Vale Music booster T-shirts, face paint, comically large pins with my band photo, and an intensely glittery sign. Oh, and big cowbells to ring when the band takes the field. The only reason they aren't band bus chaperones too is because they need to be with Kelsey . . . and because I desperately begged them not to freshman year.

"And make us proud!" Mom calls.

I droop a bit lower at her words. I'd love for today to be the time I can finally accomplish that, but I don't think the marching band gods are on my side this time. The rain morphs from a mist to a steady drizzle and my hopes sink lower. If it was a thunderstorm with a chance of lightning, they'd cancel the competition altogether, which would be much preferable. But as long as no one is in danger from the weather, we're still expected to perform.

Adding to our bad luck is our performance order. Usually it would be a good thing to go last in the hopes that you could blow away the judges and leave a lasting impression in their minds. But by the time we finally march out hours later, the soggy field is so chewed up by the other bands that we can barely see the yard lines. The rain makes the players more liable to squeak or be off tune, mud gets clogged onto the soles of our shoes, and don't even get me started with the flags. At least the others can keep their instruments off the ground, but the tips of our flags are literally swirling through the mud, which means that they're dirty, heavy, and flipping mud onto our cheeks and eyes with each drop spin and toss. It's so slippery that I even fall at one point and smear mud all over my face.

Basically, the whole performance is pure misery, and it shows in our scores.

"Well . . ."

For once, Mom is at a loss for words when I find my family again after the awards have been given out. I'm grateful that it's still sprinkling because it helps to camouflage my tears.

"You know, let's look at it this way—it can only go up from here!" Dad says. "And it'll be a performance you'll remember for the rest of your life."

I half cough, half sob. That's one way to put it. Color guard didn't even score an Excellent this time—we were given a Good. It feels the same as being rated Horrendous. I've never felt more embarrassed.

"It's only one competition," Mom says and rubs my back. "This is what success stories are made of. The hero is down and out, feeling hopeless, but then they rebound and win it all in the end. That can still be you! Think of how amazing it'll feel when you earn that Superior at your last competition. Sire will have to give you the MVM award after that!"

I wish the storm was stronger right now so lightning could strike and kill me where I stand. I'm barely holding it together and Mom is talking about me winning the MVM award? That couldn't be further from my grasp now.

"Is there a trash can somewhere?" Kelsey asks miserably and holds up her beautifully made sign. The glitter is sliding down the poster like it's crying from how bad our performance was.

I can't stand here any longer with their disappointed expressions and chipper voices. There's nothing they can say that will make me feel better. There's nothing anyone can say.

Those dreams of Superior scores and best auxiliary awards are fading further and further from view. Even worse, we haven't qualified for state yet. We *always* have a place at state by our second competition. The idea of not going my senior year is so depressing that I'm tempted to lie face down in the nearest mud puddle.

"I promised a few people I'd check on them," I tell my parents. "Everyone's pretty upset."

Dad nods understandingly. "Of course, you should be with your friends. Do you want us to wait and give you a ride home?"

"No, I'll ride back with the guard. It's the least I can do."

As soon as I'm free, I stride in the opposite direction, although I don't know where I'm going. There's no one else to talk to or check on, that was just the first excuse that came to mind. But a few minutes alone sound like exactly what I need. I head toward the Glen Vale equipment buses. Angry voices catch my attention.

"Get a grip, dude. It's not a big deal."

"It *is* a big deal. Everyone's already demoralized after tonight. You didn't need to make fun of Felix and Niko like that in front of everyone."

I freeze. That's Max speaking, and the other voice is definitely Brody. I look for them, but I don't see them anywhere. They must be around the corner of the closest bus.

"How are they going to learn if someone doesn't call them out? They both suck. They're pulling us down, and there's no way in hell I'm performing a *color guard* routine because they caused us to lose that stupid bet."

"But they're young. And they're trying. I'm pretty sure Felix's mom heard some of the stuff you said to him."

"Then it'll motivate him to make sure it never happens again."

Max growls and I can almost imagine him throwing his hands in the air. Hearing tension within the percussion section should be the lift I need to lighten my mood. If their two best players are fighting, that can't bode well for them. But I can't find any joy in this. Brody was making fun of Felix? What kind of section leader does that?

"We're never going to get better if you keep acting like this," Max argues, his voice getting louder. "People are scared of you."

"Are *you* scared of me? Because if you keep talking to me like this, then you probably should be."

I suck in a breath and push my hands into my stomach. There's a chill in Brody's voice that sends shivers down my spine.

"No, Brody." Max's voice is steady. "I'm not scared of you."

"Too bad."

I spin around and hurry away in case they're done talking. The very last thing I need is for either of them to find me eavesdropping on their argument. I've put enough space between us that I think I'm in the clear when Max calls out my name. I turn around slowly. A quick scan of the area shows me that Max and I are alone now. I take a deep breath to steel myself and raise my protective walls. It's already a horrible day. There's nothing Max can say that could make it worse.

"Look," I say, "it's been a bad day for everyone. If you're thinking about making yourself feel better by kicking me when I'm down, just keep moving. I really don't need it tonight."

Max freezes mid-stride. "That's not why I called your name."

"Oh. I just figured . . ."

He walks closer, but his posture sags. "That the only reason I would talk to you is so I could make you feel bad?"

"I mean . . . yeah. That's how it usually goes. Although, to be fair, you could probably say the same of me."

He sighs. "Why do we act like that?"

"Because our sections hate each other, and you hate me, and—"

"I don't hate you, Hazel. I've never hated you. I've been angry, but only because I wished my life was more like yours."

I nod, unsure how to respond.

"Do you hate me?" he asks quietly.

"Well . . . I hated you when we fought at drill down. And when you doused me with vinegar and gave me thawed Popsicles. And told me off when I tried to welcome you to band." He grimaces and rubs both his hands up his face and through his hair. "But I haven't hated you as much these last few days?"

One corner of his mouth lifts. "Wonderful."

"D&D was fun," I add. "Much more so than I thought it'd be."

"Yeah, it was. Felix told me he had a great time, by the way. I'm not sure he told you that."

I bite my lip, knowing I should leave it, but I can't stop myself. "I wasn't trying to, but I overheard some of what you said to Brody just now. About Felix and Niko. I'm sorry about that."

"It was so low of Brody." His eyes shine with anger. "I couldn't believe he lashed out at them like that, especially right now when they're already feeling like crap."

"We all had a bad competition," I say. "Emotions are running high. Hopefully everyone can shake it off for rehearsal on Monday." I can't believe I'm making excuses for Brody's usual dirtbag behavior, but right now it feels more important to say something encouraging to Max than to rub in how I was right about Brody all along.

"I'm glad you were here, Hazel." His gaze sweeps over my face. "It's good to have you to talk to."

"It's surprisingly good to talk to you too."

He laughs. "Another great compliment to end the night with. I'll see you tomorrow." He takes a few steps before I'm walking after him.

"Hey, Max?" Nerves claw up my throat. "Why did you keep looking at me during the Glare game?"

He stills for a moment before turning around. "How do you know where I was looking if you weren't looking back?"

"Nova told me."

"Ah." He rubs his hand along the back of his neck and shifts his weight like he's debating. Then he shrugs. "I knew you'd never look back at me. Seemed like the easiest path to victory."

The explanation makes sense, but I'm surprised by how disappointed I am from it. It's embarrassing how quickly my feelings for Max can resurface no matter how hard I push them away.

"Right," I whisper. "Well, sorry I looked that last time and wrecked your victory plan."

He shakes his head. "Actually, don't be."

Then he smiles and walks away.

Chapter Seventeen

It's been almost twenty-four hours, and I'm still thinking about Max's words from last night. What did he mean when he said *don't be*? All he cares about is winning—and, equally importantly, beating me. Had he wanted me to look at him? I can't understand why.

Well . . . that's not entirely true.

There is one possible explanation, but the idea is so ludicrous that I must be wrong. There's no way Max could be interested in me. I might have had the biggest crush on him when we were young, but he never felt the same. I'm not sure he even paid attention to the fact I was a girl. To him, I was just another friend to mess around with.

Mom pops her head into my room, forcing me to take out my earbuds for the fifth time this afternoon. She's so insistent on interrupting me that I can't even listen to my angry, angsty girl anthems in peace.

"Just heard from Melanie that she and Max are coming an hour early. And Kelsey's nagging me about going to Aunt Mary's, so I'm going to drop her off before they get here."

"They're coming early? Whose idea was that?"

Mom cocks her head in confusion. "Uh, I didn't ask. Do you want me to text her back?"

I shudder at the idea of Mom and Melanie being go-betweens for us like we're eight.

"No, it's fine. Sorry, stupid question."

"All right." She studies me. "Let me know if you need anything tonight."

I will myself to forget all my questions and thoughts about Max and focus on the game. That's what's important. We had a good first session, and tonight has the possibility of being even better, but only if I focus on being an awesome Dungeon Master and keep all this emotional baggage away from the game table.

Of course, all that goes *completely* out the window as soon as Max and his mom walk in the house. For a moment they're distracted by taking off their shoes and messing with their bags, and I get a chance to study Max. He's wearing those black jeans that are almost too tight on him and look really good. He has on a slim gray shirt that matches his eyes and shows off the definition in his shoulders and arms. I know the color gray is supposed to be boring and blah, but not when it's associated with him. The color does funny things to my heart. All those feelings from years ago are rebounding back into my mind. I squeeze my eyes shut.

"Hazel? Do you mind giving me a hand?"

I open my eyes. Mom and Melanie are still chatting by the front door, but Max is at the entrance to the kitchen with too many grocery bags and a confused look on his face.

I step forward, mentally kicking myself. "What did you bring?" I ask and peek in a bag. "More nacho supplies?"

"I figured since you're doing all the DMing work, I could bring the food again." He walks into the kitchen and drops the bags on the closest counter. "Plus I had an epic idea."

He pulls out two of the largest rolls of foil I've ever seen. His grin is way too cocky to be related to kitchen supplies.

"I'm scared."

"We're making table nachos! My mom saw the idea online." Max pulls more things from the bags. He's so animated tonight. "We're going to cover your kitchen table with this foil to protect it, then we spread out all the chips, add all our toppings, and eat them off the table like it's an enormous plate. I thought we could make enough for the whole group. What do you think?"

"That my parents will lose their minds when they see the mess."

"Nah, it'll be an easy cleanup—we just ball the foil up at the end and throw it in the trash. It seemed fitting to start each Sunday with nachos. Like you and I used to."

My skin flushes at his reminder. "Your obsession with nachos needs to be studied. But this does sound epic."

We get to work cooking the ground beef, heating up the refried beans, and covering the table with foil. I'm glad I have something to do with my hands so I have time to rein in my emotions. But I can't stop my pulse from leaping every time Max steps close to grab an ingredient or something from the cabinets.

"How are you holding up?" he asks as he rips open an enormous bag of shredded cheddar cheese.

"What do you mean? I'm fine. Everything's fine."

He cocks his head. "Really? The only thing that got me out of bed this morning was knowing we had D&D tonight."

He's talking about band. Like any sane person would assume.

"I'm . . . I guess I'm pretending like yesterday didn't happen."

"They should have canceled the competition or delayed it or something. The field was way too muddy for us to be out there. It was like marching through swampland."

"I couldn't make out the yard lines," I admit. It's so weird to be talking to Max about this like we're part of the same team instead of mortal enemies.

"No one could. It was impossible. One time I could have sworn I was on the forty, but it must have been the forty-five because Sock's tuba almost knocked me to the ground." He chuckles and pops open a jar of salsa.

"Better than me."

He turns to face me. His wavy curls are messy today. I've always had a thing for his hair. I frown and stir the ground beef quicker.

"What do you mean?" he asks. "What happened?"

"If you don't already know, then there's no way I'm

trusting you with that information. You'll turn around and use it against me Monday."

I say it in a lighthearted way, not as an accusation, but Max falls back like I shoved him.

"I wouldn't do that. Why do you always assume the worst from me?"

"Because you taught me to."

"Just tell me. I'm not going to stab you in the back." He steps closer and wraps a hand around my wrist to pull me toward him. "I told you I was sorry before and I meant it. What else do you want me to do?"

"Fine!" I take a breath and step away from him. I can't think when he's so close to me. "I fell yesterday. I was running to the sideline for one of our flag switches, and my foot slipped, and I fell. On my face. And the ground was so disgusting that mud smeared all over my chin and went up my nose, but I got my flag, and I marched back out on the field anyway because that's what captains do."

I cross my arms over my chest defiantly.

"The mud went up your nose?" His lips quirk like he's trying not to smile.

"All the way up."

"How . . ." His mouth screws up even tighter. "How'd you get it out?"

"I just kept trying to blow air out of my nose. I was able to shoot the last chunk out right before Nova's solo."

I stare him down, trying with all my might not to break, but neither of us is that strong. He bursts out laughing and I do the same. He folds in half at the waist, laughing so loudly I think he might choke from lack of air. I'm not much better. I lean against the counter and wipe tears from my eyes. Saying it aloud for the first time really puts into perspective how ridiculous that performance was. I was marching through a field with so much mud in my nose that I had to breathe through my *mouth.* If I can't laugh at that, then what's the point?

"No nachos for me," Max says when he can stand upright again. "My stomach is too cramped from laughing."

I gesture emphatically at him. "Now you know why I didn't want to tell you. It was so bad. And you'll have this information to use against me whenever you want."

"I'm not going to use the information against you, whatever that means. I can't promise the rest of my section will follow suit, especially with Brody at the lead, but I'm done. I don't want to fight with you anymore."

My heart picks up in a staccato rhythm. I don't know what to say other than to make another joke. "Be serious, you still *kind of* want to fight with me, though, right? I'm pretty sure it's in your nature."

"I wouldn't mind finally kicking your butt at Settlers of Catan right now."

"An impossible goal when you're so bad at board games. Set your sights lower."

He swallows and his eyes trail over me. "I've already set my sights very high."

Just then the front door opens and breaks the spell between us. I turn back to my ground beef—which is well on its way to burnt—and Max messes with the cheese. Li and Felix come into the kitchen, much to my chagrin.

"More Mexican food?" Felix asks as he surveys the kitchen.

"Not just Mexican food, dude. I have two words for you: nacho table."

"I don't know what those words mean in that order," Li says.

I give her a quick hug. "It's a Max thing."

"Hey!" Nova's voice calls from the front of the house. "Guess who's here?"

Nova's Old English sheepdog comes bounding through into the kitchen and right to my feet, tongue hanging out with a huge smile on his face. He's the happiest dog I've ever met. I scratch him behind the ears and then he moves around the kitchen to get scratches from the others.

"I'm so glad you brought Zoinks with you," Li says and buries her face in his fur. "I didn't realize D&D could get better, but I also didn't realize there could be dogs."

"Dogs do make everything better," Nova says.

"As do nachos," Max says. "It's time. Let's put it together."

We recruit each person for one ingredient: meat, beans, hot nacho cheese, sour cream, and salsa, then circle the table to admire our handiwork.

"This is sick," Felix says.

"Right?" Li replies and pulls out her phone to take a picture. "I've never seen anything like this."

Nova holds Zoinks back from the food and reaches out for a chip. Without thinking, I glance at Max in horror.

"Stop! You can't just . . . *eat* them!" Max says. "We each have to search for the best bite."

"Huh?" Felix says.

"The perfect nacho," I explain, while Max nods at my side. "With just the right amount of toppings, but with a chip that's still crispy and strong enough to hold everything without cracking or collapsing."

"Top Nacho," we say together.

"Uh, I'm just going to take all these," Felix says and pushes a pile onto a paper plate. The others follow his lead, but Max and I take our time, bending over and studying the table like we're professional golfers scrutinizing the topography of the land before taking a shot.

Finally I find a perfect one, stacked high with meat, cheese, and toppings, and he does the same. I raise mine in the air. "To our new game."

He gently clinks his chip with mine. "And new beginnings."

Unlike last session, when I was nervous and wishing I could claim sudden food poisoning, today I'm actually excited. This whole week I've been brainstorming and reading and jotting down ideas for encounters. Since they defeated the giant opossum last time and leveled up, it makes sense that they'll want to figure out what was going on with that. Where did those giant monstrous animals come from, and are there more of them? And that means that when they start exploring the forest, I can lead the group to the opossum's den, which just happens to connect to underground tunnels. And *that* means we can start a dungeon crawl tonight. Once we do that, it'll feel like a real D&D game.

"Are we all ready?" I ask when everyone has sat down and Zoinks is settled next to Nova's chair. I'm practically bouncing in my seat. I already have the space all mapped out in my head (and a rough sketch since I'm not an artist like Li) and I know exactly when they're going to find the traps, monsters, and loot. It's going to be so cool. I feel like a real DM—like Mom—instead of a newbie pretending to be a Dungeon Master.

"Actually," Felix says. "Li and I took your advice and worked on our character backgrounds."

I sit back. To be honest, I'd kind of forgotten about that with everything else going on. And I'm surprised Li talked to Felix without telling me. "Oh, well, that's great. What'd you come up with?"

They share a shy look across the table. They look so similar in that moment, with their glasses and fidgety hand gestures, that I do a double take.

"So, we were thinking about the fact that Ellywich is a gardener and how druids really care about the balance and sanctity of nature," Felix begins.

"And we decided that we didn't want to be related," Li adds.

"So, instead we decided we'll be from two separate families who live in close vicinity to each other, protecting and living off the land. But the reason we're here now is because a blight destroyed our crops. We can't survive there anymore, and our families are dispersed, and we don't even know where everyone is. So, we're here to search for answers to the blight and save our land and bring our families together."

Felix and Li give each other a little nod of support. I'm still processing.

"Cool backstory," Nova tells them. "Tragic backstories are always best."

Tragic backstories are great . . . except when I didn't know about them until after I already set up this campaign and have nothing built in about this. I figured they'd just decide to be childhood friends or something, not that they'd create a whole separate mystery that we'd need to solve. I swallow tightly and smile. This will be fine. It'll just be something to deal with in the future.

"Thanks for thinking so deeply about this," I say. "And now that we know that, I guess we can start. As I'm sure you all remember, we ended last session with the group defeating the giant opossum and saving everyone. However, the giant raccoon got away. Luckily, because of its size, it left a very wide path into the forest."

"Well, the obvious choice is to follow the tracks, right?" Nova asks the group. "And I wouldn't mind going deeper into the woods. All those crowds were stressing me out."

Zoinks gives a little bark next to her, and she ruffles his fur. "Well, that's too bad," she tells him in a baby voice. "I know you like people, but this is what happens when there's people. Chaos."

"Actually, I kind of agree with Zelda," Felix says. "I was hoping we could explore the city first. What's it called again? Darkthorn?"

I nod tightly and my eye starts twitching.

"I was thinking the same thing," Li says. "Felix and I—oops, I mean Elrid and I—are hoping to look for leads on what might be causing this blight. It's why we came to this area."

"Fine by me," Max says, and I clutch my hands together under the table. "I'm very gold motivated, so I'm not going deeper into the woods unless I have a good incentive. But since the four of us were so helpful, I bet we can negotiate a reward if we find someone in the city."

"Fine," Nova says with a sulk. "I hate towns, but Zelda will be beside himself with joy." She looks to me. "Okay, the party is going to go into the town to explore."

Everyone turns to face me, eager and smiling, and I absolutely freeze. What am I supposed to do now? I'd set everything up so perfectly, mentioned the tracks and the raccoon running back into the forest. Lining up the hints that should have drawn them to follow. I have everything ready for that.

My mind races. "You're sure? Right, okay, the city. Let's see . . ."

I stare down at my dungeon crawl notes and dice as if there's anything there that can help me. What does the city even look like? I clear my throat roughly.

"So, the party walks into the city. When you get there you see, um, buildings. Tall buildings. Well, not too tall, but with maybe two stories. And flower boxes."

I cut my eyes to Max and Felix, sure I'll find them rolling their eyes or smirking, but they only sit patiently. Li nods, probably thinking I'm about to say something profound or helpful, but I'm not.

"Okay. Great. So, who's in charge of this city?" Max asks after another moment.

"Uh, the . . . the duke. The grand duke of the city."

He frowns and then turns to the group. "I feel like we should seek him out. We can plead our case and ask for payment."

"What if you went to search for him, and Elrid and I started asking about the blight?" Li suggests and my stomach twists again. Now they want to split up? And talk to twice as many non-player characters that I haven't created and don't know how to role-play?

"Zelda and I will come with you, Axolotl," Nova says.

"I'd love the company."

"*No,*" I blurt, and Li jumps back in surprise, probably from how sharp my tone is. "I mean, I think you should all stay together."

"But how'll we figure out what's going on with our lands if we don't start asking around?" Felix asks.

"Well, maybe you should have told me ahead of time about your backstories rather than dropping it on me last minute," I snap and then immediately want to slide under the table. I'm totally botching this.

Felix blinks in surprise. "But you told us to come up with a backstory, so we did." He looks to Li for confirmation.

My heart is racing and guilt swirls with my anxiety so that I have absolutely no clue what to do with the group next.

"Aw man, I completely forgot that my mom brought a cake for us tonight!" Max pushes back from his chair. The others glance around in surprise before following his lead and standing up. "Well, it's mostly for the adults, but she said we could have some if we got to it before they ate it all. We should get some now before it's gone."

"What kind is it?" Felix asks.

"Chocolate fudge."

"Get out of my way," he replies with a laugh and flies toward the kitchen. Li and Nova hurry after him, and Zoinks is quick to join the party. Max lingers until we're alone in the dining room.

"Do you want a piece?" he asks quietly.

I tilt my head in confusion. "What are you doing? You were never a cake fan before."

"I don't hate it if it has enough icing, it's just not my favorite. I can choke this one down."

"But then why . . ."

I trail off as he gives me a small knowing smile. What I really need right now is a few minutes to get my bearings and figure out what comes next. I know I could explain that to everyone . . . but I *really* don't want to admit that I'm already dropping the ball as their Dungeon Master. I'm supposed to be the leader. The person behind the curtain who knows everything. I don't want them to lose faith in me so early in the campaign.

Max easily could have called me out as soon as he realized I was vulnerable, but instead he found a way to give me exactly what I need without letting the others know. The realization makes my throat tight.

"When did you become so sacrificial?" I ask weakly. "Choking down cake for me?"

"Just looking out for my Dungeon Master."

His Dungeon Master. My heart stumbles. Suddenly that one word has enough weight to render me mute.

Chapter Eighteen

"Why does it matter?" Callie complains to me during rehearsal on Monday.

"Um, why does it matter that our flags need to be parallel on count five instead of six?" I stare at her incredulously. "Because if we aren't using the same counts, then we won't be in sync."

She lifts a shoulder nonchalantly. Madisyn drops her flag to the ground. "I think what she means is why does *any* of this matter? What's the point in working so hard when it doesn't get us anywhere?"

"I agree," Devin says and sits down on the gymnasium floor.

"But we will get better, I know we will, as long as we keep working." I try to imbue my voice with conviction, but it doesn't seem to be working.

Today is our first rehearsal since that absolutely disastrous competition over the weekend, and it's clear that the guard is still dealing with some trauma from it. There's no way to sugarcoat how badly it went, but I was hoping we could breeze over those details and use that bad performance to spur us on. It looks like everyone else is taking the wallowing approach instead.

"Hazel, give it up," Addison says and sits down next to Devin. "It's not happening. We should make our peace with the fact that we're going to be cleaning up urine and who knows what in the men's restrooms here before too long."

"Yeah, thanks for that awesome gift, by the way," Rosa says. "You just couldn't rein yourself in around Brody and Max, huh?"

I clamp my mouth shut and glance at the others. Everyone looks downtrodden, even Li who usually rivals me for optimism and work ethic. A pit grows in my stomach. This isn't how things should be.

"Well . . ." I suddenly wish Faith was here right now so she could use her authority to make them stand back up or at least give them free doughnuts as a distraction. I've got nothing. "How about we take a five-minute break to relax and then get back to it?"

I get a few shrugs and grunts in return.

I'm slow to put away all the flags today. I know I should make each guard member take care of their own flags, but they're so depressed that it feels like the least I can do. By the time I get back into the band room afterward, it's completely empty. Or that's how it appears at first. However, a glance at Sire's office, which has a glass window looking into the band room, shows that Max is standing in there with Sire, Mrs. Lewis, and Mr. Jenkins, the percussion specialist. The door is closed, so I can't hear anything, but it looks like a serious conversation given the solemn expressions on their faces. I look away before they notice me gawking. Why is Max in the office alone with them? Is he in trouble? I hadn't noticed any issues during rehearsals today, but I was very focused on color guard.

I hesitate, debating what to do. There's an obvious answer, which is to go home. Whatever is happening, it's none of my business. But, on the other hand, my parents know I often stay late at school, and after last night it seems like Max and I are moving toward becoming friends again. If something bad is happening, then maybe I should stay in case he needs to talk.

After a few seconds of debate, I decide on a compromise. I won't loiter outside the office like a stalker, I'll only sit at a concrete picnic table outside. If he wants to talk then I'll be there. And if not, no big deal. This gives me time to put together my Fiona Apple playlist like I've been meaning to, plus it's a good way to take my mind off color guard.

Fifteen minutes later, Max walks through the door and tips his head toward the sky—clearly thinking he's alone—to take a deep breath. He's wearing a gray Led Zeppelin T-shirt that's slightly too tight. He certainly loves his band shirts, although I have no room for judgment since I'm currently wearing a fitted Letters to Cleo shirt I stole from my mom. Max bends backward to stretch and his shirt lifts to reveal a sliver of his stomach. The sight is enough to make my pulse leap. Between that and his gorgeous pitch-black hair, I couldn't pull my gaze from him if a meteor was rushing toward the earth to kill us both.

He straightens and almost jumps out of his skin when he sees me. "Hazel! What are you still doing here?"

I hold up my phone, embarrassed. "Um, mostly just messing around on this. But I saw you inside and thought I'd wait for you."

"Really?" He seems genuinely shocked. "You didn't have to do that."

"I know. It seemed like something a friend might do. Unless I'm overstepping?"

"No, I'm glad you waited." He rubs the back of his neck. "Actually, do you have time to hang out? I've heard there's a walking trail down there, but I haven't had a chance to explore it." Max points behind the school to the edge of a woods.

My eyes widen and I try to keep my face neutral. Clearly no one has taken the time to explain that forest to him or the implications of what he's asking. Our high school backs into a narrow strip of woods, and a long time ago the school district thought it'd be nice to make the area usable for students and nearby residents. They created a walking path through the forest, added some stones for steps, and even a few benches. Of course, as soon as the students got ahold of the space, they carved their names into the trees, sprayed graffiti onto the benches, and started using it as a "secret" place to smoke weed right off school property.

The space also got another kind of reputation. I can't count the number of couples who've snuck down there for some private time, and I don't want to know what those trees have seen. Nowadays, there'd be only one assumption if anyone saw me walk into those woods with Max. Although, no one is here to see. I peer over at the forest. Nova and I poked our heads in freshman year, but I've never been back, and I have to admit I've always been curious to see more of it.

"Um . . . okay. But don't expect much of a tour. I've never been there either," I say as we set out over the lawn and down toward the entrance.

"Really? I figured it would be popular."

"It is . . . for certain people. But you usually have to be dating someone to want to go over there."

He glances at me, and my whole body heats. I don't want to talk about dating with Max. I know he didn't ask me to do this so we can make out under the oak trees.

I'm not sure what I'm expecting to find when we step into the shade of the tree-covered path—maybe trash, or drug paraphernalia, or bras slung over tree branches? But it's just a very quiet, very pretty forest. The dirt path is wide enough for us to walk side by side, and the bubbling of the water from a nearby stream is soothing.

"So, can I ask why you were in Sire's office?"

"Wait, are you worried about me? I didn't know you cared about my well-being." His smile is teasing.

"Maybe I don't."

"Good to know. I won't waste your time, then. We can just take in all this natural beauty. Or I could tell you about this fascinating conversation from my philosophies of government class I'm taking. We're starting—"

"Max!" I snap, feeling like a little kid again. I shove his

arm, and he has to catch himself so he doesn't fall into the foliage along the path. "Fine, yes, I care. A tiny amount." I huff. "Are you happy now?"

He chuckles. "Significantly happier."

"You really do make everything into a competition. Even conversations."

"Life is more fun that way." He pauses and turns to look at the stream where it's turned into a tiny waterfall. "I was in Sire's office because I'm challenging Brody for the position of section leader. Sire and the others wanted to talk to me about it before moving forward."

I gasp. "You're *challenging* him?"

In our marching band, section leaders are chosen by Sire and Mrs. Lewis before our season begins. They've never said exactly how they make their choices, but it's pretty obvious that it's on the basis of musical skill, leadership potential, and seniority. There was no question that Brody would be named section leader this year. He's been part of the music program here since fifth grade, just like me. He was first chair in symphonic band last spring, and he's been the de facto leader of percussion since then. And once you're named section leader . . . that's it. I can't remember a section leader ever being ousted mid-season. It would shake up the entire section and obliterate Max's relationship with Brody.

"I'm challenging," Max repeats, his voice low and calm. "They already made it clear how unusual this is, but once I explained what's been happening when they aren't around, they agreed that a change might be needed. They're going to discuss it more, and talk to Brody, and then give us a final decision on Wednesday."

I run my hands through my hair, trying to smooth my curls and my thoughts even though I know it won't help. "But . . . Max, are you serious? Do you know what this will mean?"

"This isn't my first year in band, even if I'm new here. Brody is furious, and he'll be even worse if they side with me. And if Brody gets to stay as section leader, he'll never let me live it down. I'll have to hear about it every day for the rest of the year."

I gape at him. "Then why would you do it?"

"Because he's a bad section leader and the group deserves better." His eyes narrow and his expression darkens. "Brody thinks the way to get the best out of people is to ridicule and shame them. He's constantly calling out the younger players when they get out of rhythm or miss their marks on the field, and he encourages the rest of us to laugh along with him while he makes fun of them."

"I could have told you that. In fact, I think I tried."

He winces. "I know. And I was a stubborn idiot for not listening. But he was cool with me, and, I guess, I wanted to believe you were just biased against him." Max shoves his hands into his pockets and starts down the path again. It narrows and weaves slightly upward so that I have to shuffle very close to him to keep at his side. "What's the real deal with you and Brody? He told me a few things, but I'm pretty sure they were lies."

"I'm sure they were."

"Did you date him or something?" His voice is uneven.

"Wow, you really have no respect for me at all, do you?"

I shiver with disgust. "I would *never* date Brody. He's hated me ever since freshman year when I won the Most Valuable Member award, and he was sure he deserved it more. I think if Nova or someone else had won, he'd have let it go. He did during sophomore and junior years when he didn't win. But since a color guard member beat out all the band members, he was livid. He loves pointing out how much we suck, as if that'll prove that I never should have won that award to begin with."

"That story sounds way more plausible than anything he told me." Max winces. "I'm so embarrassed that I believed he was a friend. I think he was only chill because he realized I could be a threat if I wanted to be. And now I do."

"You and I have never seen more eye to eye. I almost believe you've turned over a new leaf. No pun intended," I say and gesture at the trees.

"Yeah?" He stills and turns to me. It's so quiet here, with only the gentle rustle of the branches and the trickle of water. I understand why couples come here to be alone. "I'd like to make it up to you. I'll do whatever you want me to do."

Out of nowhere, an image of him kissing me fills my mind. My breath quickens and I look away. When I was young, I spent an embarrassing amount of time imagining what that might be like, but I know kissing is the last thing I should be thinking about. Max and I have only taken the smallest steps toward rebuilding our friendship. I shouldn't be throwing other emotions into the mix when we aren't on steady ground to begin with.

"The best thing you can do for me is replace Brody.

Assuming Sire actually chooses you as the new section leader." I give him a teasing smile in the hopes that it masks any other emotions that might have been flitting across my face.

"You don't think they'll choose me?"

"I don't know. I guess we'll have to wait and see."

Max's jaw flexes and I have to bite my cheek so I don't burst out laughing at his expression. I'm pretty confident that Max is about to be the new section leader, but the way he tenses when I question him is too funny to ignore. He makes it *so* easy to mess with him.

He takes a step closer to me. "Fine, we'll make a bet out of it."

"Of course we will. And what will I get when I win?"

"We don't need to worry about that since it's clear you'll be losing." He glares at me, but there's no heat to it like there used to be. Or, at least, there's no anger in his expression. His eyes drop to my mouth for a moment, and a whole other kind of heat fills me. "And when you lose—which you will—you have to buy me ice cream before the home football game next Friday."

I wasn't expecting that. My cocky swagger drops away and I shuffle backward. We're going out for ice cream together now? Is he . . . asking me out on a *date*?

Chapter Nineteen

I linger after school on Wednesday even though we don't have band practice. I know it's silly—it's not like my hanging around will have any effect on Sire's decision about the percussion section leader—but I guess I want to be nearby to find out the news as soon as possible. I tell myself that's for the sake of the guard, so I can be prepared if Brody is on the warpath tomorrow, but that's not the complete truth.

Either way, I take my time outside, rolling the competition flags just so and storing them in our outside shed, making sure to keep my new key close at hand. There's no way I'm making that mistake again. By the time I walk back into the school, I'm one of the last people here. Brody, Max, Sire, and the assistant directors are all huddled in the back of the band room.

Sire's head whips around to me. "Sorry, Hazel, the band room is closed right now."

"Oh, sorry, my fault." I point to a stray practice flag that someone left leaning against the wall. "I just wanted to, um, get a little more practice in. I'll go to the gymnasium."

"I'm pretty sure the cheerleaders are practicing in there this afternoon. But you could try the auditorium stage. There shouldn't be anyone there."

"Oh, okay. Thanks."

Brody eyes me warily, and Max gives me a small nod. I cross my fingers behind my back and hurry out.

I don't really need to practice, but I head to the auditorium and wander around. I've never been on this stage before because we don't practice here, but it's actually not a bad space. The ceilings are super high, so we could practice tosses, and I even notice mirrors along the back wall, hidden by heavy curtains.

It feels kind of weird lurking in this empty cavernous space, but I decide to stay for a while in case Max comes to find me when he's done. Twenty minutes go by while I mess around with some harder flag tosses and try to fill my mind with thoughts of our D&D campaign. I'm just starting to think that I misread this situation and Max isn't coming, when the door at the back of the auditorium squeaks open. Someone steps inside, silhouetted by the bright light from the hallway. I catch my flag with a snap, then lower it to the ground. My heart thumps uncomfortably in my chest. I don't need to see his face to know it's Max. Somewhere along the way, I seem to have memorized the outlines of him—long legs and broad shoulders and the perfect waves of his hair.

"How'd it go?" I ask.

"Bad news," he calls from the back. He strides down the aisle until he's close enough that I can make out the smirk on his face. "We share a common enemy now. And you owe me ice cream."

I yelp. "It happened? You're section leader?"

Max jumps up onto the stage with me. "I am."

I don't think, I just throw my arms around him and squeeze. He squeezes me back, holding so tight that my feet almost lift off the floor before he releases me.

I step away, a little shaky. "Congratulations!"

Max sits down on the edge of the stage, and I lower myself next to him, careful to leave enough space between us that he couldn't suspect how my pulse has sped up since he came in.

"Thanks. I was getting worried that Sire and Mrs. Lewis would be reluctant to make the change so far into the season. I have a feeling Brody didn't react well when they talked to him, though."

"They know how talented you are. Actually, I've been wondering, how did you get so good at the drums?"

He snorts. "I feel like I should take offense. Are you that surprised?"

"Let's just say I don't remember you being entirely diligent when we were younger."

"One of the best things about our move away was that the new house had a soundproof basement. My parents weren't always fighting, but there was enough tension that I liked to hang out down there and practice. It's amazing how good you can get at something if it's all you do."

Oof, now I feel like a jerk. The last thing I want to do is bring up more drama about his family now that we seem to be moving past that. "I'm sorry. I shouldn't have said anything."

"No," he replies immediately. "You can ask me whatever you want. In fact, it's kind of nice to talk about it with someone. I couldn't really talk to my friends at my last school about stuff like this."

"Well, in that case, how's your mom doing? I barely saw her on Sunday."

"She seems . . . better. Not perfect, but getting there. I'm still a little worried about her, but I think her D&D game is helping. It gives her something to look forward to every week."

"And you're . . ."

"I'm okay." He turns so he's facing me instead of the auditorium seating. "Really. After you and I talked, I sat down with Mom again. We'd never really delved into everything, and she tried to explain why she felt like she needed to leave. I could tell she left some stuff out for my sake, but I got the basic idea. I hadn't known how controlling my dad was." He clenches his hands in his lap so hard that the tendons are visible on his forearms. "I'm glad she did it. And I'm glad I came here with her."

I nod, not sure what to say. I can't quite believe he's being so honest with me.

"You're a really good son for moving senior year to be with your mom," I say quietly after a moment. "I'm sure it means a lot to her. I don't think everyone would do that, even if it gave them a chance to join the best high school marching band in Ohio."

That makes him laugh, which was the goal.

"You've caught me—that *was* my main motivation." He messes with his fingernails. "How are things with you and your mom? Didn't you say there was some tension?"

I snort. "Yeah, always."

"Is that what led you to go into color guard? You're amazing at it, by the way. I never told you. But I figured I'd come back to find you as first chair trumpet."

"My parents would have *loved* that. I think the first time I broke their hearts was when I decided to play flute instead of a brass instrument in fifth grade. Every year they hoped I'd change my mind. And when I decided to try color guard freshman year, I thought they'd both keel over in shock. I still play flute in symphonic band, and I enjoy it, but . . . I guess I just wanted to do my own thing. I thought maybe there would be less pressure if I did something different." I shake my head. "Joke's on me. They're set on me winning the senior MVM award like Mom did."

"But *you* still want it too, right? So it doesn't matter what your parents want as long as it's something you care about."

"Right. Plus, I can't let *you* win it." I smile a little too brightly.

I can't admit to him that I'm not sure anymore if I want it or even deserve it. It's an odd realization. Growing up, I wanted to win everything all the time, no matter what. I put so much pressure on myself to be the best. The best dancer, the best performer, the best daughter. And I told myself it was worth the work because the payoff was so big. But now . . . I don't know. Life didn't change after I won the award freshman year. It's not like I could suddenly relax and be carefree for the rest of high school. And is it even fair to vie for the award again when I've already won it once? Mom would adamantly say yes since she did exactly that, but more and more I'm having a hard time caring. Mostly, I just want the guard to be happy. Well, I want that *and* to win our bet against the percussion. But I don't think we'll win unless I can find a way to help the guard members enjoy our practices.

"I can't deny it'd be pretty cool to come into this band as the new kid and then steal the title away from the rest of you."

"Oh my god, you never stop. You'll have a great shot at it, though. It's obvious that a lot of the percussion section already loves you. They'll rally around you." I shake my head. "I don't know how you did that, though. I'm—" I cut myself off when I realize I'm about to say too much.

"What?"

"Nothing." I mimic locking my lips. "Insider secrets."

"Color guard secrets, you mean? You can tell me. I'm not Brody, you know. That's kind of the whole point."

"But Brody will still be part of percussion. And it's not even about Brody, it's just . . . we're competitors, Max. Our sections don't get along, and it feels wrong to tell the section leader anything that could give you leverage over us."

He leans back on his elbows with a furrowed brow and

stares out into the auditorium. "I can't promise that everything is going to change with me as section leader. We're still going to fight to win our bet. The others are going to revolt against me if they're forced to perform your guard choreography in front of everybody. We'll still want more Superior ratings than you, and more compliments from Sire."

I lean back as well, mimicking his position. Nothing he's saying surprises me, but it's still disheartening. "I know."

"But that doesn't mean I'm going to sabotage the guard." He shifts. The side of his pinky finger barely touches mine, and I can't tell if he meant to do that or not. "I want to win, but that's only going to happen by me bringing the percussion together and getting us to perform at our best. Whatever's going on with the guard doesn't change that."

I glance over at him, trying to read his expression and whether or not he could be lying to me. It's still hard for me to trust him completely, but maybe I can look at this as a test. If he uses this info against me in the future, then I'll have my answer.

"It's just, I'm struggling. I want everyone to love the guard the way I do and to be excited to perform and for us to feel like . . . I don't know, a family? That's really cheesy, sorry—"

"It's not cheesy," he says, his expression kind. "I get it."

I take a relieved breath. "And I can't figure out how to make that happen. Sometimes I even wonder if they hate me a little bit." I whisper the last sentence. I'm being way too forthcoming.

"It's impossible to hate you, Hazel. Believe me, I've tried."

I turn back to him and his smile is warm. And maybe a little mischievous.

"I don't know if I have good advice for you," he continues. He tips his head up to the ceiling like he's thinking. "It's going to be an uphill battle for me now with Brody insulting me whenever he sees an opening. But, at least for me, it helps that some of us have bonded over video games and quoting LOTR lines to each other. We've even started playing *Helldivers* together in the evenings. And we talk music. There's this drummer I'm obsessed with—El Estepario Siberiano—and now we're constantly sending each other clips of him playing. Do you have anything like that with your guard members?"

I slump. This is such a basic thing—bonding over our shared interests—but I have no idea what most of the others enjoy. Even those of us who were in guard together previous years never hung out outside of band. And this year, we've been so busy rehearsing that I rarely get to talk to them about what else is happening in their lives.

But then I remember our section dinner and how we all made characters. It was silly, but we had a good time. Maybe that's exactly the type of thing we need more of. We need something to bond us together.

I nod slowly. "That's really helpful. Thanks."

"You can pay me back with ice cream." He jumps to his feet. "Actually, now that I think about it, you have to pay me back . . . since you lost your bet." His smile is wicked. "To *me*."

"I knew I'd lose."

He blinks in surprise. "Then why'd you take the bet?"

"Because it's really fun toying with you." My grin matches his as I make little puppet master movements with my hands.

"I'm eating double the ice cream just for that."

Chapter Twenty

"I have a few ideas to shake things up," I tell the color guard at practice the next day. I spent last night thinking about Max's advice, and I want to try putting it into action. "The first thing I thought we'd try is rehearsing in a new space." I gesture around at the auditorium stage.

Madisyn, Addison, and Devin look around dubiously. "Why?" Madisyn asks. "We've never done this before."

"That's exactly why," I reply and walk to the back of the stage. Faith isn't here since it's a weekday during her work hours, but I got permission from Sire to try this out. "I thought a change of scenery might be nice, but mostly we're here for this."

I dramatically pull back the enormous dusty curtains that cover the mirrors along the back wall.

"Everyone knows the routines at this point, so now it's a matter of getting as synchronized as possible. I figured if we could all watch our own reflections, we might be able to catch things quicker."

The others quietly inspect themselves without arguing. I'll take it after the last few rehearsals we've had.

"And I had another idea—what do you think about having one person each day act as our DJ for warm-up? You can pick whatever music you like, and we have to warm up to it." There's a burst of chatter. "But there's one caveat," I continue. "You have to play music that you think your D&D character would like."

"What, why?" Rosa asks.

I shrug. "For fun? Plus, I was thinking more about it, and sometimes performers feel better when they have an alter ego that they tap into while they're performing. It's like they turn their regular self and all their anxieties off and let this other character come out. You already have alter egos, so why don't we use them?" I walk slowly around the room. "You three chose fighters as a class." I nod at the seniors. "You can tap into that power during the performance. And I remember you chose to be an elf," I say to Keira. "Elves can be elegant and graceful, so you could put that energy into your performance."

"What about me? I was a rageful barbarian orc—does that mean I can knock over the tuba section if they get in my way?" Yori asks, and the whole group bursts into laughter.

I smirk. "Let's not go quite that far, although I like your spirit."

"Use your rage against the percussion section," Callie says.

"Speaking of that," I say. "I don't know if you've heard

the news yet, but Brody is out and Max is the new section leader. I'd recommend staying out of Brody's way until he calms down about it."

A murmur spreads through the group. "He's going to be on the warpath," Devin says.

I nod. "This could be good for us. There's going to be so much chaos in the percussion section that I bet they won't have time to mess with us. And I think Max might be more chill about that as well."

Rosa snorts. "Yeah right, he was just as bad as Brody."

"He's worse," Callie argues. "All that stuff at band camp was his idea. Who knows what else they'll think up now that he's in charge?"

Li and I exchange a quick uncomfortable glance. Like me, she's seen a different side of Max during our D&D games. But that's a whole other world from here. I'm starting to trust Max—it's why I'm suggesting all these guard changes, after all—but I'm not entirely sure how he's going to act as section leader. Will things actually change between our sections? I guess we'll have to wait and see.

"The best thing we can do for the next few weeks is ignore them and focus on getting to our absolute best. That's the way we really put them in their place." To my surprise, a few guard members nod resolutely. Maybe I need to lean harder into motivating them with spite. "I know we aren't close to that best auxiliary award yet, but we have everything we need. Our show is creative, we've got beautiful flags, fun choreography, and—most importantly—a group of really talented members." I put out my hands toward them. "Don't you think we should at least try?"

A few nods, and small smiles grow as they all look around at each other.

"I can tell you that Lyra Stormclash would never take lip from some scrawny percussion players like Brody or Max," Madisyn says.

"Huh?" Rosa asks.

"That's my fighter!" Madisyn replies with an eye roll.

"My orc would flatten them. Easy," Yori says.

"And then my elf could elegantly dance over their flattened bodies," Keira adds.

There's a small prick of guilt at hearing them trash the percussionists, but I push that away. No matter the motivation, the guard sounds excited. Determined, even. This is exactly what I've been hoping for.

"This is great!" I exclaim. "Let's keep the talk of 'flattening' people away from Sire and Faith, but I love this momentum. We *can* win this—we just need to dedicate ourselves. Which means we better get started. Which of your characters is going first as DJ?"

Yori raises her hand immediately. "I already searched on Spotify and found a whole playlist for my orc. Rage Against the Machine feels appropriate for the first song."

I nod appreciatively. "Perfect choice, Oof."

The changes aren't immediate, but each day I notice small differences. Members self-correcting when they see they're off from the group, drop spins that are in sync for once, and even Callie and Keira practicing throws without me asking.

By the time we get to our home game the following Friday, I'm actually excited. And more importantly, the others seem excited as well.

Of course, that could be because our homecoming game is tonight. Students are going all out—wearing school colors and face paint and decorating the halls with balloons and garlands. Our show tonight is easy since we're basically just standing in formation and performing to Ariana Grande while the homecoming court walks across the field.

"Hazel, are you going to homecoming tomorrow?" Li asks as we leave the band room for our break between school and the football game.

I shake my head. "Not this year. Nova wasn't interested and I didn't have a date, so we decided to skip. We're going to spend tomorrow shopping, watching movies, and eating too much food."

"Oh, that sounds fun!" She nervously adjusts her glasses. "I'm going with a few friends."

"You'll have a great time."

"What are you doing now? Do you want to hang out?"

"Um, actually, I'm going to grab some ice cream with Max. But only because I lost a bet to him and I have to pay him back," I add when she lifts an eyebrow.

"I thought you could barely tolerate Max?"

"That's usually how it feels."

Li eyes me. I always think of her as young and naïve, but she might be more observant than I realized. "So the fact that you aren't going to homecoming has nothing to do with the fact that Max refuses to go?"

"What? No." My stomach flutters at the news. Max isn't going? Up until this second, I haven't thought at all about whether Max was attending the dance or not, but now I want to know everything. "How do you know what Max is doing for homecoming anyway?"

She shrugs. "I heard people talking about it. I guess girls keep asking him and he's refusing everyone. He wouldn't even get a smoothie with Erika."

Li's gossip has the same effect on me as marching during a freezing-cold downpour. Girls are asking him out? I shouldn't be surprised. Max is the hot new guy in band. And even though he's the same age as us, knowing that he takes college classes during the day makes him seem older and cooler than all the other guys we've grown up with. Still, I didn't realize that so many people were interested in him. I'm mortified by the way jealousy claws up my throat at the mere mention of it.

"He and I don't talk about that kind of stuff."

She grins. "But you do go out for ice cream together. Even though he doesn't go out with anyone?"

"Oh no, don't start. I'm paying off a bet, that's it." My cheeks are red, and she knows she's got me. "Speaking of, I'm supposed to meet him now."

She giggles. "Of course you are."

"Oh my god," I groan. "Listen, please don't say anything or make a big deal about it with the guard members, okay? It seriously means nothing, but I don't think the guard will like it if they find out."

"They'll hate it, for sure. But I promise I won't say anything." She gives me a knowing wink and my cheeks warm even more.

I can't get Li's words out of my mind as I climb into Max's car a few minutes later. I already wasn't sure what to make of this outing, and now my mind is spinning with possibilities. I try to push the questions away. It's entirely possible that the girls who asked Max out weren't his type and that's why he said no. Or maybe there's still someone from his old school that he's hung up on. There are a million explanations that don't involve me and Max together, and it's not doing me any favors to let this get to my head.

Max drives us to a DairyFreeze on the side of the road about ten minutes from school. You can't even walk inside, it's just a tiny box with a window where you can walk up and order. There's exactly one person working—a girl named Hayley from my history class.

"What can I get you?" she asks with an extremely wide grin for Max.

"Hmm, what should I have . . ." He taps his chin thoughtfully and shoots a grin my way. "What's your most expensive ice cream?"

Hayley squints in confusion. There aren't real ice cream choices at the DairyFreeze. You get soft serve from the machine and you're happy about it.

"That was not part of the arrangement," I remind him and cross my arms over my chest. "I'm not made of ice cream money."

"All right, fine, I'll take a vanilla and chocolate twist. But make it the largest size you can do, please."

I shake my head and step up to the window. "I'll take the same, but a small."

"You never have any fun," he whispers.

Hayley comes back a minute later with my regular cone and another one as long as my forearm.

"Whoa," Max says.

"You said you wanted the biggest cone I could make," she says with a wink. "Happy to oblige. Let me know if you need anything else."

Looks like it's not only the girls in band who are noticing Max.

"You're going to be so sick," I tell him when I've paid and we're seated at a plastic table next to the window.

"When are you going to learn to stop underestimating me?" He takes a big bite. "I can finish this, no problem."

"There's literally no way you can finish that. She probably used all the ice cream in the machine to give you that."

"She was really nice."

"She was flirting with you."

He glances back at the window. "Was she? I couldn't tell."

"Are you going to homecoming tomorrow?" I blurt before I can stop myself.

He freezes right as he's about to take another bite. "Uh, nope." He studies me. "Are you?"

"No. Nova and I are hanging out instead."

He bobs his head, and we sit in silence. Okay, that was super awkward, but now I know for sure that he isn't going. Not that it's a big deal or matters at all to my life.

"Your hair looks especially good today," he says and takes an extra big bite of his ice cream cone.

I jolt at his unexpected words. "What? No, it doesn't."

"I said what I said."

"My hair almost never looks good," I argue. "It's impossible to control."

"You're just biased against it. I think it looks great even if it's 'frizzy.'" He says the last word with finger quotes, as if frizzy hair is a made-up concept that only I believe in. I can assure you, it is not. "It reminds me of when we were younger, and you'd have to constantly push it out of your face when you were playing a board game."

"Yeah, another added bonus of the curls. They make me look perpetually thirteen."

His gaze dips to my mouth and back up to my eyes. "You don't look thirteen anymore, Hazel."

His words send heat racing through me. What is going on with us? At least when we were at each other's throats, I knew what to expect. He'd be rude and I'd be rude right back. It was simple. Now, I barely know how to have a normal conversation with him.

I take a bite of my cone so I can refocus. "So, um, how's Brody taking his demotion?"

He rolls his eyes. "Pretty much like you'd imagine. He's decided to simultaneously stop caring about everything related to percussion while also pointing out my every flaw to the rest of the section. He thinks he's being subtle, but it's so obvious that he's trying to turn the section against me. The others have been cool, though. I took a few of the younger players aside after practice earlier this week and did some more rehearsing. I think it helped. How about you? Are you feeling better about guard?"

"Yeah, a little."

"More guard secrets?" he asks with a small smile. "That's fine, I won't pry." He takes another bite. "Actually, I'm curious about your take on Felix and Li."

I shake my head in confusion. "What are you talking about?"

"Well, I probably shouldn't say anything, but it seems like Felix is very . . . aware of Li. There's been a few times I thought he was staring off in the distance during practice, but then I realized he was watching her."

"Whoa, really?"

Today is full of surprises. I'm grateful that Felix hasn't been rude to Li or the rest of us, but it never occurred to me that he might be interested in her.

Max tilts his head thoughtfully. "I don't know, I haven't talked to him about it. Maybe it was a coincidence. But those two could be cute together. You should give them more D&D homework so they have a reason to talk."

I laugh in surprise. "Are you *matchmaking* right now?"

"You make it sound like we're living a hundred years ago. I'm not matchmaking, I'm just saying they have some common interests and they're both younger band members. Plus, you said Li is a bit of an outsider in your section, like Felix."

"That's matchmaking," I repeat, grinning. It's adorable that his mind would even go there.

"Never mind, forget I said anything."

"No, I think it's cute, I'm just not getting involved in anyone's love life. If there's something between them, they'll figure it out."

"Maybe." He leans forward. "But sometimes people never figure it out, even when all the evidence is right in front of them."

Suddenly, I'm not sure if we're talking about Li and Felix anymore. Instead of replying, I take another bite of my ice cream cone and hope it cools me down, since I'm pretty sure my temperature just skyrocketed.

Chapter Twenty-One

On Sunday morning, I wake up to a text from Max, asking if he can come over before D&D today so we can catch up on homework together. It's the first text he's sent since before he moved away. Honestly, I wasn't sure he even had my number anymore.

I'm shocked by how elated I am at the idea of spending more time together. Last month I was dreading his visits with my entire essence, and now I'm counting down the minutes until I can do homework? What is happening to me?

"Hazel, stop tapping your foot like that." Kelsey glares at me from across the dining room table. "You're making the table shake and I can't line up my stickers right."

We're sitting together while she works on her latest sticker book craft and I (pretend to) read for my English class while I actually watch the clock on my phone. I force myself to stop and shake out my limbs.

"Sorry."

"Why are you so twitchy?"

"Just bored. Wait until you're in high school and then you'll understand."

"It's because Max is coming," she says without looking up. She's too busy placing her stickers just so to form a unicorn.

"No, it's not. And how do you know that?"

"Mom told me. She said they might take me to Aunt Mary's house early today since you'd have a friend over. Your friend who's a *boy.*" She waggles her eyebrows.

There's a short knock on the front door and then I hear it creak open.

"Hello?" Max's voice calls from the hall.

I stand, but not before Kelsey has flown out of her seat and toward the front door. I hurry after her.

"Hiii!" she says and beams up at him. Today he's wearing a black Weezer shirt and his book bag is slung over one shoulder. My tension releases as soon as I lay eyes on him.

"Hey. That's a nice way to be greeted." He smiles down at her, and she stands even taller.

"That's because I'm way nicer than Hazel."

I sigh. "You're not way nicer—just nosy."

He crouches down so he's eye level with Kelsey. "Is she in one of her grouchy moods?" he asks in a stage whisper.

"When is she not?"

The two of them laugh and I cross my arms over my chest. "You know I can hear you two, right?"

Kelsey looks over her shoulder. "We know! We just don't care."

Max snorts. "You're way more fun than you were when I used to hang out over here."

"I don't think that's how I'd describe it," I mutter.

"Maybe Hazel should go to our aunt's house tonight instead and we can hang out here together," Kelsey says conspiratorially.

Max's shoulders shake in silent laughter, and he meets my gaze over the top of Kelsey's head. His expression is so relaxed that I can barely associate it with the downcast, miserable guy standing in this same hallway back in August. He looks so much like my childhood friend that it takes my breath away.

"Did I hear—oh, Max!" Mom walks into the hall, looking frazzled. "I thought I heard the door open. Sorry, there's so much going on between work and volunteering and this campaign that I can barely keep my head screwed on tight."

"No problem." Max straightens. "Thanks for letting me come over early. And, uh, sorry if I ever acted rude or anything before. I was just . . . going through some things."

She blinks in surprise. "Of course, it's already forgotten. We're always glad to have you here."

I gawk at Max. That was unexpected.

Mom pats Kelsey on the shoulder. "Are you ready?"

"Do I have to go?" she asks with a lingering glance at Max. I might be watching her form a crush on him right before my eyes.

"Well, Aunt Mary did mention something about making homemade ice cream and having a sundae party with the cousins, but if that doesn't sound fun, then—"

"We're making our own *ice cream*?"

Mom winks at me and hustles Kelsey toward the door.

"How quickly I'm forgotten," Max says as he follows me back into the dining room.

"As if anything can compete with sundae parties. Much better than homework." I nod toward his book bag.

"Truth."

We both pull out our laptops and settle into a rhythm. I keep my eyes strictly on my screen, though it's hard to focus knowing Max is right across from me. I'm hyperaware of his every sigh and shift of weight. Could he be paying attention to what I'm doing too? Or is he actually working like a good student? I can't tell, but I try to be as still and quiet as possible just in case. We're like that for fifteen minutes before he stretches and pulls out a water bottle. I take the opportunity to ask something that's been on my mind.

"So . . . what was going on with my mom back there?"

He shrugs and takes a drink of water. "It just felt like something I should do. You know, clear the air and all that. Especially if I'm going to be coming over here all the time."

A smile spreads across my face. "Is that your plan?"

"Yeah. If you're okay with it."

"Hmm." I tap my finger on my chin. "I'm not sure. Are you going to insist on us watching Lord of the Rings movies whenever we have free time?"

"That depends on whether you'll listen when I tell you about Christopher Lee."

"I won't. *But* that's because I already know all the lore. You forget how many times we watched those movies back in the day."

"I haven't forgotten anything."

Our eyes meet and the warmth of his gaze sends fire sparking down my veins. Then he grins. "Did I ever tell you that Viggo actually broke his toes when he kicked that helmet in *The Two Towers*?"

"I will throw this laptop at your head."

He chuckles and holds up his hands in defense. "All right, all right, back to work."

By the time the rest of our group arrives, Max and I have plowed through a mountain of homework. As happy as I am to see everyone, especially Zoinks with his big doggy grin, my anxiety for tonight quickly rises. I should have done more to prepare.

Last week we had to cancel our session because Felix was sick, which gave me a much-needed reprieve from figuring out how to handle this campaign, but I still haven't done anything about it. I could blame my packed schedule, but really I've been procrastinating. That backstory and added mystery from Li and Felix really threw me. I can't work out how to incorporate everything smoothly, but I also don't want to tell them they have to change it.

I start the game again where we left off last time, with their characters exploring the city and throwing out miscellaneous suggestions of what they'd like to do next. I have no real plan for them.

But, when in doubt, throw a monster in their path.

"Ha!" Max yells after successfully attacking the harpies, our latest monster, once again. "I do thirteen points of damage."

His yelling gets Zoinks worked up. The dog puts his paws on the dining room table and barks loudly.

"Thank you, my thoughts exactly!" Max calls to him.

Zoinks trots to Max for pets, then goes around to each of the rest of us for scratches and attention, which we happily give. I *love* having Zoinks here. Not only is he incredibly adorable, but playing with him kills a lot of time and keeps people from fully realizing how dumb this campaign is.

"Now you know why Zelda—and Zoinks—is such an extrovert," Nova says, almost aggravated, as she gives Zoinks a kiss on the head. Her turn is next, so she has her ranger throw a dagger at a harpy for more damage.

"Li, what would you like to do?" I ask gently when Nova's finished. She hasn't said much since we started playing. Usually she's so enthusiastic.

"Um . . ." She frowns and flips through pages of the manual in front of her. "I'm not sure. I guess Axolotl needs healing, right? I could do that."

"If you want to," I reply.

"I kind of wish I would have chosen another class," she says after healing him. She picks at the food Mom made for everyone tonight. "I guess I didn't realize how much fighting there was in D&D. Max, you were smart to pick fighter as your class."

"I'm thrilled to be in a party with two druids," Max tells her. "That means two people who could heal me when I almost kill myself for the fifth time this session." He laughs, but her returning smile doesn't reach her eyes.

Sure enough, Max finishes off the harpies after a couple more rounds but gets down to his last hit points and needs to be healed once again.

"There are certainly a lot of monsters descending on this city," Nova says to the group when everyone is dusted off and ready to continue on. "What do you think it means?"

That I'm a boring Dungeon Master, I think to myself and squeeze my dice behind the screen.

"Maybe there's something here they want?" Felix says.

"Or something is drawing them here?" Nova replies.

"Do we see anyone around we could ask about these things?" Li asks me.

"Um . . ." My foot is shaking under the table. "You're on a main thoroughfare in the city, so there are many established businesses surrounding you. However, when the harpies came, the people on the roads ran for cover and the business owners all locked their doors and hid away."

"It's impossible to get information in this place," Felix complains, and Li nods back at him.

"We just have to know how to ask," Max says. "Is the road we're on slanted?"

"Yes." I have no idea why he's asking, but I can't keep shutting everyone down or they really are going to abandon the game.

"Perfect." He leans forward toward the other players. "What we need is to talk to someone in charge. The city has now had three major encounters in a row and we're the ones who keep saving the day. We deserve answers and compensation for all this death-defying work."

"It wouldn't be so death-defying if you didn't keep charging into battle," Felix says with a shake of his head.

"Well then, I wouldn't be doing a good job role-playing because that's exactly what Axolotl and his axes would do. So, here's my thought. We start walking up this road—"

"Until we come to whoever lives at the top of it," Nova finishes. "Brilliant. Rich and powerful people always live on top of hills."

Everyone nods their agreement and turns back to me. I don't know who lives at the top of this hill, but I better figure it out pronto.

"Right. Okay, you all walk up the road for twenty minutes. During that time you pass only a few people, who avert their gazes and hurry past you. Eventually you see a large structure at the top of the hill. It's a . . ." I roll a d20 in my hands mindlessly and try to pull something together. "It's a citadel. Two guards are posted at the entrance."

"We go up to the first and ask what's been happening in the city lately," Li says immediately.

I clear my throat. "The city is being overrun by foul beasts, day and night," I tell them in the deeper voice of the guard. "We used to be on the streets constantly, battling them back, but our ranks were diminished and now our leader doesn't send us out."

Nova frowns. "But if the city is under siege, why did you have a musical festival only days ago?"

I cringe. It's literally painful discovering in real time how bad I am at this.

"Uh . . . well . . ." I look down at the table and back up. "Our ruler thought that it would be a good idea. To bring more people to the area."

"More people to be slaughtered, it sounds like," Felix says.

"And to support the local businesses," I continue. "That's why he planned the festival for outside the city. And to give the remaining townspeople something to look forward to. They have so little."

"And they'd have even less if it wasn't for us," Max retorts, but at least the group looks mollified by the answers.

"Do you know if any other elves have come here for refuge?" Li asks my guard. "Or any information about a blight in the lands to the east of here? We're searching for information."

"No other elves have come, or at least they haven't made themselves known to me," I reply in my deep voice.

Li droops a bit and my stomach twists in guilt. I hate seeing her this way, but I don't even know why this city is under siege (except that encounters with monsters are easier for me to throw together).

"Zelda steps into the guard's personal space and growls," Nova says and pats Zoinks on the head. His tongue flops out into a huge grin and we all laugh. He couldn't intimidate a mouse. "You don't seem like the kind of man who has a lot of answers, and since that's all we need right now, I think we're done with you. We want to speak to your ruler."

If I wanted to, I could refuse to take them, or make the party persuade my character to do their bidding, but I don't have the heart to do that. I've already given them enough pushback.

"Oh my god, I'm sorry to interrupt, but your dog is precious! Can I pet him?"

We look up to find Melanie standing in the doorway to the dining room. The rest of Mom and Dad's group walks up the basement stairs, and it's clear the night is done. We didn't accomplish very much other than fighting, but the party didn't revolt against me, so that's something.

Li is especially quiet as everyone packs up and heads out. She doesn't even laugh when Zoinks stands on his hind legs to give Max a lick on the cheek.

"Doing okay?" I ask her quietly.

"Yep. See you tomorrow." She waves, but my stomach clenches at her monotone. I'm letting her down as DM, that much is clear. Felix is quick to her side. The two walk out, talking in hushed voices, and I'm left in the doorway with my worries and self-doubt.

Chapter Twenty-Two

Max: Do you have time to go to a game store with me after school? I thought we could pick up some D&D miniatures for the game.

I blink and reread the message as I walk to my sixth-period class, still getting used to the fact that Max and I text now. It's Wednesday, the one day each week when we don't have extra band practice after school, so technically I'm free this afternoon.

Hazel: Where? We don't have anything in town.

Max: I know, it's one of the worst parts about living here. I found one about forty-five minutes away though. I can drive us.

I squeeze my phone a little tighter. A whole afternoon with Max *and* a game store? There's no way I can say no to that.

I'm outside as soon as he pulls into my driveway after school. My heart speeds at the sight of him.

"Hey," I say as I climb into his car. I'm proud of how normal my voice sounds. "This is unexpected."

"I know." He backs out onto the road. "But I was thinking about it, and the game doesn't feel legit without some miniatures. I think it'll help us to be able to visualize the layout of the city."

Mental note that *I* need to figure out the layout by Sunday.

"I was going to order some online," he continues, "but I figured it was probably smart to include the DM in the process."

"I appreciate that."

I sneak a glance at him. Is that the only reason he invited me—so that he wouldn't overstep in the game? Or was he looking for more ways to spend time alone with me too?

"So, what should we listen to on the drive?" He runs a hand through his hair, looking almost self-conscious. "I have some pretty great playlists. I even have some classics on them, which I know you'll like."

I take his phone and scroll through his Spotify. Okay, I'll admit there are some nineties bands on there like Nirvana, Nine Inch Nails, and Stone Temple Pilots that I like. But there's not a single female artist on any of the lists. I sigh and hand it back to him.

"I think we need to broaden your horizons. I've got the perfect playlist." I have about two billion, but the one I'm thinking of is a little less angry than my usuals. More "Lovefool" from the Cardigans and less "You Oughta Know" from Alanis Morissette.

I'm expecting to get some side-eye from him when the first song starts playing, but instead he smiles lightly and relaxes against the headrest. We listen quietly to a few songs before Max sits up abruptly.

"*Now* we're talking." He leans forward to turn up the volume. "You know I love a good drum opening."

"This is one of my favorites."

It's a cover of "I Want You to Want Me" from Letters to Cleo, one of my favorite nineties bands. They played this song on the rooftop at the end of *10 Things I Hate About You,* and it was absolutely perfect. I can't help singing along, and it seems Max is incapable of listening to music without using the steering wheel as a makeshift drum. Soon we're laughing and bopping along as we zoom past cornfields.

"See, this is what happens when you listen to more female lead singers," I tease him.

"Fine, fine, you've made your point," he concedes. "But I'm not giving up Nine Inch Nails."

Eventually we switch from music to listening to *Don't Split the Party* so that we can be properly inspired before we get to the store. We make it to Scottsville and Max pulls into a parking lot that's seen better days. The game store, Sword and Board Games, is in a neglected shopping center next to a pizza shop, a nail salon, and an off-brand dollar store. It's not exactly inviting.

I give Max a dubious look. "Are you sure about this?"

"I've heard good things. We should at least check it out."

We're a few steps from the door when two teenage girls walk out. The South Asian girl is wearing purple d20 earrings I wouldn't mind owning, while the white girl next to her is decked out in a green paisley maxi skirt and tank top with a ton of long beaded necklaces. They're laughing and talking quietly to each other, completely oblivious to us. I'm honestly surprised to see other girls my age here. I haven't been to a lot of game stores, but when my parents have taken me in the past, I've always felt a little out of place.

"—tell Logan how much jewelry they bought from us," the necklace girl says to her friend as they walk past.

"I know, I can't believe it, Quinn!"

I do a double take and look over my shoulder at their backs. That's . . . weird. Weren't some of the livestream players named Logan and Quinn?

Max pauses at the door. "Ready?"

I shake my head so I can focus and turn my attention back to him. The interior is way cozier than I'm expecting. Large wooden shelves fill most of the space, with a long checkout counter along the left-hand side. Behind it is a man wearing a Monty Python shirt. In the far back, I can see a door to another room. There's quiet chatter and laughter coming from there that makes the store feel welcoming.

We aren't in a huge hurry since we both told our parents not to expect us home for dinner, so we slowly meander through each aisle. When I turn the corner, I laugh and look over my shoulder.

"Uh-oh. You might not want to come over here unless you'd like to be reminded of your epic loss."

This aisle is dedicated to board games, and many of the

shelves closest to me are filled with various versions of Settlers of Catan.

Max comes to my side and examines the shelves. "You did not win that game."

"Keep telling yourself that. I schooled you constantly at board games."

"You did not," he argues, but he's smiling. "Anyway, I could take you now. I've changed a lot since we played last."

Yes, you have, I think, and allow myself a quick glance of appreciation. "Actually, I've been thinking about that."

"About how good I am at board games? I like to reflect on that too."

"No," I say, rolling my eyes. "About how you're different now than you used to be."

He stills. "For better or worse? Actually, never mind. I don't want to know."

"That answer depends on when you ask me," I tease. We leave the board game aisle behind and move into Warhammer. "But you seem, I don't know, more self-confident. And popular. Every time I see you in band, you're laughing with someone or making a ridiculous bet—"

"My bets are not ridiculous—"

"Or people are hovering around you. You didn't used to be like that. You were a nerd like me."

He gently grasps my upper arm. I stop walking and turn to look at him. "You say that like being a nerd is a bad thing. Do you know how excited I am for our game Sunday? Or how many notes I've taken on my phone about Axolotl and his hobbies? By the way, he has an artisan background and likes to spend his free time forging intricately designed weapons and little metal sculptures. One of my favorite things about being back is getting to be a nerd with you again."

My breath hitches. I missed this—*him*—more than it's safe to say.

Max clears his throat. "We should probably find the D&D section, yeah?"

D&D merchandise fills the entire right-side wall of the store. It's both impressive and intimidating to see how much they have. There are rule books, spellbook cards, battle mats, and even themed greeting cards. I skim the seemingly endless rows of painted and unpainted miniature figurines. You could play for fifty years and not even get close to playing each possible character type.

"I don't have a ton of money, but I want to make sure we get miniatures for Felix, Li, and Nova too," I say. "And maybe some terrain?"

"Look, a dragonborn fighter!" Max says and holds up a miniature.

I scrutinize it. "Is that how you pictured him, though? I didn't think he had red scales."

"Yeah, true . . ."

I find elf druid minis for Li and Felix, but they also don't look the way I'd imagined their characters.

"What do you think?" I ask and show Max. "Will the others be disappointed if these don't match their character descriptions? Li already knows every detail about how Ellywich looks."

"We can't afford to have custom characters made for everyone. But, if you're worried, we could get unpainted miniatures. That is, if you think we'd be up for painting them? It would be time-consuming."

That sounds like another excuse to hang out together, and I'm not going to fight it. "We could have a nachos and painting party some afternoon. Then surprise everyone with their minis at the game?"

He nods. "Sounds like a perfect idea."

We decide we'll each buy two—I'll buy the ones for Li and Felix and he'll get the others. We take our time picking out the four characters, and Max grabs a ton of different paints. It's expensive, but he insists on paying for those.

The man at the register earlier has been replaced with a girl my age. Her blond hair is piled on the top of her head in a messy bun, and she's wearing a bright orange shirt covered in strawberries along with dangling Pop-Tart earrings.

"Hi, did you find everything okay?" she asks Max as he hands her the items.

"I think we found too much stuff, actually."

He pays, then leans toward me and puts a hand on my lower back. "I'll be right back," he whispers. He's gone in an instant, but it's like he's sent an electric jolt through me. He walks to the other end of the counter where lots of open boxes sit in rows.

I push my items toward the employee. "We could've easily spent a few hundred dollars here if we had the extra money."

"My friends and I have the same problem. It's a constant struggle even with my discount."

"Sounds like a workplace hazard. I love your earrings, by the way."

She smiles softly and touches one. "Thanks. They were a gift from my boyfriend."

I glance over at Max, wondering what he's doing, and see he's now chatting with another guy. Max is holding some card packs, but I can't tell what kind. The girl hands me a small shopping bag.

"Hey, do you know what cards they're looking at?"

She squints. "Those are Yu-Gi-Oh! cards."

I laugh and shake my head. I walk to Max's side, and she comes around the counter to follow me.

"Have you been holding out on me?" I ask him. "Do you still secretly play Yu-Gi-Oh!?"

He winces. "I mean, maybe. Kinda. And I make extra money selling cards online." He holds up his bag of paints and minis as if to explain how he was able to afford them.

The guy next to him adjusts his black glasses. "You can make good money doing that. I keep thinking I should try it."

"With your abundant spare time?" the blond girl asks in a teasing voice. "Remember, stage crew is going to be no joke this year."

"Especially with you as director." He leans over and kisses her on the temple before turning to us. "You know, if you're interested, we run a weekly tournament and you're welcome to join. I'm Nathan, by the way. I probably should've started with that."

"Riley," the girl says with a little wave.

Max glances longingly at the cards. "We're from out of town, so it'd be hard to get over here every week. We just came for D&D figurines because I'd heard good things."

"I'll be sure to let my dad know," Riley says. "What characters are you playing in your game?"

We tell them, and Nathan and Riley nod their heads approvingly.

"Very cool," Riley says to me. "DMing seems so intimidating."

"You're not wrong. It's been a bit of a struggle."

Max nudges me with his shoulder. "Don't listen to her, she's doing awesome."

Riley opens her mouth to say something else, but just then the door opens. Two more teenagers walk in, hand in hand, and I'm suddenly really sad that we don't have a place like this in our town. It would be cool to have a store where we could hang out rather than being in my dining room.

"Hoshiko!" Riley exclaims and waves. She looks back to us. "Sorry, we should go. Our senior class trip to NYC is coming up and there's so much to plan. But good luck with your game!"

"She means there are so many Broadway shows to squeeze in," Nathan says and takes her hand.

She grins. "Same thing."

He chuckles. "You're always welcome at our tournaments or if you want to play D&D here. There's plenty of space."

With that, they wave goodbye and head for the back. Nathan lifts Riley's hand to his lips as they walk to their friends, and the sight makes my chest ache. It's surprisingly heartwarming to see a couple my age look so happy. I've barely dated myself, other than a few dates for school dances and an occasional movie, and Nova's sworn off dating altogether until she gets to college. Is there a version of reality where Max and I could ever act like that? I sneak a glance at him. I'm probably getting way ahead of myself.

"They were cool," Max says as we walk back to his car.

"Totally. I'm glad you suggested we come. Otherwise, I never would've learned you're still a huge Yu-Gi-Oh! nerd."

He groans.

"I just can't believe you didn't tell me."

"And now you know why I didn't."

We get into his car and head back toward home.

"Now I *really* can't wait for D&D this Sunday," Max says. "I loved fighting off those harpies before. Are there going to be more?"

"I can't tell you. That would compromise my integrity as a Dungeon Master." I try for a playful tone, but it falls flat.

"You sound less than excited."

I heave a sigh and lean back into the seat. "It's just . . ."

I study his profile, wondering how much to say. As a DM, I should be keeping my ideas for the game secret, and also . . . I'm still a little nervous about being vulnerable around him. He already knows my struggles with color guard. Does he really need to know about another area of my life where I'm failing? But, to his credit, he hasn't once thrown my worries as section leader back in my face. Hopefully I can trust him with this too.

"Running the game is harder than I thought it would be," I admit. "And I already knew it was going to be tough."

"But you've done great."

I deflate. "I only threw a bunch of monster encounters at you all in the city because I didn't know what else to do and didn't take the time I should have to prepare. I wasn't even planning on the group going into the city."

"Really?" He looks away from the road for a split second. "Isn't that where you were leading us? You had the festival right outside of the city."

I laugh. "The opposite actually. I had an entire dungeon crawl planned out in the forest with hidden doors and treasure chests." My fingernails press painfully into my palms. "I'm too rigid to be a DM. When that plan didn't work out, I just kind of . . . froze. And I'm pissing everyone off."

Max shakes his head so forcefully that I'm not sure he can see in front of him. "Did Nova say that?"

"No, but I don't think Li and Felix are having a good time. I totally blew off the backstory they made up for their characters."

"You're being too hard on yourself. We wouldn't be playing at all if it wasn't for you." He taps the steering wheel. "Can I help somehow?"

"Do you want to take over as DM?" I ask, only half joking.

"I mean, I guess I could give it a go. It'd be a shame to lose Axolotl from the group, though. And to lose such an awesome DM. I don't think you should give up."

I press the heels of my hands into my eyes. "*Or,* hear me out, what if I devote myself to *Yu-Gi-Oh!* instead? I can't imagine how many shows I've missed since I stopped watching."

"Yeah, I don't think so. You should talk to Li. She seems open-minded, I bet you can work it out."

"Ugh." I blow an errant curl from my forehead. "Thank you for your stupid, logical advice, I guess."

"Anytime. Thanks for trusting me enough to tell me." He glances over at me again. "I'm glad you didn't give up on me."

My pulse thrums at his words. "I'm not sure I'm capable of giving up on you. Not really." I bite the inside of my cheek. "Although sometimes I did want to pour thawed Popsicle juice on your head."

He scrubs a hand over his face. "I'm never living that one down, huh?"

"There's *a lot* you're never living down. But this afternoon was a step in the right direction."

Chapter Twenty-Three

"What are you all doing?" Faith asks Friday afternoon when she walks into the auditorium, which the guard has taken over like it's our second home. This evening we have an away game, so we're prepping in here before we load up the buses and head to Coshocton High School.

Yori looks up with a huge smile. "We thought we'd get our hair braided and paint our nails together before the game."

"Oh." Faith glances at me in surprise. "Well, that sounds great."

I do a last swipe of green nail polish onto Devin's pinky. He inspects it and nods in approval. "Thanks, Hazel."

"No problem." I stand and walk to Faith's side.

She leans closer. "So, this is a . . . surprise."

I cross my arms over my chest and take in the scene. Some members are still sitting in groups of twos and threes (I don't think I'll ever be able to split up Madisyn, Addison, and Devin), but more people are sitting together. I'm happy to see that Rosa and Yori are hanging out with Li so she's not perpetually alone in our group. There's nail painting, French braiding, and lots of chatter. A small voice in the back of my head argues that this is a waste of time, and that we'd be better off reviewing some choreography before heading out, but I push that voice away. I need to see how this method works before dismissing it.

"Sire's been talking about how there's something different with the color guard lately, and now I see what he means," Faith says quietly.

"You talk to Sire?"

She lifts an eyebrow. "I know I can't be here every day, but I'm still the color guard director. He gives me a daily update."

"Oh."

"Don't worry, like I said, they've been positive comments. Yesterday he said I might be out of a job if you keep this up."

My cheeks warm, but I try not to look too pleased with myself. "I've been thinking more about what you said before. And I've been watching the other section leaders too. I thought I'd switch it up some."

"Good switching. This is the way to win Superior ratings." She nods approvingly. "And best in show awards."

Just the possibility ignites the competitive fire inside me. This time, I think she might be right. The members have really embraced DJing our warm-ups and they've even taken to calling each other by their character names. That's certainly helped the morale of the group, but practicing in front of mirrors is what's made the biggest difference. I barely have to call out the corrections anymore when we're practicing inside because they can see it for themselves.

I turn to her. "Do you think you'll be here for our practices this coming week? I'm sure having you here would motivate the others even more."

"I'll try my hardest," she says, but she doesn't look confident. "But like I said, I'm not even sure you need me."

I swallow down a sigh. I know there are some perks to this arrangement with Faith. It gives me a lot of control over the guard without an adult to constantly answer to. But if I want the guard to have a successful end to the season, then I'm the one who is going to have to make that happen. I wish the knowledge wasn't suffocating, but sometimes it feels hard to take a deep breath.

Thirty minutes later, the whole band heads outside to load onto the buses. Nova makes a beeline for me.

"What's wrong?" she asks.

"Just a frustrating conversation with Faith."

I look around the crowd to make sure Faith is far away before I say more. Instead, I see Max laughing with Felix and a few other percussion guys. As usual, he looks happy and relaxed. He's fallen into his role as section leader so easily, it's like he's been with our band for years. There's a pang in my chest knowing that he's standing so close, but there's no way I can go up and talk to him without making everything weird. Felix might be cool with me joining their group, but I'm sure the others wouldn't be.

"Uh, Hazel, hello? Did you hear me?" Nova waves a hand in front of my eyes, then follows my gaze. "Girl . . ."

I spin and put my back to Max. "Sorry. It's not what it looks like."

"Like you're pining over him? Because I'm pretty sure it's exactly what it looks like."

"I was just thinking that it sucks how Max and I are friends, but we don't hang out at band."

"I hope you're not thinking about kicking me out as seatmate on the bus."

"No, of course not," I reply quickly. We'd probably spend the entire ride bickering if Max and I ever sat together. Or maybe we'd sit in silence because we'd run out of things to say to each other. Of course, a lot of couples don't use the long bus rides for talking . . .

My cheeks heat and I shut off those thoughts immediately.

Nova shakes her head. "Listen, I'm happy you aren't at each other's throats anymore, but you need to be careful around Max. I think you should stick to playing D&D with him, instead of whatever this other game is."

"What are you talking about? We're friends now."

"You can fool everyone else, Hazel, including Max and maybe even yourself, but you *can't* fool me. Whatever childhood crush you had on him, it's coming back in full force and denying it isn't going to make it go away." She looks between us. "I just don't see how anything between you two will work out when you can barely acknowledge each other in public. I don't want to see you get your heart broken."

I put my head on her shoulder. "That's not going to

happen," I whisper. But my voice doesn't come out as confidently as I'd hoped. Nova knows me too well.

I wait until Max lines up for a bus and then make sure to ride the other one so there's no awkwardness. And once we arrive, there's no time to think about anything but getting ready for the football game. It's always disconcerting being at a new school. Yes, high school football fields are the same size, but they *feel* different. There's something comforting about stepping out onto a newly painted thirty-yard line knowing that this is the exact same grass you've been on a hundred times before. Here, nothing feels quite right.

The first two quarters go smoothly, but I'm nervous as we walk to the field for the halftime show. Faith walks through the guard, squeezing our shoulders. I catch the eye of a few members and smile encouragingly, although I notice that Li always seems to be looking in a different direction when I turn toward her. This isn't the place to have a real conversation with her about the D&D game, but I need to do it soon.

We walk along the length of the football field between the crowd and the pit, where the larger percussion instruments sit. Up ahead, other sections are pumping each other up with their chants. The clarinets and flutes each yell theirs, and then the saxophone section screams, "We love sax!" followed by a chorus of laughter and squeals.

"I should've played saxophone just so I could go around screaming that," Callie tells the rest of us with a smirk.

Out of the corner of my eye, I see Brody standing in the pit with three or four other kids from the percussion section. It's an odd place for him to be lingering since he doesn't play a pit instrument. Something about this doesn't feel right. I glance around, looking for Max, but he's not anywhere I can see.

My steps slow as Brody and Kyle unfurl a roll of paper and lift it above their heads. Gasps and laughs trickle through the band and up into the stands as people begin to notice.

It's a printed banner that says:

Glen Vale Color Guard Toilet Cleaners

And on either side of the words is a picture of a toilet bowl . . . with our faces inside the toilet. A picture of each member of the color guard has been photoshopped so it looks as if we're floating pieces of poop.

Keira screams, as do Madisyn and Addison. My whole body goes rigid, my hands balling up into fists, and I swing around to take in everyone else's reactions. The whole band has frozen to read the sign. Some are laughing while others glare at percussion. *Everyone* is whispering about it, and already I see crowd members pulling out their phones to take pictures.

"We wanted to make you something special to cheer you on for the rest of the season!" Brody calls in our direction.

I step forward. I'm going to knock this kid unconscious with my flag pole. I don't care how many witnesses are here.

Devin grabs my arm to pull me back at the same time that Mrs. Lewis, Mr. Jenkins, Faith, and Sire push through the band toward Brody and the other percussion members.

"The entire crowd just saw my *face* in a toilet!" Rosa cries in horror.

"All our faces!" Yori adds. "You know everyone's going to post photos."

Addison drops her face to her hands. "Just when I think I can't hate them more, they always prove me wrong."

All the band instructors look thunderous. Sire rips the paper banner from their hands and gives it to Faith, who crumples it into a ball. I'm still shaky and adrenaline is pouring through me, but Sire's and Faith's rage is soothing. I'm too far away to hear what's being said, but it looks like that group will be suspended from the performance tonight.

I shake myself and turn away from the scene. I will not let Brody get to me. And I'm not letting him get to the rest of the guard either.

"Do you think Max knew about that?" Li whispers from my side.

I shake my head. Brody only had a few kids with him, and Max was nowhere to be seen. It's much more likely that Brody concocted that show all on his own.

"I don't think so," I tell her, then call out to the whole group. "Hey, everyone? Huddle up for a second."

Reluctantly, the others circle around me. A few, like Li, still look shaken. The others look mutinous.

"We already know Brody is a bully and a jerk," I say fiercely, "which means the only way we let him win is by letting him get in our heads. I don't want to give him that power. We've done a lot of work over the last few weeks, and it's time we show everyone just what we can do."

Rosa and Deja nod and Yori claps her hands. "You already know what Oof would do to Brody."

I point to her. "Then let's use that to put all our doubters in their place for once. In fact, I've been playing with a new chant of our own, and I think tonight is the right time to use it." I had been planning on pulling out this new color guard chant for our third competition, but right now is the time to light a fire under us. I whisper the words to them, then take a step back.

I call out: *"Show up!"*

And they respond: *"Show out!"*

"All in!"

"No doubt!"

I put my hand in the middle and the others join me. *"Glen Vale Guard!"*

We scream the last words and lift our hands triumphantly in the air.

Our field commander blows her whistle to call the band to attention. Brody and the others may think they know what we're capable of, but they have no clue.

Everything about tonight's performance feels different from the moment we step onto the field. We're performing the last song of our competition show tonight, since this is mostly a crowd who's never seen it and we always need the practice. I march to my starting position and see that Brody and several other percussion players are indeed standing on the sidelines. I smile serenely and stare into the faces in the crowd with pride.

The performance begins and energy flows through me as the guard transitions through our choreography, moving from our windmill moves into butterflies. It's a cool night and quiet enough that I can hear our flags ripple in unison. When we hit the drum break, the guard members run from our various places on the field to line up on the fifty-yard line. Right on cue, we begin one of our hardest pieces of choreography—staggered pop tosses starting from the front of the line and rippling back to the last person. But tonight, I don't need to call out our musical counts or hold my breath in fear. I know we're hitting the choreography dead-on, and I'm not sure I've ever been prouder of anything.

We get a big round of applause from the crowd when we're finished, which is impressive since it's an away game . . . and they just saw our faces inside of toilets. We high-five and Faith comes running over for hugs.

Sire calls us to attention on the sidelines. "Nicely done to those of you on the field tonight. However, I want to say that while we might not be here in an athletic capacity tonight, any unsportsmanlike conduct is *absolutely* unacceptable. We expect much better of you, and if we see anything again like what we saw before the show"—he cuts his eyes to Brody—"individuals will be removed from this band. Understood?" Sire slowly meets our eyes. "All right. You can grab food during third quarter, but be back at the stands by the time fourth quarter starts. I'm not in the mood to go searching for people. And color guard—"

My stomach jumps into my throat.

"Good job tonight." His eyes meet mine. "That's the kind of improvement I'd like to see from the whole band."

I bob my head and try to play it cool. Li, Rosa, and Deja high-five me with huge grins. "Nicely done!" I whisper to them, my whole body vibrating with excitement and relief. I'm embarrassed that my eyes are stinging from the threat of tears. It's a small thing, this compliment, but Sire's approval feels like an award.

Fingers graze my elbow, and I turn to find Max at my side. His expression is strained.

"Can I talk to you?" he asks quietly, his voice low and tense. "Alone?"

"Percussion doesn't deserve your attention," Callie tells me.

"Your section is pitiful," Madisyn growls at him.

I look between the guard and Max. I can understand their reactions, but I need to talk to Max.

"It's okay, just give us five minutes," I tell them. "I'll be fine."

They cross their arms and glare at Max, but no one argues. Max leads me toward a quiet area behind the bleachers. It's not exactly private, but most everyone is standing in line for concessions, so we have the space to ourselves for now.

"I'm sorry, Hazel." The words rush out of him. "I know you don't have a reason to believe me, but I *swear* I didn't know they were planning on doing that."

"It's okay. I know you didn't know."

He stares at me in shock. "But . . . I figured you'd . . ."

Everything about him is so rigid. It's clear he's freaking out about my possible reaction. Li was quick to wonder if he was behind it, and it makes sense that I'd assume the same, but the possibility hadn't occurred to me. As soon as I saw Brody, I knew Max had no part in it.

I shrug, trying to think of how to explain my reaction to him. "I didn't assume anything. I guess I just trust you now."

He takes a deep breath. "Hazel, there's . . ." He trails off, tugging at his uniform. His hands clench and then unclench.

"What? Is something else going on?"

"No, it's nothing." He runs a hand through his hair. "Only that I'm glad you aren't mad."

"You can't be expected to control Brody, especially when you're nowhere around him." I smile lightly. "And honestly, there's nothing like rage to motivate people. That's probably the best we've performed all season, and now the guard knows they're capable of performances like that. I almost feel like I should thank Brody for making us better. I'm not going to, of course, but I could."

"If you thank him, please let me be there to witness it." He shakes his head in disbelief. "Wow, I really thought we were about to get into a huge fight. I was preparing a whole speech in my mind about why you should forgive me."

"I'd like to hear that."

He steps closer, and his nearness sends sparks up my spine. "I could still give you the speech. It includes a lot of pleading, in case that's of interest."

It's always of interest, but I'm still wrapping my mind around the fact that he cares this much. Speeches? Pleading? It's obvious he's more worried about my opinion of him than I'd dared to guess before. Am I the biggest fool in the world to trust him like this? But the fact is that I *do* trust him now, without question, whether or not I should.

"Well, if we're not going to fight, then do you want to get some food?" Max asks.

I'm hesitant to leave the security of the bleachers with Max still by my side. I don't want any more attention, or for the guard to think I'm a traitor, but I'm hungry and I want to hang out with him. If they get mad, I'll just explain he had nothing to do with it.

We head to the concession line and skim the menu sign while we wait. "Why don't you save your speech for the next time Brody does something stupid," I say. "It'd be nice if we could schedule that for directly before our third band competition since it's such a great motivator for my guard. Not that we'll need help blowing you out of the water with our upcoming best auxiliary trophy."

"There are the fighting words I've been waiting for," he says with a smirk. It's amazing how attractive he can look while sporting a green-and-white band uniform and a hat with a big white plume. "Now you're motivating me. I might need to call an extra rehearsal."

"I've already called two."

"And maybe more section dinners for extra bonding."

"I booked a five-night cruise to the Bahamas for our bonding sessions."

Max laughs. "Hand me a flag, then. I'm officially joining guard."

We make it to the front of the line. I order a slice of pizza and Max orders nachos, of course. When we step out of line with our food, he holds out the plastic container to me.

"I think we can both agree you deserve first dibs tonight."

These aren't nearly as impressive as the ones we made together before our first D&D game, but the hot nacho cheese sauce smothering the chips still looks pretty tasty. My eyes rove around the pile, and I find one on the edge that looks pretty good.

"Nope." He plucks the chip from my hand. "Not one of the sad nachos. Take the one at the very top." He gazes at me like he's imparting real wisdom. "Top Nacho, Hazel. Never forget you're Top Nacho."

His words are silly, but butterflies flutter in my stomach, nonetheless. It's dangerous how much I'd rather eat mildly stale nachos with him than do anything else in the world.

Chapter Twenty-Four

Saturday I'm scheduled to work a shift at the Glen Vale High food stand at our county fair. The fair is a *big* deal around here, and we make most of the money we need for the rest of the year from the proceeds, so shifts are pretty nonnegotiable.

Despite the fact that it's late September, it feels like July. It's in the mid-eighties and sunny, and no place in the fairgrounds has air-conditioning. When I arrive, I'm happy to see that Max is also working the same shift as me and Nova. She and I are given positions as servers, so it's our job to pick up orders at the back counter and then take them out to the tables. It's not a hard job, and people are always happy to get their food, but I'm sweating within minutes. I shouldn't complain, though, since it's nothing compared with Max's job.

"Ahh!" he cries, not for the first time. I lean over the counter toward the back kitchen.

“How are you holding up in there?” I call to him through the little window that separates the serving station from the cooks.

“What is *wrong* with this doughnut baller! Every time I make a new batch, I end up burning myself!”

“At least they taste good?”

“That’s probably because each order comes with a small shard of my soul,” he mutters. “And my skin.”

All the seniors know to stay away from the doughnut baller. It’s a countertop deep fryer that makes mini doughnuts very quickly, but it’s tricky to use without a lot of experience. Usually a parent will unwittingly volunteer, but none of the adults argued when Max asked to do it. Plus, all the cooks with hair more than a few inches long have to wear a hairnet for food safety. Since Max’s hair is long enough to cover his eyes, he got that supercool accessory as well. I’ve already taken a dozen pictures of him on my phone—secretly, of course. We’re friends, but it never hurts to have blackmail material just in case.

“Three more orders, Max!” calls Nova’s dad from the cash register with a smile that’s a bit too big.

Usually my parents try to sign up for the same shift as me, but this year they’re caught up with 4-H, which is an organization that helps kids connect with the community and learn practical skills. I did it when I was younger, and now Kelsey is involved, which means that—of course—Mom volunteered to be the adviser for her local 4-H club. It keeps her busy all year, but during fair time it might as well be another full-time job. Both of my parents are practically living at the fairgrounds—which isn’t unheard of if you’re showing farm animals—and I have no idea how they're doing it all. Luckily, they haven't roped me into any extra activities for the afternoon.

Nova comes up next to me. "Still struggling?" she asks with a nod toward Max.

"He's not very happy." There's another yelp before I can say more.

She chuckles. "You didn't think to warn him?"

"And take away his bragging rights? Now no one can say he isn't part of Glen Vale."

When we're released at the end of our (very long) three-hour shift, we walk out onto one of the main thoroughfares lined with carnival games and food stands and pull off the Glen Vale Knights shirts we're required to wear over our clothes. Max rips off his hairnet with pure glee.

"How do I look?" he asks me with a serious expression and shakes out his hair. I want to tease him, but the reality is that he looks so hot right now it's hard to pull my eyes from him.

"Stop fishing for compliments," Nova tells him. "Everyone knows you've got great hair."

"I'll stop fishing when you stop giving." He runs his hand through it like he's a model. "And people say you're rough around the edges."

I shake my head in warning. "Don't make her mad."

"I'll sic Zelda on Axolotl tomorrow if you aren't careful," Nova says.

Max laughs. "I'm gonna be honest with you, I'm not too intimidated by Zelda. Or Zoinks. The worst I'm likely to get is dog saliva on my face."

"We'll see what the dice say," she retorts without heat. "Should we walk around?"

I'm happily surprised that Nova's including Max. She and I have been to the county fair every year since we met, and over the years, we've perfected our routine, including stops for lemon shake-ups (the ratio of lemon to sugar needs to be just right), the perfect fries (thin, greasy, and covered in salt), and our favorite sandwiches (Italian sausage and peppers from the stall at the entrance to the Dairy building).

"Yes! I could use a lemon shake-up first. Do we want to—" I break off when I see Li in the distance. She's all alone and walking in the direction of the education and art barns. I still haven't had that conversation with her. There never seems to be a good time for it . . . which is why I keep putting it off. If I don't talk to her today, then we'll be back in the same position at the D&D game tomorrow.

I bite my lip and glance at Max. He nods subtly.

"Actually, I just saw Li and I've been meaning to chat with her about the game." I turn to Nova. "I think she's upset that I haven't included her backstory more."

"I'm not sure she's capable of being mad at you. You're clearly her idol. But Max and I can hold our own, right?"

Max bobs his head. "Do you like corn dogs? I saw a vendor selling them down by the grandstand."

"I do not. But I like fries, and the best ones are in the same direction."

They nod in unison and I glance between them. Are Nova and Max actually friends? The idea is both weird and endearing.

"You're going to lose her if you don't go now. We'll find you later." Nova shoos me away and I jog in Li's direction with a backward wave to them.

"Li?" I call when I get closer.

She spins around at her name, but I catch the moment of hesitation when she sees that it's me who's calling to her.

"Hey," I continue. "Do you have a second to talk? That is, if I'm not interrupting your plans?"

"I'm just wandering around until my shift," she says. "What's up?"

We fall into step with each other, though we occasionally need to dodge strollers and wild bands of middle schoolers running past us as we walk. I think I see Felix ahead of us in the distance, and I'm tempted to call him over just to put off having this conversation for a little longer, but I know I have to stop doing that.

"I was hoping to chat about D&D before the game tomorrow."

Her face falls. "Oh, okay."

It hurts me to see how disheartened she looks at the mere mention of the game.

"I want to apologize," I say. "I'm sorry I've been such a bad Dungeon Master, and I understand if you don't want to play anymore, but I hope you'll stick with us and give me another shot."

She glances at me with a furrowed brow. "You're not kicking me out of the group?"

"What?"

I'm so surprised that I stop walking and someone immediately bumps into me from behind. We need to get someplace calmer, so I steer her into the dim quiet of the 4-H barn and then face her.

"Of course I'm not. Why would you think that?"

She sighs. "I could tell you were annoyed with the backstory Felix and I gave you for our characters. Clearly we went in the wrong direction with it. And I've been thinking you'd probably have more fun with people who are more experienced or are at least the same age as you."

"Omigod, no!" I shake my head adamantly. "You didn't go in the wrong direction with anything. You *can't* go in the wrong direction—those are your characters. You can do whatever you want with them." She starts to argue, but I keep going. "Listen, we're all new to this, especially me. I promise I'll make sure to have you and Felix feel more included."

"Really? Because I don't want to stop playing with you all. I really love it." She looks like she's about to cry, and it's breaking my heart, so I pull her into a hug.

"I promise, you're not going anywhere. So, we're good?"

She gives me a joyful, but watery, smile. "Yes, definitely."

"Oh, thank god." I breathe out a sigh of relief, although it's occurring to me that Max is totally going to gloat when he hears his advice was helpful. "Now that I know we're good, I need to clear the air with Felix too. I just saw him a few minutes ago. Do you want to help me search?"

"Right now?" Her voice raises an octave. "You saw him?"

"Um, yeah." I lift my brows. "Is everything okay with

you two? He hasn't been rude, right? Because I won't stand for that."

"It's . . . um . . . maybe the opposite?" She adjusts her glasses. "We were chatting yesterday at the away game, and then all of a sudden he squeezed my hand in this way that made it feel like *something* could possibly be going on between us—although that's probably all in my head—but the thing is that maybe I'm starting to kind of have feelings for him, and now everything feels so weird and—"

"Li." She's speaking so quickly I can barely understand her. "Take a breath. You don't have to search for him with me if you don't want to."

"Thank you. I know I'm being delusional. He's a sophomore and so cute and popular—there's no way."

I bite the inside of my cheek to keep from smiling too widely. Felix is a nice guy as far as I can tell, but the way she's talking about him isn't exactly based in reality. Max invited him to play with us because he was having a hard time making friends with the rest of the band. As far as I'm concerned, he's lucky to be friends with Li, let alone anything else.

"I won't claim to know what's going on in Felix's brain, but it seems like you both have some things in common. Maybe you should try spending more time with him?"

"The idea totally freaks me out . . . but I also keep fantasizing about it." She giggles. "In fact, I had this ridiculous idea that maybe if I wandered around the fairgrounds enough, we'd run into each other and he'd ask me to hang out."

Omigod, she's so adorable I want to squeeze her.

"Okay, well, we cou—" I glance over her shoulder and freeze. "Stay cool when I say this . . . but I'm going to need to steal your manifestation skills for our next band competition because Felix is actually walking up to us right now." I smile and wave to him like we're having the most casual of chats. "You've got this," I whisper.

A second later Felix steps to Li's side, looking way happier than I normally see him. He's generally a guy of few words and fewer facial expressions, but he's practically beaming.

"I didn't expect to find you two in the 4-H building of all places."

"I was just about to go looking for you," I say. "I was apologizing to Li about how the D&D game has been going lately. And that apology extends to you too. I promise I'm going to try to bring Elrid and Ellywich into the game more."

If Felix is taken aback, he hides it quickly. "Huh. Thanks, Hazel. That's really cool of you. And, just so you know, I had nothing to do with that stunt Brody pulled last night. I'm sorry about that."

"Don't worry about it. I'm glad we ran into you." I eye him in mock suspicion. "Though why are *you* hanging out in the 4-H building?"

Felix shrugs. "My two younger brothers are in it, so I came to see their stuff."

"My mom advises the club my sister is in," I reply and glance around. "I should probably see the exhibit while I'm here or they're going to kill me. You guys want to come too?"

Each 4-H club in the county has a large display space to show off the various projects that members have been working on. A lot of people show animals in the fair, but others like Kelsey complete projects on sewing, computer science, cooking, and photography. We walk up and down the displays until I finally find the "Blue Ribbon Bandits," the group Mom supervises. Of course, even in 4-H, the focus would be on winning every competition.

"Mom's done it again," I mutter as I take it in.

Compared with the other displays, which look cluttered, bare, or haphazard, Mom's club's looks like a professional showpiece. The walls artfully display the different photographs and drawings that members turned in to the fair, while the base of the display has arrangements of handmade clothes, robots, and baked goods. And, unsurprisingly, there are more blue ribbons on these projects than any other color. Kelsey got two this year alone. I sigh, knowing Mom will expect me to perform at the same level. The best auxiliary award at our upcoming competition, Superior ratings at state, another Most Valuable Member award. Lots of opportunities to let her down.

"Your mom advises the Blue Ribbon Bandits?" Felix asks, and I nod. "Ah. That figures."

I frown. "Why would you say that?"

"Everyone knows that group. They're big on winning. And it's obvious how competitive you are."

"Oh." I don't love that, but it's the truth. I'm my mother's daughter, whether I like it or not.

"It's not a bad thing," he reassures me with a small smile.

"It's the reason the color guard is better this year. Well, that and Li."

Li looks at the ground and smiles.

I glance between them. Li isn't wrong, there *is* something here, but they're both so shy that it might not become more without a little push. I know I told Max I wasn't going to get involved, but I just can't help it.

I pull out my phone and make a big show of frowning at what I see. "Argh, I'm so sorry, but I promised I'd meet my parents soon and walk around with them." I take a step back. "You two are welcome to tag along, but I think you'll have more fun by yourselves. Li, weren't you saying you wanted to get an elephant ear?"

Her eyes go wide, but then she nods enthusiastically. "Unless you don't want to, Felix?"

"As if I'd ever turn down fair food. They're selling them at the midway. Do you want to go look?"

Li's practically skipping as she and Felix leave the barn, and I'm tempted to run up behind them and pinch their cheeks like I'm their grandma. I'm just about to text Nova and Max when Li comes flying back into the barn alone. Her arms arc around me before I have time to worry.

"Thank you!" she whispers in my ear. "You're seriously like the best big sister!"

Then she's running back in Felix's direction without a backward glance. If I'm not careful, I might cry.

I text Max and Nova to find out where I should meet them. I haven't made it far before I see Max strolling my way holding a huge paper cone of fries. My heart twists at the sight of him. He's the perfect mixture of handsome and adorable, with that goofy grin on his face, and I have a sudden urge to take his face in both my hands and kiss him.

"You and Nova weren't messing around with these fries," he says and stretches the container out to me. "I got them for you, but I think we're going to need to share."

I happily take a few, grateful for the distraction so I can get my impulses back under control.

"How'd everything go with Li?" he asks.

"Really well. Thanks for pushing me to talk to her"—I point a fry at him—"although you don't need to be so cocky about always being right."

"I didn't say anything!" He lifts his free hand in surrender.

"Yeah, well, I didn't finish yet. You also *might* have been right about Li and Felix being a good fit. I can see a spark."

He has the gall to do a triumphant victory dance next to the funnel cake stand.

"Don't drop the fries!"

"As if." His expression is pure elation. "Ooh, you hate it when I'm right."

"I do not," I retort. "I hate it when you *know* you're right and do uncoordinated dances in my face."

"Uncoordinated? How dare you. I've got all kinds of moves." He does a spin, and I can't help laughing at how dorky he's being.

"Where's Nova? Not that she'd hang out with us if she saw you dancing."

"We ran into some people by the rides. I told her I'd come find you while she holds our place in line."

"Let me guess," I say with a smile. "We're going on the Zipper first?" Nova and I ride it every year and spend the whole time screaming and laughing so loudly you can hear us on the other side of town. I always swear I'll never get on it again but immediately relent the following year.

"Um . . . yeah, that's the one," he says, looking surprised. "You two are very in sync."

I shrug and take a few more fries. "Standard best friend stuff."

We walk through the midway where fair barkers yell for our attention. Max moves closer to my side. "Actually, before we get back to everyone, I have a question I've been meaning to ask you."

His serious tone sends a spike of adrenaline shooting through me, but then I mentally kick myself. It's very possible he's about to ask whether it's cool if he hangs out with his percussion buddies instead of me. I shouldn't jump to conclusions just because I wish we were here together as more than friends.

I slowly turn toward him.

His jaw works back and forth like he's debating something. "Do you have fair plans with Nova this evening?"

My pulse speeds higher and I shake my head. "I think there's a tractor pull tonight, but we usually skip that kind of stuff. Why?"

"There's someplace I'd like to take you. Just the two of us, if that's okay?"

My breath hitches at the intimate way he's studying my face. People are streaming past us, barkers are shouting mere feet away, but all I can focus on is him. He could tell me he wants to go bathe in cow manure this evening, and I'd still agree to try it out one time. I'm so lost for this boy, it's not even funny.

"Yeah, okay," I whisper. My voice is unsteady. "Sounds like a plan."

Chapter Twenty-Five

We have a great rest of the day eating too much food, visiting all the baby farm animals, and riding so many rides that I'm at risk of losing my voice from screaming so loud. But the whole time, there's a tight ball of anticipation in my stomach, wondering what Max is planning for this evening.

I drop my car off at the house after leaving the fair and take a moment to text Nova. She seemed very understanding when I told her about our plans, but Max was with us, so I can't be sure of her reaction. A second later she texts back.

Nova: Totally fine. Have fun with Max!

An exclamation mark? About Max? That's weird. I shake my head and put my phone back in my pocket.

A few minutes later, Max pulls into the driveway.

"So, can you tell me where we're going?" I ask after climbing into his car. "Or is that a secret?"

He rubs his hands down the steering wheel. "This is going to sound strange, but have you heard of something called forest bathing?"

My eyes widen. "Is that like . . . skinny dipping?" My mind whirls with possibilities. I really like Max, but going from friends to skinny dipping overnight is a little fast for me.

He laughs and backs out of the driveway, though his neck turns a bit red. "Uh, no. Forest bathing is this Japanese practice my mom learned about. It just means spending time in forests, basically. She's been taking a lot of long walks at this nature preserve outside of town, and she always comes back happier and more relaxed." He glances over at me and then at the road, and I realize Max is nervous. He's twitchy, his left foot bouncing as he drives, and he's speaking faster than usual. "You've been working so hard—we *both* have, actually—and I thought some serene time in nature might be nice. Sorry if you thought we were doing something fancy."

"No, this sounds fun. I'm officially intrigued."

"Yeah? Okay, cool."

Max drives us out of town to the preserve. I've heard about it, but I've never been there. Mom might be a superwoman, but she and Dad aren't nature people. When we step out of the car, I'm grateful to see that we won't be roughing it—this is clearly an accessible park made for everyone. Several wood-planked paths break off into the woods, and there are shelters and barbecues.

He raises his eyebrows questioningly to me.

"Oh no, this was your idea. I'll let you lead the way."

He takes me down one of the paths, and I have to admit that as soon as the woods close in behind us, a sense of calm fills me. Although it's evening, the sun doesn't set for another hour. These woods aren't densely packed, so I can see through the trees to the fallen logs in the distance and the squirrels scampering along tree branches. And because we're raised off the ground a few inches on this wooden pathway, I don't have to worry about walking through poison ivy or thistles.

We walk quietly together, and it's nice to not feel required to speak constantly. I notice that quite a few trees along the path have become time capsules for past relationships, their trunks filled completely with carved initials and hearts. A lot of couples must have been coming out here for a lot of years to fill up so many trees. It makes me think back to our walk in the wooded area behind the high school. Did anyone ever tell Max the reason most people go back there? I sneak a quick glance at him. Could that possibility be on his mind now?

He catches me looking. "Getting tired?"

"No, this is great."

"Good, because I'm actually leading us somewhere else. But it involves a few flights of stairs."

"Stairs? In the middle of the forest?"

He laughs. "Trust me. Come on, we're almost there." He picks up speed, which kind of kills the chill forest vibes, but after a few more minutes a huge set of steps comes into focus ahead of us. They must go up at least two stories, and at the top is another wooden pathway, except that path goes through the treetops.

"Whoa," I whisper.

"Right? My parents used to bring me here when I was young." His expression dims just slightly at the mention of them, but he pushes through. "It's not nearly as popular as it once was. I'm hoping we'll have it to ourselves, especially with the fair going on right now."

He takes my hand for a moment, just long enough to tug me in the direction of the stairs, but it's enough to set my heart beating quicker.

I know it's disingenuous to feel this way about Max and not tell him. He deserves to know where my head's at . . . but the idea of putting myself out there makes me want to leap off the top of these weird forest stairs. He might not be interested in me. Or maybe he isn't interested in serious relationships at all. I know plenty of guys like that, but I'm not sure I could do something casual. *Especially* not with Max. We have too much history.

I swallow and take a few deep breaths—mostly from this line of thought, but also because these stairs are steep and I'm getting winded. I remind myself that everything will be fine no matter what. The worst-case scenario is that I tell him how I feel—how I've always felt—and end up leaving the forest with a broken heart and never-ending embarrassment and misery and then have to run an hours-long D&D game across from said heartbreaker.

Very doable.

A little laugh escapes me as I reach the top of the stairs.

"You're laughing after that?" he asks. "I need to up my cardio."

"Just laughing at how, um, how wild this all is. Climbing up into the treetops like this."

Yep, I'm a total chicken.

We walk along the elevated path, and I'm awed by the tree limbs within arm's reach. Luckily, they built very high, sturdy railings, but I don't stray from the middle just in case.

"You know," Max says, looking over his shoulder since I'm lagging behind, "last night I was thinking about all those games we used to play at your house when we were younger."

"You mean, when you'd cheat at Mario Uno?"

His mouth drops open in outrage. "I did not cheat at any version of Uno. I was clumsy when I was young and accidentally knocked the cards from both our hands onto the floor."

"Then why did I have different cards after we picked everything up? You weren't even smooth about it. You totally snuck some of my cards."

"I would never."

We glance at each other and laugh, and my nerves fade away. Max holds my gaze for a moment, then turns and gestures in front of him.

"We're here."

"We're where?" My eyes get big, and I take a step back. "Because I'm not stepping foot on *that*."

The path through the treetops has led to a wide expanse of netting that's been stretched over the forest floor below. The netting is the same material as the woven rope hammocks you might find in someone's backyard . . . except it's square and pulled taut along all four sides where it attaches to the walkway that encircles it. It's also absolutely enormous. The rope netting must be as wide as my living room. It almost reminds me a bit of a trampoline, if the trampoline was made of rope, wasn't bouncy . . . and was two stories off the ground.

In other words, the whole thing is absolutely terrifying.

The gray in his eyes sparkles mischievously. "You're definitely getting on there with me. That's the whole reason I brought you here."

"There's no way. We're too far aboveground. And those are *ropes*—my feet could fall through the gaps! I'm not dying in this forest."

He points to a sign nailed onto the railing. "Look, it's literally weighted to hold two tons. Fifteen grown men can lie on there at once and still be perfectly safe. It's only you and me."

My head starts shaking back and forth of its own volition. "I'm not a fan of heights."

"I guess I should have figured that out from your ear-splitting shrieks on the rides this afternoon." He looks down at the rope netting and back at me, his eyebrows knotting in worry. "Huh . . . this isn't exactly the relaxing outing I had planned."

"Maybe because you planned an outing with the sole goal of making me hyperventilate."

He puts both hands out like he's trying to calm me before I bolt in the opposite direction. Little does he know I'm frozen with fear and going nowhere.

"I'm not going to force you to come out there with me. Or, like, pick you up and toss you into the center."

My eyes flare wide with horror.

"Oh, believe me, it's happened. I saw a guy do that to his girlfriend once. *But,* I will ask you to trust me. We'd go very slowly, one step at a time, and we'd stop as soon as you said." His expression grows serious, and he turns his palm up to me. "What do you say? Will you trust me, Hazel?"

I take a breath, my eyes flicking to the woven rope and back to him. The ropes are thick and tightly laced. And everything looks well maintained.

And, most importantly, I do trust Max.

"Yeah," I breathe. "Okay."

"Good." He wraps his hand in mine and walks me over to the edge of the netting. I take a step onto the rope, which gives under my weight, and I jump right back off.

"What if we sit down and scoot on our butts?" he asks.

"Maybe." My heart is still beating out of my chest at the fact that I can see through the ropes straight down to the forest floor far below, but I force myself to keep my eyes up. I sit down next to Max and start scooting, creeping toward the center until finally he stops.

"You okay?" he asks.

His expression is so gentle that I feel calmer from looking at him. "I'm shaky, but I'm not dead yet. And as an added bonus, I'm sure I look really cool right now."

He chuckles. "We're close enough to the center now. Try lying back and looking up at the sky."

I do it very gingerly. The ropes dig into my back a bit,

but the breeze is cool, and the netting is stable underneath me. A moment later, I open my eyes and take in the swaying treetops dappled in sunlight, and the touches of blue sky visible through the leaves. Begrudgingly, I realize he was right. It's kind of . . . amazing.

Max cautiously lies back next to me and puts his hands behind his head. We stay there, breathing and listening to the birds until my heart has slowed to a normal rhythm. Finally, Max shifts to look at me.

"What do you think? Are you still pissed that I made you come out here?"

"Not anymore."

He smiles faintly. "I'm glad." He's quiet for a moment. "Because I brought up those game nights for a reason."

I look over at him in confusion.

"I've been thinking about how boring or miserable those nights could have been when we were younger. Being left at a random house every weekend while my parents had fun downstairs, having to kill time with some kid I didn't know. When they first brought it up, I begged Mom to let me stay home alone instead. But then we hung out, and I never complained to her again. It was anything but miserable hanging out with you." His eyes rove over my face. "We're competitive and stubborn, but it worked between us anyway. We've always worked, Hazel."

My heart speeds again. Max turns onto his left side and I turn on my right, but the netting is awkward and we both tip into each other, as if we were lying together on a regular hammock.

I giggle nervously and try to scoot back so I'm not pressed against him, but he puts a hand on my hip to stop me.

"If you aren't interested in me as more than your competitive friend, then that's okay. But I've missed everything about you. There's no one else in the world like you, Hazel. I'm still hoping there's something I can do to win you over."

It's as if his words are an electric jolt, racing through the length of my body. My world narrows until all I can see is his face. I can barely believe this is happening. I've spent the last five years waiting for these exact words.

"You won me over when I was twelve," I whisper. "I've just been waiting for you to notice."

His eyes flare wide in surprise at the same moment that I lean a bit closer to him. The netting pushes us together farther, and our lips brush. His hand squeezes my hip, and he deepens the kiss. Fire rushes through me, hot and wild and electric. Kissing Max is what I expected in the best possible way, and also so much more. The slide of his hand up my back, his breath in my mouth, the sound he makes when I shift closer against him. It makes me feel like I'm floating. I think I am.

A few moments later I pull away, although it's hard to do that when the hammock material seems designed to tip us closer together.

"Are you okay?" Max asks breathlessly. His gray eyes are warm, and his expression is hungry, but it fades as he studies me. "Do you need off of here?"

He moves to sit up.

"No." I put a hand on his chest. "I don't want to go.

Actually, I wanted to tell you that this netting thing was a really great call. Although I wouldn't call it relaxing. My heart won't slow down."

His mischievous expression returns. "Sorry, but I don't think I can help you with that one."

Then he leans closer and presses me back, and everything but him fades from my mind.

Chapter Twenty-Six

I can't stop smiling for the next twenty-four hours. I probably look scary. My parents keep giving me sideways glances and even Kelsey asks me why I'm so happy all of a sudden. I just shrug and say I'm in a good mood. And I am. My time with Max plays on repeat in my mind. The way he looked at me, as if he couldn't possibly believe his luck. As if I was what he wanted the most in the whole world.

I'm staring down at my bagel sandwich with a stupid smile on my face when Mom clears her throat and points at the calendar hanging on the kitchen wall.

"I can't believe October is around the corner. Soon you're going to have your last regional band competition and then state."

That wakes me up from my blissful stupor. "If the band qualifies for state, you mean."

"Of course you'll qualify." Her lips press into an aggravated frown. "Glen Vale has performed at state every year for the past eighteen years. This isn't going to be the moment it all falls apart. Not when you're a senior."

A wave of nausea rolls through me, and I push my sandwich away. I wish Mom's grim determination was enough to guarantee us a spot. Going into this year, making it to state hadn't even been a concern for me. But now, with only one competition left, all the pressure is on. Devastated doesn't begin to describe how I'll feel if we don't qualify.

"It won't fall apart, Mom," I say quietly.

"I know it won't. You won't let it. How are those synchronized drop spins coming?"

"They're coming along."

Translation: At least one person is off almost every time we practice, *but* that's better than several people being off.

"And how about the Most Valuable Member award? I can't think of anyone more deserving."

With everything going on, I've barely thought about my chances of winning that award . . . and honestly, I don't care as much about it now. It would certainly be an honor, and Mom and Dad would be over the moon, but do I need it? I'm not as certain as I once was.

"Right now I'm trying to focus on prepping for our last regional competition," I finally reply.

She reaches out and pats my hand. "Spoken like a leader deserving of that award."

"Are you meeting Dad and Kelsey at the fair this afternoon?" I ask, mostly because I'm desperate to get off this conversation.

"Yes. Wait, where are my sunglasses?" She spins in a circle.

"I swear I'm so busy I can't keep track of anything nowadays." She rustles through her large bag and pulls them out triumphantly. "Are you coming too? I ran into Nova yesterday evening and she said you and Max had left."

"Uh, yeah, he and I walked around a nature preserve. It was . . . really fun." An image of his fingers combing through my hair rises in my mind and I smile again before I can help it. Am I blushing? I think I might be blushing.

"Ooh." Her voice rises in pitch. "So, you and Max are spending time alone together now? That's very interesting."

"It's not interesting. It's mundane. We saw trees."

"You saw trees. Right." Her smile widens. "I was wondering why you couldn't stop smiling all last night."

"It's really not a big deal, so don't make it into a thing, okay?"

"Okay, okay."

She studies me, possibly waiting for me to say more, but I take a bite of my sandwich instead. Max and I haven't talked about what comes next, and I don't need her embarrassing us as soon as he walks in the door. As it is, I'm already sure we'll be a topic of conversation downstairs during their D&D game tonight.

"Well, just so we're on the same page, I will say that I think you and Max would be adorable together and I'm already on board. Melanie and I always wondered if there might be something between you two. But"—I try to interrupt to no avail—"make sure you're keeping your focus and attention on what matters. Marching band season is almost over. No regrets."

"No regrets," I mumble. I'm definitely having regrets about this conversation, though. I should have eaten lunch in my room.

It feels like an eternity until Max and his mom arrive Sunday evening for the game. I'm curious how Max will act around me with his mom next to him, but he's just the same as always until Melanie is safely downstairs with my parents and we're alone.

"Hey." His voice is hopeful.

Nerves and anticipation flutter through me. "Hey."

He takes my hand and pulls me into the dining room. "How are you? Are you freaking out?"

"Are *you* freaking out?"

"No, except I'm worried you might be second-guessing us."

Us. My heart tugs at the word. There was a tiny part of me that was worried about how things would go today. What if yesterday hadn't meant as much to him as it had to me? What if he'd had his fun and now he was over me? But the realization that we both have the same worries allows me to take a breath. I lean into him, and he pulls me to his chest without hesitation.

"I'm not second-guessing anything," I whisper.

"Good, because I really missed you. I haven't been able to think about anything else." His hand rubs up my back and through my hair. "Have I already told you how much I love your hair?"

"If you have, then you should say it again."

"I *really* love it." He leans back so he can see my face. "We probably should have discussed this yesterday, but what's the likelihood of canceling the game so we can spend the night together, just the two of us? I'm thinking movie, popcorn, the two of us under a thick blanket . . ."

I laugh and step out of his arms. "The others will *riot*."

"We could take 'em." Strands of hair fall over his face. I push them out of the way so I can see his eyes, and my heart almost bursts with the knowledge that I'm allowed to do that now.

He squeezes my hand. "Speaking of the others, have you thought about what you want to do tonight? Are we telling them?"

I bite the inside of my cheek. "It's not that I'm embarrassed or ashamed or anything—"

"No, me neither."

"But it's going to be a big *thing* when we tell them. Especially with our color guard and percussion history—"

"And it might distract from the game—"

"That's true. Though I don't want to mess anything up between us."

He steps closer. "You won't. We can do whatever makes you more comfortable. If you'd rather not say anything, then we don't have to, it's okay."

"Well . . ."

I stare down at our hands. His thumb is tracing circles across my skin, and that small movement sends electricity racing up my arm and through my body. Part of me loves the idea of screaming the news to the others as soon as they walk in the door, and holding hands during the game tonight, and kissing him whenever he rolls well. But to say that would change the dynamics of the game is an understatement. We're still not on steady ground as a group. Having the Dungeon Master dating one of the members could throw everything off even more.

"It's really okay, Hazel," Max murmurs.

I glance up to find an unflustered expression on his face. He already knew what I was going to say before I could figure it out.

"Yeah? We'll just . . . play it cool, then?" I ask. "We don't need to pretend to hate each other or anything, but we'll just act the same as always."

"The same as always?" He smiles. "Then we better start making nachos."

"Actually, I already have that part figured out." I lead him into the kitchen and hold up a bag of flour tortillas. "I have two words for you."

"Missed you?"

"Dessert nachos!" I throw my arms open wide in excitement.

He chuckles. "I thought it couldn't get better than *missed you*—well, maybe *kiss me* could work nicely—but *dessert nachos* has a nice ring to it. Though, uh, what exactly are they?"

"We cut the tortillas into triangles, brush them with butter and cinnamon sugar, and bake them. Then we top them with chocolate syrup, whipped cream, and strawberries. I got restless this afternoon, so I decided to search for nacho recipes we haven't had yet. What do you think?"

He steps up behind me and wraps his arms around my waist. "That I've never been happier I convinced you to let me join your game."

"I think I could make you a tiny bit happier." I twist around in his arms so I'm facing him.

"Really?" He gives me a skeptical look. "I'd like to see you try."

I lift onto the balls of my feet so I can reach his ear and whisper, "*Kiss me.*"

He doesn't need more convincing. His lips are on my neck at the same time that he takes a step forward so my back is pressed against the kitchen counter. I suck in a breath. Just then the front door opens with a bang and the telltale sound of nails clicking on hardwood alerts us that we're not alone.

"Hello!" Nova calls.

Max jumps back from me as Zoinks bounds into the kitchen. My heart races, but an Old English sheepdog is a great distraction. I bury my face in his fluff.

"Oh, you're just the cutest!" I tell him. "Wait, I have presents for you, buddy." I grab a shopping bag from the kitchen island and pull out each item for him. "Two squeaky potion bottle toys, a squeaky dragon for him to chew on, and . . ." I pull the last dog toy out with a flourish. "His own d20."

Zoinks starts mouthing and sniffing each of the toys.

Max picks up the d20 and inspects it in awe. "You found D&D *dog* toys?"

"They make dog toys of everything in existence, so it wasn't too hard. It only seemed fair to include him a little more. Who can play D&D without a d20?"

"I'm mildly annoyed you didn't get *me* any presents, but

these are too cute to ignore," Nova says with a shake of her head.

Soon, Li and Felix arrive—together—and the oohing and awwing start all over again. It's a full thirty minutes before we can speak about anything other than Zoinks, but I'm not complaining. No one can notice any changes between me and Max if we're all too busy fussing over our favorite member of the D&D party.

Nova gives an exaggerated sigh. "You know, if Zoinks keeps getting this level of love on game nights, then he's not going to want to leave your house."

I rub my hands together maniacally. "Then my plan is finally coming together."

Zoinks barks in response.

"I think he's just anxious to get playing," Li says with a laugh. She seems much lighter and happier than she did last game, which is a good sign. I sit down behind my trifold screen and glance at my notes for tonight, written in my beautiful calligraphy to make them feel more special. I really want to make the game welcoming for the whole group, and hopefully today is a new beginning for that.

Last session we finished with the party demanding to meet the ruler of Darkthorn, so I pick up exactly where we left off.

"Thank you for your tireless work defending this city," I tell the group as the duke. "We have been trying to hold off the wizard, but we can't withstand his bombardment much longer."

The others shift in their seats. "There's a wizard?" Nova asks.

"That's what we believe, although I've never set my eyes on him. From what we can tell, his ambition is to rule this city and all the lands around it. We believe he's currently living somewhere in the surrounding forests and using his magic to create these monstrosities that he sends here."

"Do you know any more?" Li asks. Her eyes are bright with interest.

"That he's a coward," I reply. "Otherwise, he would come here himself. And he clearly has no capacity for empathy. Not only has he killed many of my people, but I've heard rumors that his experimental spells have led to other ill effects on the surrounding lands."

I'm hoping Li and Felix will pick up on this clue and ask for more information, though I can hardly blame them if they don't, given how I shot them down when they tried to learn more in the past. However, Li leans forward and asks, "Can you tell us more about these ill effects?"

"I don't know a lot," I reply as the duke. "We've been too overwhelmed here to venture out and see what's happening, but stories have come back that the land has turned black and nothing will grow or survive. I don't know what happened to the people who used to live there."

"We're those people," Felix says. "We've been searching for answers about what caused this blight. Our people have had to flee and are spread across the surrounding kingdoms now."

"I can't give answers, but the stories of the blight—as you call it—began the same time as the attacks on our city, so I imagine they're related."

Max gives me a small smile and I take a breath. Felix and Li are both sitting up straighter and seem as interested as I've ever seen them, so I think this is working pretty well.

"You said you think the wizard could be living in the forest?" Nova asks.

"We're almost certain of it, although none of my men have been able to track him down. Or, at least, I assume they haven't because they've never returned. I've stopped sending them."

The four of them look at each other wordlessly and each gives a short nod. My heart twists with happiness to see them like this. United and attentive and on the same page with each other. I wasn't sure we could get to this place, but I might be on the verge of turning this campaign around.

"I have a proposal for you," Max says. His eyes have narrowed, and his shoulders are set. It's Axolotl I'm dealing with now—not my cute boyfriend, if I can call him that. "I am a fighter by trade and quick with my axes. One of my party members is a ranger and she and her dog are both talented trackers. And these druids will stop at nothing to save their homeland. We are willing to travel into the forest, search out this wizard, and defeat him. But we will need compensation."

I slowly look to each of them before turning back to Max. "Our coffers have been depleted by the attacks, but if you can bring back proof of defeating this villain, I can promise you each a title and land of your own. And, if you are willing, I will gather a search party to help these druids find their dispersed families."

The four look to each other again, this time with grins on their faces.

"Let's go track a wizard," Nova announces, and the others whoop in agreement.

Everyone sits back, looking excited. "Love the way you pulled this together, Hazel," Nova says.

Felix bobs his head. "Totally. Did you know this backstory with the wizard from the very beginning?"

I could lie, but I don't want to run a game where I have to pretend to be someone I'm not. "Nope!" I say and the others laugh. "I was as lost as you all at first, but I found my way to it eventually. Thanks for sticking with me."

"I love color guard, but this might be my new favorite thing," Li tells me.

"Your DM loves it," I tell her, "but don't let your guard captain hear you talk like that."

She grins. "I'll be sure to keep it a secret."

Max stretches and stands. "Can we take a quick break for snacks before we start tracking this wizard? In addition to killing it on the DMing and captaining fronts, Hazel also discovered dessert nachos that I'm dying to try."

I smile as the others pass me on their way to the kitchen, but my brain is fuzzy. I feel almost disembodied. Did Max kiss me earlier in that same kitchen? Are we actually dating now, after all the daydreams I've had about this exact thing? It feels like the universe must be screwing with me or that I've twisted everything in my mind. But when I glance at Max, trying to decipher if he's feeling the same way, he returns the look with such reassurance that I can take a deep breath.

"Good?" he asks softly. Hopefully.

Oh, wow. One word and my heart goes tumbling.

"Great," I whisper back.

"Then let's go eat our weight in chocolate-covered tortillas."

Someone gasps behind me. Nova points to me, then to Max and back to me. "Wait. Are you two . . . did something . . ."

"Shhh!" I wave my hands wildly in her direction.

"Oh my god, you two are totally together!" she whispers. "I knew something was up at the fair!"

"You did?" Max asks.

She crosses her arms in annoyance. "You were so eager for time alone with Hazel you were practically vibrating."

"I wasn't *that* obvious." But Max's neck is red and it's so cute I might burst.

"That explains your use of punctuation yesterday. You never use exclamation marks when it comes to boys."

"I'm nothing if not a supportive friend." She pulls me into a hug. "But I need to know *everything* ASAP," she whispers in my ear.

"I'll text you as soon as we're done here," I whisper back.

Chapter Twenty-Seven

"If I can have your attention," Sire calls Monday afternoon after everyone has filed into the band room and gotten settled in their seats. "We've got two weeks until our last local contest, which means that another important event is coming up in October: the Most Valuable Member awards. These awards are granted to one person per grade level. They're voted on by peers, in conjunction with ratings from myself and the other assistant directors. We'll be opening up the ballots this Friday, and I know they mean a lot to students, so please make sure that you vote. Also, remember that this is not a popularity contest, but instead a way to acknowledge students' hard work and dedication to our marching band. Please vote accordingly."

Sire stares around the room like he's forcing his words into our minds, but let's all be real, *of course* it's a popularity contest. Just hearing his speech reminds me of why I was so set on winning at the beginning of our season, but that's more of a long shot than ever, no matter what Mom wants to believe. We already know there's one section that will not be voting for me.

As soon as Sire releases us, the guard heads to the auditorium for our rehearsal. All the members bunch together, whispering, and I join them hesitantly. Hopefully they aren't angry about anything happening with guard. I'd really thought we were coming together as a group.

"I've been seething about it all weekend," Callie says.

"Seething about what?" I ask.

"About the game on Friday," she replies incredulously. A few of them nod in agreement. "I assumed you were too."

I blink, momentarily confused, and then remember the stunt the percussion section pulled before our halftime show. After everything with Max this weekend, the football game wasn't even on my radar. I get the impression that's not what they're expecting to hear, though.

"Uh, right, absolutely," I say and roll my eyes like I'm so upset to be reminded of it. "Although it's obvious Brody's only organizing this stuff because he's bitter and frustrated. We should keep ignoring him."

I bite my lip, wondering if Max is having a similar conversation right now with his section. Not that I could ask him while we're still on school grounds. We didn't talk about it officially, but I'm assuming we're continuing with the "play it cool" strategy today.

"Hazel, what's with you?" Devin asks.

"What do you mean?"

"We thought you'd be extra fired up today," Madisyn replies. "Devin was already complaining about all the extra drills you were going to have us do since the competition is coming up."

"Who cares about drills?" Rosa says. "What we need to do is figure out a way to put percussion in their place once and for all. God, I can't stand them."

"I had to wash my shorts four times to get that vinegar smell out, and sometimes I think I can still smell it," Yori says. "Those were my favorite."

"We should do something," Deja says.

"Maybe pour some vinegar in their hats so they have to smell it the entire time they're marching."

"Or hide all their performance gloves. Or their drumsticks! Sire will lose his mind."

The others laugh, except for Li, who looks tense. I know she must be thinking about Felix. This is getting way out of control.

"Whoa, let's calm down a bit on the vindictive streak," I tell them. "That's not going to do anything except have us sitting on the sidelines when Sire finds out what's going on. We have to keep focused on what's really important."

But even as I say that, I know I'm not following my own advice. Devin was right—usually I would have spent any downtime during my classes deciding on which drills we needed to do today. I'd have every minute planned out, along with the rehearsals for the rest of the week. Instead, I spent my time imagining what Max was doing today in his college classes and wondering how everyone would take it if we announced we were dating.

I guess I have my answer to that second question.

The rest of the guard continues to grumble around me,

muttering about how we need to destroy percussion. I appreciate their loyalty to this group, but I don't like seeing them angry. And it isn't true that the entire percussion section is out to get us. Maybe telling them about me and Max could turn down the tension between our two groups? It might humanize the percussion section for them . . . or blow up in my face.

We work on hand placement for our windmill tosses, but I'm grateful when Faith shows up twenty minutes later. She's trying to get here more now that our biggest performances are coming up, and for once I'm happy to hand over the reins and take a step back.

When practice finishes for the day, Nova finds me. She's wearing her favorite black shirt that says *Dogs > People*. "Hey, so Max told me to tell you that you should meet him in one of the individual practice rooms before you leave." She frowns when she notices my beaten-down energy. "Is everything okay?"

She and I texted all last night as I caught her up on me and Max. I was worried she might be critical after her earlier concerns about us getting together, but she was only supportive. Of course she has no idea about how the guard is feeling. I groan and push my hair out of my face.

"Yeah, the guard was just reminding me about how much they hate the percussion section. It made for a very uncomfortable rehearsal."

"Oof, sorry." She gives me a playful nudge. "But I think some time in the practice room will help."

I find Max in the second of three rooms off the main band room. The practice room is small, just big enough for a chair and music stand, and the walls have foam tiles to help with sound insulation. The only way to see into the room is a small window in the upper half of the door, and not many people come in this hallway unless they're using one of the rooms. This is the perfect place to be alone for a few minutes.

"How are you?" Max asks as soon as the door is closed behind me.

I shrug and look away. "Meh. The guard is still seething about Friday."

"Brody really knew how to time that perfectly, huh?" he replies with a grimace. "So you didn't tell them about us?"

"I assumed we weren't doing that, right? Did you tell your section?"

"I haven't said anything to anyone." He smiles reassuringly at me, but I don't feel better.

"Is it dumb to keep it a secret?"

"I don't think so. Like we talked about yesterday, it makes sense with everything going on. Although I wish I was allowed to do this more often." He leans in and kisses me softly on the temple.

"Sire would kill us."

"Maybe we need to go check out that forest walk behind the school again." He lifts his eyebrows in a silly yet suggestive way that makes me laugh.

"I see you finally found out why people go into that forest."

"I've known since I got here."

My stomach drops. "You *knew*? The whole time?"

"Brody was quick to taunt me about how many times he's gone back there with girls."

I quickly push that gross thought from my mind. "Then why did you suggest we go there together?"

"Because, well . . ." He studies my face. "I thought you knew why! Did you think I wanted to go walk in the woods because we were *friends*?"

"I mean . . . yes?" My jaw might become unhinged from my skull, I'm in such shock. "We were barely getting back on good terms then, so there was no way you had any interest in me and—"

"Hazel, I've wanted to kiss you ever since you jabbed your finger into my chest and told me off. You were so gorgeous I could barely breathe. I was sure you'd shoot me down when I asked you about the forest." He looks both morose and amused as he runs a hand through his hair. "When nothing happened there, I was convinced you weren't interested."

I slap my hands over my mouth in shock. "I didn't know! I didn't even think something like that was possible!"

He leans back and groans, which makes me laugh. His expression has morphed to pure agony.

"Are you telling me that if I'd made a move in the forest, you would have been open to it?"

I think back to that afternoon and the way my mind had immediately gone to kissing him when he told me he wanted to make things right.

"I'd describe my past self as *exceptionally* open to it."

This groan is more agonized than the last. "You're killing me. All that time I was worrying about how to convince you to take a chance on me and it was all for nothing."

"Not for nothing." I step closer to him. "We're here now."

"We *are* here now," he murmurs slowly, and my heart speeds. "And you're happy about that?"

"I'm more than happy."

The corner of his mouth lifts in a smile. "Then come here."

He raises his hands to either side of my neck and kisses me. This time feels different than Saturday. I sink into his chest and revel in the feel of his mouth against mine and the fact that all this time that I've been wanting him, he's been wanting me too. It's incredible. We're finally here together and I don't want anything to ruin it.

Chapter Twenty-Eight

With our last regional competition (and hopefully state) coming up, Max and I don't have time for more stolen moments during band practices. In fact, we barely see each other all week. I'm happy for any excuse to be with him, so I jump at the chance to come to his place Saturday to paint D&D miniatures.

"This is nice," I say when I walk into the apartment he shares with his mom.

He shrugs. "I guess. Mom tried to do what she could with decorations and plants."

It's a basic space with plain white walls and dated carpet, but Melanie was able to liven it up some with bright pops of yellow and lots of houseplants. Still, standing in his living room, which also serves as the dining room and Melanie's office (given the messy desk shoved in a corner), I can understand better where his resentment from before might have come from. This apartment is certainly very different from my house—or, I'm guessing, the house he left behind when he moved here.

I walk to a round kitchen table where he's laid out all the paints. I pull out the miniatures I bought, along with more paints and brushes Mom and Dad had in a box in the basement.

"Are we ready for this?" I ask, picking up the model that will serve as Ellywich and seeing how many tiny details there are to paint.

"I don't know. I hope this wasn't a horrible idea."

"Why don't we start with some of the terrain you bought." I pick up a building that's supposed to serve as part of Darkthorn. "We can't mess these up too much."

"Let's hope not."

I study him as he sits down across from me. Something about his tone isn't quite right. There's an edge to his voice that I haven't heard since band camp.

"Is everything okay?"

He doesn't look at me. "Fine. I'm just tired."

I bite the inside of my cheek and pour out some brown paint. The minutes tick by as we work in silence, and my tension ratchets up. He hasn't been this quiet around me since August. Maybe our secret is affecting him? I know it's been harder for me than I was expecting. I'm constantly monitoring myself, making sure that I don't give anything away to my parents or the rest of the guard. I can't even meet his eye during practice, for fear that I'll accidentally smile and someone will ask what's going on.

I keep going over it in my head, trying to decide on how we should handle things moving forward. I'm not eager to hear everyone's opinions, but we can't keep this secret forever. The first few days made sense because it was so new, but at some point people will start getting upset when they find out we've been lying. And I still think we have the possibility of bringing color guard and percussion closer through this. Maybe we could even invite both groups to get pizza together or something. It makes me smile, the idea of Li and Felix getting to hang out together. If we're going to be good leaders for our sections, the least we can do is be truthful to them.

I'd like to talk to him about all this, but not if he's already in a mood.

Finally, after ten minutes, Max sighs and his shoulders slump. "I'm sorry," he says softly. "I'm just in my head about my dad."

I let out a breath. I don't want him to have struggles of any kind, but I'm relieved he's not upset about us. "What's going on?"

"I don't know if you've noticed, but he hasn't come to any of our football games or competitions this season. I know it's a drive for him, but I figured he'd be there for at least one. I was expecting him next Saturday for the regional." He slumps lower. "But Mom heard from him last night, and he said he's not coming to that or state. I guess he already has plans with friends those weekends."

Seriously? Anger surges in me. It would be one thing if his dad had to work, but how can he choose his friends over his son like that? Max has been in band for years, so it's not like his father wouldn't understand how important it is or how much work goes into our season. Especially when Max is a senior. This will be his dad's last chance to see him on the field.

"Mom made excuses for him," Max continues, "but he's angry with me, I know it. He wanted me to stay with him when they separated. He didn't understand why I'd leave when I already had a life there." He rolls back his shoulders, probably trying to come across as nonchalant, but he's anything but that now. "The longer I'm away from him, the more I realize Mom and I should've left sooner."

"Max, I'm so sorry. What he's doing is . . ." I try to think of the right words without cursing out his dad. "It's not right. He's your dad and he should be there no matter what. You didn't do anything wrong."

"Yeah."

"Is your mom doing better?"

That brings a small smile to his face. "She is. I know Dad's trying to make everything more difficult for her, but she's so much happier now."

"Good. And don't second-guess your choice to move back with your mom. She needed you."

"I know." He rubs his free hand down his face. "This is probably irrational, but now I want the percussion to perform even better just to rub it in Dad's face. I want him to know that I don't need him there cheering me on in order to do well. That I don't need him at all."

Hesitantly, I reach across the table and squeeze his hand. He gives me a grateful smile and entwines his fingers with mine.

“Thanks for being here. Sorry I’m not very good company today.”

“That’s okay,” I reply. “I’m happy to be here when you need someone to talk to. We haven’t had much of a chance to do that lately.”

“I know,” he says. “Band practices have been so intense this week.”

“Actually, I wanted to talk to you about that. All week I’ve been thinking about how we’re keeping this secret from everyone.”

He sits up straighter. “You have? I’ve been thinking about it too.”

I sigh in relief. Thank god we’re on the same page. I’m sure it’s been just as hard on him as it’s been on me. And once we tell everyone, we can actually spend our spare time together during practice. We could even ride the same band bus to the competition next Saturday.

He squeezes my hand again across the table and scoots his chair so he’s a little closer to me. “I’m so glad you suggested we keep things quiet.”

My body goes cold.

“I wasn’t sure at first, but now I see that you were thinking much more clearly than me. Can you imagine how much our sections would freak out? The last thing we want to do is distract them right now.”

He looks at me expectantly. I’m so surprised that I can’t think of how to respond.

“Percussion . . . it’s not going well, Hazel.” He sits back, pulling his hand from mine. “We’re splintered. I’m trying my best to bring the section together, but if Brody, Kyle, and some of the others found out about us, they'd use it as another thing to give me grief over. I'm just really glad we agreed to focus on what's most important for now."

What's most important.

It's as if his words are tiny daggers embedding deep into my flesh. Yes, I know how competitive Max is, how competitive we both are. And, yes, I was the one who decided I didn't want to tell anyone else about us . . . but not because color guard was more important to me than he was. It was because I didn't want to ruin what was happening between us by having everyone else's opinions in the mix.

"Honestly, I don't think I'm up for painting today. Would it be okay if we postponed and did something else?" He stands and stretches. "Mom's shift isn't done for another four hours, so we have time to watch a movie if you want. If we watch LOTR, I promise I won't inundate you with more factoids."

His gaze is so soft that my worries seem baseless in the face of it. I just wish I could feel totally secure in this new relationship. Can I even call it a relationship when no one else knows we're together and we barely see each other? It doesn't feel like it. But we get so little time together, and I don't want to ruin this afternoon.

"Don't make promises you can't keep," I tell him, working hard to keep my voice steady. "You know you won't be able to stop yourself from talking through the whole movie."

His gaze falls to my lips, and he grins playfully. "I can think of a few things that could keep me from talking."

That's all it takes to make my pulse skitter. No matter my

hesitations or worries, there's no denying how Max makes me feel. I could lose out on our bet, the MVM award, even state, and I'd still be happy as long as Max was with me. But could he say the same? I know he really cares about me. He just cares about band more.

Chapter Twenty-Nine

The whole D&D group comes over early on Sunday, and I love it. It's required at this point; there's no way we can play, eat, get enough time with Zoinks, *and* still catch up on the other things happening in each other's lives. Although there are some topics I'd rather avoid.

"Ugh, I don't want to talk about it," I complain and bury my face in Zoinks's thick fur.

Felix raises his hands in surrender. "Calm down, I was only curious about how you voted for the awards."

Voting for the MVM awards started Friday. Once student voting ends, Sire and the other directors will cast their votes and calculate the scores. I feel a little sick imagining it. Each year it's nerve-racking, but this year it feels impossible. And god forbid Mom overhears us and wants to join in on the conversation.

"Well, I know we're not supposed to say it aloud—" Nova starts but is cut off by our laughing. The whole band talks incessantly about who they voted for. "But I'm happy to say I voted for you for freshman member, Li. I think you really deserve it."

Li's eyes pop open wide behind her glasses. "You did not."

"Of course I did," Nova insists.

"I did too," Max says.

"You *know* I did," I tell her. "No competition—and not because you're the only freshman in guard this year."

"Without hesitation," Felix adds. His expression is affectionate and brings me an extra surge of happiness. The only downside is that Max is never going to shut up about his matchmaking abilities.

"I . . ." She glances around the room with tears in her eyes. "I can't believe you all did that. Did you get together and plan it?"

We all shake our heads. "No planning needed when it's the objective truth," I say.

She swallows and wipes at her eyes. It makes my heart so full to see her like this, though it's only what she deserves. "Thank you all. I mean, I definitely won't get it, but knowing I have your four votes means a lot to me."

She's being too humble. I know for a fact that she has more than our four votes. The entire guard is voting for her, no questions asked, and I'd be shocked if Felix wasn't lobbying some of the percussion section as well, though he hasn't said anything. But I've noticed Li talking to a few of the younger percussion players, Jamila in particular. Maybe this next generation won't carry on the animosity from our year. I think she has a real shot.

There's an awkward pause. Usually, we might go on to

announce who else we voted for, but it's a lot harder when Nova, Max, and I are all up for senior member. I've been struggling for the last week trying to decide who to vote for. I feel guilty, and might take the secret to the grave, but ultimately I voted for Nova over Max. It's not that he doesn't deserve it—I'd argue we each deserve it—but Nova has been a loyal, talented player for all four years, and she's never won a thing. She doesn't bring it up, but I'm sure she wants it. And Max will have (almost) the entire percussion section to give him votes, plus every girl in the band holding on to their crush on him.

"Actually, I have something for each of you," Li says and lifts her bag. She pulls out a handful of papers and glances at them shyly. "I finished your character sketches." She hands one to each of the players, and it's comically adorable how their faces each light up with joy when they take a look. Nova screams with excitement, which makes Zoinks bark, and then the whole table laughs.

"Li, these are incredible. *Look* at Stump and Zelda together!" Nova says and brandishes the paper so we can see it.

"Um, Nova?" I blink at her in shock. "Are you crying?" I'm not sure I've seen Nova cry once in all the years I've known her.

"No. I mean . . . not really." She wipes her eyes. "I've just tried to imagine what Zelda would look like in the game, but I'm not very visual, and this is . . . It's more perfect than I could have imagined."

Li is also looking teary-eyed now, and if I'm not careful then they're going to make me cry. Li gives her a hug and Nova squeezes her back so hard she might pop Li's head off.

"Axolotl has never looked so cool," Max says appreciatively. "Seriously, thank you for doing this."

"You're *really* talented. You should do more with your art," Felix says seriously, his expression almost imploring, and Li glances down at her hands.

"Oh, well, it was nothing. Just something fun to do in the evenings between homework. Hazel"—she turns to me—"you don't have a real character, but I thought you might enjoy this."

She hands me a sheet of paper. On it is a girl who has my curly hair, but is wearing a billowing green robe, pointed green hat, and holding a flag pole rather than a wizard's staff. I remember the way Li described me as a wizard during our color guard sectional dinner here—she's captured the idea perfectly.

"Ahhh, Li! I'm getting a frame for it and hanging it in my room."

"Same," Nova says. "I barely want to touch it, I'm scared of ruining it somehow."

"And now we know how each of our characters look, so that'll help with role-playing," Max adds. "Speaking of . . ." He glances at me.

"Max and I got the idea that everyone should have a miniature of their character for the game," I add. "They still need to be painted and we haven't made much progress yet, but these portraits should help out immensely."

"That's awesome," Nova says.

"And we'll need to find a miniature Zelda—the shop didn't have anything that gave off his floppy-tongued energy," Max says.

"Or his floofy fur."

"I'll do some searching," Nova replies.

"Well, we better start. You all need to get back to hunting down this wizard," I say.

We gather around the table, and I'm almost giddy that I get to use some of what I came up with for our dungeon crawl.

"After your progress through the forest during the last session, you now find yourselves outside of an enormous cave. The entrance is as tall as the second floor of the citadel you just came from. You see tracks on the ground, some mounds that give off a stench like rotting meat, and not much else. It's silent, almost eerie."

"What kind of tracks are they?" Max asks.

"Zelda sniffs around the cave as if he's very suspicious. Can I roll a survival check to learn more about the tracks?" Nova asks.

"Definitely," I reply and continue once her skill check is successful. "Stump, you discover that these are the same type of tracks as the giant opossum you fought at the music festival."

"I guess we're going into the dark creepy cave, then?" Felix asks.

"Aren't elves supposed to be brave?" Nova asks.

"I don't know, but I'm not. I like to play music and eat good food. It's the main reason I was sad about the blight."

"Not because you lost your home and family?" Li asks with a raised eyebrow.

"That's where the good food was kept," he tells her with a laugh.

"When we get this solved, remind me that I don't want my family interacting with yours."

"I will not. I'm hoping our families will be spending a lot of their time together once we've found a way to save our lands. I'd like to introduce you to my parents."

Felix and Li smile at each other for a moment as if no one else is sitting there, and I can practically feel Li's delight from here. Mental note for future sessions: Find ways to bring those two characters even closer into contact. There's definitely going to be some in-game love happening.

My phone buzzes with a new text.

Max: I TOLD YOU

I laugh before I can help it and then bite my lip. Felix and Li sit back and resettle themselves.

"I'm thinking that Zelda and I will take the lead and go deeper into the cave tunnels to track for scents," Nova announces.

"I'll come with you," Max says immediately, and he and Nova share a ghost of a smile across the table.

"Shouldn't we all come?" Li asks.

"You two can hang back and guard the tunnel," Nova advises.

I almost feel bad because I'd like to give their characters a little alone time rather than moving on to what I have planned next. But then, one of the fun things about being DM is that I get to mess with their plans and special moments, just the same as they get to mess with mine.

"As you begin your descent deeper into the caves, you hear the scrape of claws against stone."

They all exchange glances.

"My time to shine," Max says and mimes brandishing his huge axes.

Felix eyes me. "You aren't going to let us get close to the wizard for a while, are you?"

I grin mischievously. "If I did that, the campaign would be over sooner. None of you want that, right?"

They shake their heads.

"Bring it on. I could use some more experience," Felix says.

It turns out the claws are attached to an owlbear, one of my personal favorite monsters. The battle is a hard one and the owlbear is almost strong enough to overpower my group since they're still a low level. Luckily both Li and Felix can heal because everyone is going to need it.

The rest of the session is excellent. I'm able to take them down a series of passageways, throw another encounter at them, and even include the classic "treasure chest that's actually a mimic." Maybe it's been done a lot, but it's never been done by me.

Unlike usual, Melanie and Max leave quickly at the end of the night because she has an early shift the next day. Li and Felix also leave together, so Nova and I get some rare time alone.

"Are they dating now?" Nova asks and sits down on our sofa in the living room. Zoinks follows and curls up on the ground next to her.

"Li and Felix? I don't think so. Or, at least, Li hasn't said anything official to me about it."

"So, knowing this group, they've been dating for weeks and are keeping it a secret as well. You all are doing a great job of reminding me that I shouldn't date until college. Or maybe grad school, I don't know."

I drop down on the other side of the sofa. "Don't be dramatic, it's not that bad."

"Maybe, but it's weird. I was expecting you and Max to come clean this evening. I understand why you didn't want to talk about it last week at the game—you two had barely been together for twenty-four hours. You needed a minute to feel settled. But now it's been over a week and you're still keeping it a secret from everyone?"

I mess with my hair rather than look her in the eye. "If we tell everyone, things will get so complicated. Our sections hate each other."

"Who cares? They don't get to decide what you do with your life."

"I know, but it's been such a struggle getting color guard to bond. Now that we're finally coming together, I don't want to be the one to splinter or distract us."

She raises an eyebrow. "And I'm sure Max is more than fine keeping you a secret."

My stomach churns at how easily she can predict the truth. Still, I don't like her wording.

"What are you saying?"

"I'm not saying anything other than I'm worried about you. I know you've fallen for him already, no matter what you tell me, and this whole arrangement is making me nervous. I don't like that he can kiss you in secret and then deny you're together in public."

"But it goes both ways," I argue stubbornly. I feel the need to defend us even though I have the same reservations as her. "I'm doing the exact same thing."

"But *is* it the same?" she asks quietly. She sits up straighter and looks me in the eye. "You really like him."

I deflate. It's clear what she's implying—that Max might not feel as strongly about me as I feel about him. I want to keep fighting her, but a small voice reminds me of our conversation yesterday. Percussion is still his priority. I lean back and stare up at the ceiling, wishing I knew for sure whether he's as serious about us as I am. The obvious solution is to just ask, but that's terrifying.

I lift my head to look at Nova. "I kinda hate this conversation, FYI. But thanks for caring anyway. Even if it is in your cynical and pessimistic way." I roll my eyes good-naturedly.

"I hate it too. And you're welcome." She nudges my leg with her foot. "Now let's go raid your kitchen for dessert before I have to go back home."

Chapter Thirty

Today is the day. Our third and final regional band competition, and our last chance to qualify for state. I'm so nervous that I wake up nauseous, and I'm pretty sure I'm going to stay that way for the rest of the day.

I finish the final touches on my French braid and check myself out in the bathroom mirror at the house. The guard decided to wear green satin bows in our braids for this competition, and I want mine to be pristine. Downstairs, I can hear dishes clinking and hushed voices as my parents get ready. Mom, Dad, and Kelsey are driving to the competition even though this one is close to two hours away. I'm sure I'll find them in their band T-shirts with matching buttons, face paint, and pom-poms at the ready.

"Ooh, I love your bow," Kelsey says when I walk into the kitchen. "Can you do my hair the same way?"

"Uh, sure," I reply, a bit surprised she cares. "I have an

extra ribbon I can use." I pull a hair tie from my wrist where I always keep extras and run my fingers through her curls to separate them into thirds.

"Does Max like ribbons?" she asks over her shoulder.

Ah, there it is. Now I see why she's interested in my hair-style.

"I've never asked him about his opinions on ribbons."

"How are you feeling about today?" Mom asks, a steaming cup of coffee in her hands. She's dressed as the quintessential marching band parent, just as I expected her to be.

"Great," I reply, trying to exude confidence. "The guard has really come together over the last month, so I'm feeling good."

Dad nods over his mug. "You've put in the work and now you get to enjoy the benefits. You can go out there and just have fun."

The briefest hint of annoyance flickers across Mom's face. Honestly, I kind of feel the same. I wish that going out and "having fun" was enough for me, but it's not. I've had too many years growing up in this house for *fun* to be my goal.

"Now is the time to really go after it," Mom adds. "You can relax tomorrow. Winners never let up."

"She's already done so much, Lauren," Dad says reproach-fully.

"I know," she tells us both. "I'd just hate for you to have regrets, especially with band awards around the corner. I know how much all this means to you."

My eyes drift toward the living room bookshelf where both Mom and Dad display their band awards from high school and college. They were so happy to add my freshman award to the shelf. They pushed all their things to the back so my award would be front and center. I've never won anything else important enough to add to the shelf, so it's sat there ever since, alone and gathering dust. But I'm feeling sick enough from the pressures of our show today. I can't think about anything else.

"Five, six, seven, eight!" Faith calls.

We're warming up at Twin Valley High School, and Faith is drilling us on a super difficult piece of choreography in our show. Not only does it have two flat tosses, but also a backhand spin series that's really tricky. I've done it so many times now that it's as easy as walking for me, which means I can rehearse while also letting my eyes wander back toward Max.

He looks so cute with his plumed hat on. I can't hear what he's saying to the rest of his section, but I think he's giving them a pep talk. Unfortunately, this week has been just as hectic as last week, so we haven't spent much more time together. I'm anxious for today to be over for many reasons, but one of them is that I've decided we need to come clean with our sections after today. I won't say anything to Max now, but—barring another horrible competition like last time—I plan to tell him this evening. I know he was hesitant before, but it's been two weeks now and I want to spend the rest of our time in marching band together. I'm sick of trying to pretend he doesn't exist when all I really want to do is run over and give him a good-luck kiss on the cheek.

"Stop, hold up." Faith waves her hands. "Not everyone was on count. Let's try that again."

I glance around, wondering who was off this time. Maybe Yori? She struggles with this part.

"Hazel, are you ready?" Faith says and lifts an eyebrow.

"Of course, I'm always ready."

Callie snorts. "Then try being on count this time."

I open my mouth to argue before realizing that Faith is nodding subtly. Oh my god. I squeeze my eyes shut and push everything else from my mind. I can think about Max *after* today's performance, not before.

The rest of warm-ups goes smoothly, but I can feel Faith's eyes lingering on me. When we take a break, she comes over to me directly.

"Is everything okay? You don't seem like your usual self."

"I'm fine. Ready for this afternoon."

"Good. I need everyone to be on task today." She nods her head and her blond ponytail flips around her neck.

"Seriously?" I mutter.

I know Faith is my color guard director, but right now all I can see is a girl barely older than me who blew off more rehearsals than she attended. I don't think she's in the position to be lecturing me on taking this seriously.

"What?" she asks with a frown.

"Nothing."

"It seems like you have something you'd like to say."

I huff out a breath. "Faith, you've barely been around. I know you come for our games and competitions, but for the most part it's just me. And when you do come by, more often than not you're bribing everyone to love you with treats and unearned compliments. I'm sorry I was off count earlier, but I don't think I deserve a lecture when I've been the one holding this group together."

As soon as the words are out of my mouth, I freeze in shock. I can't believe I just said that. Yes, I've been frustrated, but I meant to stuff those emotions inside me, not spew them all over my color guard director right before the biggest competition to date.

Her face pales and I'm positive she's about to tell me I'll be standing on the sidelines rather than performing today. Instead, she slumps.

"You're right," she says quietly. "I know I haven't been there for you like you needed."

I shake my head. "No, Faith, I'm sorry. I shouldn't have said that. You've been great."

She laughs sarcastically. "I haven't been great. I thought I could balance it all, but getting to the rehearsals with my job has been way harder than I expected. Even when Sire asked me, I knew it was a bad idea, but I didn't want to let everyone down. The idea of Glen Vale without a guard . . ." She shakes her head sadly.

Her words throw me. "What are you talking about?"

"I was Sire's last resort, and I mean *last*. He knew it was a bad fit, but neither of us wanted to take guard away from you all, so I tried to do my best. I'm sorry that you feel like I failed you."

It takes me another few moments to fully process what she's saying. We were that close to losing color guard altogether? I try to imagine it, but my heart lurches and I push the thoughts away. Instead, I throw my arms around her and pull her into a hug.

"I had no idea, Faith. And you didn't fail us! We're here and we're going to kill it today, I promise."

She hugs me back. "I know you will. Now go get the rest of your guard as pumped up as you are."

I jog away, still in shock that there was a very real version of my life where I didn't get to be in color guard at all this year. I debate telling the others, but I don't want to distract them right before we're about to go on. There will be time to do something for Faith later. Now is the time to prove that it was worth keeping color guard around this year.

"Circle up, everyone!" I call. "Are we ready?"

I put my hand in the center of the circle and everyone else does the same. I start the chant, yelling as loud as I can.

"Show up!"

"Show out!"

"All in!"

"No doubt!"

"Glen Vale Guard!"

We give each other quick hugs, take deep breaths, and then get in line to march onto the Twin Valley football field.

"Glen Vale High School," the disembodied voice of the announcer booms. "You may begin your warm-up and/or preplacement."

Chapter Thirty-One

We've got this. We can do it.

My stomach wobbles as we all head to our starting positions. I look from side to side as I go through the motions of stretching and placing my flags, catching the eye of whichever guard members are close enough so I can give them a nod of reassurance.

Our field commanders call us to attention, the percussion hits their first note, and my mind goes blissfully blank. The next seven minutes fly like I'm fast-forwarding a TV show at 2x speed. One second we're swinging our lightning bolt flags to mimic a storm during the opening moments of *Night on Bald Mountain,* then we're nailing our pop tosses during the drum break, and suddenly I'm lifting a huge stained-glass flag in our final pose. I distantly register the cheers and the cow bell my parents bring to each competition. Dear god, my parents are extra.

We march off the field, my heart still on fast-forwarding speed.

"Did we kill it?" I ask Faith as soon as I find her waiting on the sidelines.

"Yes! Absolutely phenomenal!" She claps and waves over the rest of the guard. "You all gave me goose bumps. It's the best I've ever seen you!"

"Eeeeee!" Li squeals and throws her arms around me. Madisyn and Addison pile onto our hug, and soon the entire guard is one massive squealing huddle.

"This is what hard work can bring you!" Faith exclaims. "Now go relax in the stands and enjoy the other band performances. And hey"—her voice gets more serious—"no matter what happens, you all should be very proud of yourselves. You represented Glen Vale color guard very well."

We make our way to the bleachers to await the awards ceremony at the end of the competition. Max is already there, surrounded by friends. He catches my eye and mouths *nice job.* My heart aches to sit down next to him, give him a huge hug, and analyze every minute of the performance. I want to eat crappy nachos by his side, and talk about our chances as we watch the other bands perform, and kiss him whenever I feel like it. Instead, I walk right past him and remind myself that soon we'll be able to do all those things.

Nova climbs up a few bleachers from her clarinet friends and sits next to me. "How do you feel?"

"Like my heart is about to beat out of my chest. But Faith said it's the best we've ever performed, so I'll take it. Your solo sounded as amazing as always."

“Thanks.” She shrugs. “It’s not a hard piece of music.”

She’s definitely deflecting. I know the solo is hard, especially when all eyes are on you, but Nova is self-effacing to a fault, so I let her have that.

“And, even better,” I say, “Brody was noticeably silent when the guard passed him on the bleachers, so it feels like we already won.”

Nova applauds me. “If you can shut him up, then you deserve every trophy they have. You’re definitely my hero.”

A roar of laughter comes from the percussion and Nova slips her arm through mine and squeezes. “I have a good feeling about this awards ceremony.”

“I’m going to puke from waiting, so don’t sit close to me.”

Four other bands perform, then there’s a break so the judges can calculate their scores, and *finally* the disembodied voice of the announcer returns to say that the award ceremony is about to begin. Li sits down at my other side, looking almost as nervous as I feel.

“And now what you’ve all been waiting so patiently for: our award winners.”

I immediately tense and Li grabs my left hand while Nova leans into my side on my right. The announcers go through several other categories before getting to ours.

“The award for Best Overall Percussion goes to . . . Oak Grove High School!”

For a moment, I’m elated. Percussion officially lost our bet. Still, it’s hard to feel pure joy when the entire percussion section deflates a few rows in front of me. Brody might be sitting there, but Max and Felix are there as well. I know how much Max wanted it and how hard he worked. I can't find it in myself to celebrate his loss.

"Next up is the award for Best Overall Auxiliary." I curl over in a ball and hold my breath. Nova and Li both lean closer against me. "And the award goes to . . . Glen Vale High School!"

Screams erupt all around me. Hands grab my arms and shoulders, shaking me so hard I might fall off the bleachers.

"We did it!" Li screams. "We did it! Best in show!"

Nova throws her arms around me and squeezes tightly. "Ahh, congratulations! I'm so proud of you!"

It takes me another second to fully comprehend before I can jump up and scream with them. The announcer keeps talking, but I can't hear a thing except screaming. All of a sudden, the rest of Glen Vale jumps out of their seats and our section of the stadium fills with more cheering.

I turn to Yori, who is now the closest to me. "What's going on?" I call.

"The band got a Superior rating—we're going to state!"

My screams raise another octave. I grab on to any band member I can see, shaking them and giving them hugs as my eyes fill with tears. It doesn't feel possible. Of course I wanted this to happen, and I'm so incredibly relieved that we're going to state, but the best in show award? We *actually* did it? We won the bet? I can't believe it.

When the awards ceremony is done, the guard half jumps, half runs down the bleachers. People yell out congratulations as we pass, and Sire stops us at the bottom to tell us how proud he is. None of us can stop shrieking and laughing as we make our way back to the band buses. Even Callie, who has always seemed the most apathetic, is beside herself with excitement.

"Hazel!"

I spin to find Mom, Dad, and Kelsey running toward me. "My god, Hazel! You did it!" Mom gushes and pulls me into a hug.

"Thanks, Mom," I breathe into her neck. "We're all freaking out, we're so excited!"

"Of course you are! And you deserve to be! Oak Grove was stellar today. But not as good as you." She hugs me again before passing me to Dad and Kelsey.

"Great job, honey," Dad says more quietly. "So proud of you."

"You guys were way better than last time," Kelsey tells me.

I laugh. "Thank you, I guess?"

"But it's the truth!" Mom cries. "And it's just the beginning for you. Today is best auxiliary, next is the senior MVM award and Superior ratings at state! I can already see it!" She's so excited she's literally jumping up and down. Unfortunately, her excitement has the opposite effect on me. I haven't even processed our win yet, and Mom is already talking about the next thing?

Dad rubs my back and gives me a small smile. "There's time to think about all that later. For now, go celebrate with your friends."

I race off, happy to get some distance from Mom and spend time with Nova. Although, now that I think of it, an even better idea comes to me. Max and I should tell our sections right now, before we get back on the buses. Then he and I can sit together, along with Felix and Li and Nova, and we won't have to hide anymore. It'll be the perfect end to this incredible day.

I wave goodbye to my family and go in search of Max so I can tell him my plan. But another possibility pops into my mind as I scan the crowds and peek down each row of school buses. What if he doesn't want to see me tonight at all? I'm sure he's upset, maybe even a little angry, that guard beat out percussion. I hesitate. Maybe I should give him some space for now.

"Hazel!"

I spin at Max's voice. We're both standing between two school buses, shielded from view. For the moment, we're alone.

"Hey, I've been looking for you," I call and walk in his direction. "I'm sorry about percussion—"

But I don't finish my sentence because Max sprints headlong toward me. When he reaches me, he wraps his arms around my waist and twirls me in a circle so that my feet fly off the ground.

"Hazel, you *did* it!" he cries. "You won!"

He puts me back down, and I stumble. My throat tightens with emotion at his reaction, and I struggle to say, "I can't believe it."

"I can. I always knew how great you guys could be."

"And . . . you're not mad?"

He grimaces. "It's not your fault we couldn't bring home the win. Percussion is feeling defeated right now, but we'll bounce back. I bet some of us will even have a good time learning your guard choreography."

Relief floods through me. "Max, listen, I've been thinking and . . . what if we told our sections about us now? Tonight. I don't want to keep us a secret anymore."

He leans back. "You want to tell them?"

"Yeah, I do." I take his hands in mine. "Aren't you sick of trying to pretend we don't care about each other? I know the guard will be shocked, but they'll get over it."

"Max?" someone asks. "What's going on?"

Max jerks his hands from mine. We both turn to find a small group of Glen Vale percussion members walking toward us. At the front are Jamila, who plays the snare drum with Felix, and Niko, a cymbal player. Behind them are a few other percussion players. Thankfully, Brody isn't with them.

Max takes a small step away from me. It's probably not more than a few inches, but it might as well be a mile. "Hey guys, what's up?" he asks casually.

"We were coming to look for you," Niko says slowly. "Jamila's mom suggested we grab milkshakes to make up for this horrible competition and we wanted you to come." He frowns and glances between me and Max. "Or are you already busy?"

"Not busy. Just congratulating Hazel on winning our bet."

The others look less than impressed at that statement. Jamila gives Niko some side-eye and crosses her arms over her chest. "Yeah, we saw. That was quite the congratulations."

"Don't be a sore loser," I snap.

"All right, everyone calm down," Max says. "Hazel and I go way back. We're old friends."

"Huh," Niko replies. "Because I could have sworn I was picking up on some *other* vibes."

More band members join the fray, probably curious about why we're all standing around. I see Felix and Li, and Nova's there wearing a stony expression.

"What's the holdup? Are we going or not?" Brody's loud, grating voice cuts through the group. He pushes his way to the front and rolls his eyes. "Are you seriously wasting precious time talking to Hazel? Let's *go.*"

"Who are the toilet cleaners now, Brody?" I smile maliciously. "I bet it must be so hard knowing you lost. Although, to be fair, you do already have a lot of experience with being a loser." I know I'm not helping matters, but I can't resist rubbing it in *just* a bit.

Brody turns his glare on me, but Niko interrupts. "Actually, I don't think Max is going to hang out with us tonight after all," he tells Brody. "He's already got a date."

A few people snicker. My heart speeds as I turn to Max. I lift my eyebrows slightly, urging him to rip off the Band-Aid and tell them. It's his section, so I'm not going to do that for him, but it's clear that the time for secrets has passed. They've already guessed anyway.

But rather than pulling me close and announcing his feelings, he's quiet. Tense. *Tell them,* I think desperately. *Say the words.*

Yes, I'm dating Hazel.

Yes, I care about her.

She's important to me.

Max clears his throat, his eyes wide and harried. He looks to his section and then back at me. His Adam's apple bobs as he swallows, and then he turns so he's fully facing them.

He shakes his head derisively. "Are you kidding? Me and

Hazel? Of course we don't have a date. I was just trying to be the bigger person and congratulate her—something the rest of you could stand to do more of."

I fall back a step.

"The bigger person?" Brody says with a snort. "Please. I know you still have that equipment shed key."

The shock of the words is so sudden that I really think I might be sick. He has the key that I thought I'd lost? I turn to him. "What the hell? Max?"

He pales and waves his hands in front of his face. "It's not like that. We were never really going to do anything."

A few percussion players scoff, as if they beg to differ with his version of events, but he rounds on them. "*Not. Now.* I'm not getting milkshakes tonight, so you can head out." He turns to me. "Hazel, don't freak out, just listen to me."

The others linger, probably hoping to see us blow up in a huge fight, but my jaw is clenched too tightly to say a word. Felix ushers his section away with a nervous glance back at us. Only when we're alone again do I have the strength to say something.

"You *stole* my key?"

Max looks sick. "It was for a stupid bet, back in August, before our first football game. But I never really meant to go through with it."

"But you thought about it? About . . ." I can barely get the words out, imagining what they must have had planned. "About vandalizing our equipment? Ruining our flags?"

I know I'm right when he squeezes his eyes shut. "For like a *second*. I know I can be competitive, but I wanted to win on my own merits, not because I sabotaged my competitor."

I take a jerky step backward. "I just . . . I can't believe you did that. I would never have done something like that to you or anyone in percussion."

"I know . . ."

"I was livid with myself for losing it, and Sire was so disappointed in me," I whisper. "But it turns out it was never my fault to begin with. You stole it from me." I shake my head in disbelief. "And you never *told* me, Max. How can I possibly trust you?"

"Because it was almost two months ago," he pleads. "Things have changed so much—*I've* changed so much. I swear I would never hurt you. That's why I couldn't go through with it. I imagined seeing your face when you opened that shed and I knew I could never do anything like that to you."

I wrap my arms around my stomach and stumble backward a few more steps.

"I should have told you, but I was scared that if I did, then *this* would happen." He gestures between the two of us. "I couldn't risk losing you. You're the best thing in my life—you always have been. Even when we were kids, I loved your giant curly hair, and how your laugh was louder than anyone else's, and how competitive you were, and the way I could say whatever I wanted and you always understood what I meant. And now"—he gestures to me again—"you're so much more than even that."

"I'm the 'best thing in your life,' but you can't admit we're dating? That's not how this works."

"That's not fair," he says quietly. "They caught me off guard. *You* caught me off guard. I thought we'd decided we were going to keep things a secret and I wasn't prepared . . ."

The same nausea from this morning is back, burning my throat and making my stomach swim. “You already made it perfectly clear that percussion is the most important thing in your life. Isn’t that what you told me when I came to your apartment? Well, you’re in luck, they’re going for milk-shakes right now. Why don’t you go spend the rest of the evening with them? Because you definitely aren’t spending it with me.”

I turn and walk away.

Chapter Thirty-Two

We don't play D&D the next day. Maybe I'm being childish or emotional, but the idea of sitting next to Max for an entire evening feels more than impossible. I text the group Sunday morning to tell them I'm not feeling well. I know I'm not fooling Max, or any of them, but they don't push me on it. I finally clomp down the stairs to the kitchen around one p.m. when I'm too hungry to hold out any longer.

"Hey, there you are!" Mom says brightly. She's at the kitchen table with piles of green fabric spread around her, while Kelsey is putting together a Lego set in the living room. "I was going to wake you up hours ago, but I got a text from Melanie that you aren't feeling well?"

Of course she found out from Melanie before I even came downstairs.

"Yeah, just a little under the weather."

"And I was thinking you'd be on top of the world after

the amazing day you had yesterday. Are you still buzzing from it?"

"Yep," I say flatly. "Totally buzzing."

Kelsey pokes her head into the kitchen. "Did you get Max sick? I was hoping he was going to come over today so I could show him what I'm making."

"I'm not sure how he's feeling."

That part is the truth at least. Max hasn't texted and I have no intention of reaching out beyond my single group text this morning. I'm not even mad at him. Or, at least, that's not the main emotion I'm feeling. It's more that I feel so heavy I can barely lift my feet off the ground or my head off the pillow. I'm surprised I can support my own weight right now.

"You should eat something. You look pale," Mom says. "But first come look at what I'm working on!"

She lifts a dark green long-sleeved shirt to reveal that she's ironed an absolutely enormous picture of my face to the front of it, along with the words *Glen Vale Marching Knights* and *Color Guard Captain* onto the back.

"What do you think? I'm making enough so the whole family can match at state. Grandma and Grandpa should be coming along with Aunt Suzanne and Uncle Bill, and I didn't want to leave them out. And don't ruin the surprise, but I also made a shirt for Melanie with Max's face on it. She's going to love it!"

I stare in shock. I know I should be grateful that she cares enough to make themed clothes, and that my extended family cares enough to come to state, especially given the conversation I had with Max about his dad. But my face is so *big* on the shirt. She didn't even include my neck or shoulders. It's just a stark oval cutout of my face. Somehow, she's also managed to choose the most unflattering photo from this season—my hair is extra frizzy, my face is pink and shiny with oil, and at least one pimple is highly visible. I'm mortified at the idea of them all walking around with these shirts on. They might as well also wear neon hats that blink *My Daughter Is a Huge Dork!*

"It's . . . uh, it's a little much, don't you think?"

"Absolutely not! There's no amount of cheering or excitement that could be too much for this moment. This is *state.* The end of your high school marching band career. The end of an era." Her eyes glisten with tears.

Wow, this is not the conversation I was wanting to have when I walked down those steps. I take a deep breath and remind myself to keep things in perspective. Okay, *yes,* Mom is determined to embarrass me by wearing a shirt so ugly that I may need to wear a mask to the competition. But at least she's planning to come. I never (ever) have to worry that she'll stop attending my events or won't be interested in what I'm doing. And that's something to be thankful for . . . right? Even if her tears and "end of an era" speeches make my nerves spike again?

I rub my fingers along the hem of the shirt, rather than look at her. "What would happen if the color guard didn't get Superior ratings at state?"

"Don't even think about it. Your group is so talented this year, I'm sure it'll be fine."

"But what if something happens? What if it's windy, or muddy, or one of the members gets sick, or we just make mistakes? Any of those things could happen. I can't control all that."

I hold my breath, hoping she'll say she'd be proud no matter what happens. She stands and comes around the table, taking both my hands.

"It's totally normal to be anxious," she says. "It's a lot of pressure being captain. I remember from when I was the trumpet section leader. A lot of people are looking to you and I can understand why all these worries would be going through your mind. But you already know what to do: Lock in and practice harder than you ever have before to build up that muscle memory. It's hard now, but it'll be worth it in the end. I know you won't let us down."

She smiles reassuringly, but her words don't soothe me the way I was hoping they might. Instead, everything feels even heavier now. All I want is my bed.

I'm in a horrible mood when I get to rehearsal on Monday afternoon. This might be the first time I've ever truly dreaded going to band. But I'm obviously on my own with that sentiment.

"Hazel!" Rosa cries as soon as she spots me. She and Yori start dancing. "I'm still on such a high from the competition! I never thought I'd care this much about color guard, but now I see why you've been so competitive this whole time. Winning feels so good!"

Deja and Callie join us. "Yeah, it does. I didn't really believe we could get Superior ratings at state, but now I'm pumped," Callie says.

This—exactly this—is what I've wanted all season long. And now that I have it, I can't enjoy it. It's not fair. I deserve to be joyful with my group, dammit. But I don't want to pull them into my drama, so I try my best to put on a happy face.

"You were all absolutely awesome on Saturday," I reply. "Thanks for sticking with it."

"Right back at you," Callie replies. "I know I didn't make it easy."

Sire walks to the front of the room and calls us to attention.

"First off, a huge congratulations to everyone for your hard work and dedication this season. It took us some time, but we did it. We're officially state-bound!"

The roar of cheers is so loud my ears ring when we're finished.

"Don't forget that voting for the MVM awards ends this Friday, so please cast your votes. Now, just because we're coming off a great competition doesn't mean the work is over. State is next Saturday, and there are still things we can improve in the coming days." There are a few playful jeers and boos at this news, which Sire ignores. "We're going to spend the first part of rehearsal watching back the recording of our performance and analyzing where we can improve. Before we begin, though, I also want to give a few well-deserved shout-outs. Eric and Nova, excellent work on your solos. You both sounded terrific. And can we all give an extra round of applause to our color guard, who not only earned straight Superior ratings on Saturday, but also brought home the best auxiliary award? The last time that happened was seventeen years ago! It's a tremendous achievement."

To my surprise, the cheers from the band are almost as loud as they were a few minutes ago. The guard members jangle my arms, and I smile and wave self-consciously, although I'm careful to keep my eyes far away from the percussion section. No one is booing, so that's a good sign, but I don't want to see their half-hearted applause. And I don't want to see Max's face at all. I'm not sure I can handle it.

The color guard sits down in a cluster of chairs in the back corner while Sire preps the performance film. "Oh, that felt good," Devin says.

Li studies me. "Are you okay?"

I shrug and give her a watery smile.

"Are you sick?" Addison asks. "I was expecting you to be the most elated out of all of us. Where's the choreographed victory dance? And matching T-shirts declaring us winners over the percussion?"

I laugh, though it's a bit strangled. "Would you be shocked to hear I played with some designs on Canva last night?"

"I'd expect nothing less," Madisyn replies.

"Girl, we've been together for four years," Devin says. He puts his hand gently on my knee. His green nail polish from the competition is pristine, whereas I've already chewed and chipped mine off. "Don't tell me this is your real reaction. What's actually happening?"

At the front of the room, Sire is still messing with the video and lights.

"Nothing. Don't worry about it."

"Nope, nothing means it's something. We're a team." Devin glances around at the group. "We can't have our leader falling apart on us now. Tell us."

"You wouldn't like me much as a leader if I told you."

They all exchange surprised glances.

"We'll love you no matter what, Hazel," Li whispers.

I bite my lip. I could make more excuses or refuse to tell them, but honestly, what does it matter now?

"Max and I . . . we were kind of . . ." I swallow down my nerves. "Well, we were together and now we're not. I'm still getting over it."

"You and *Max*?" Keira squeals loud enough that I'm sure other people overhear. I squeeze my eyes shut in embarrassment.

"Sorry!"

"I'm so sorry, Hazel," Li says. Unlike the others, she doesn't look surprised. She's more resigned than anything.

"Did he do something?" Yori asks. "Say one word and I'm bringing back my orc barbarian persona. I'll knock him out with a flag pole on the field."

"He doesn't deserve you," Callie says.

Rosa sighs. "You can't trust boys."

"Hey!" Devin complains. "I mean, having dated a few, I can't argue. But I still take offense."

"Thanks, everyone. I'll be okay. I just . . . I really liked him." Some of the emotion I'm desperately trying to hold back seeps into my words, and they all sit back at it.

"Color guard?" Sire's voice is stern. "I know you're coming off a successful weekend, but no one in this room is perfect. I expect you to pay attention to the film with the rest of the band."

We all sit up and train our eyes on the screen.

Five minutes later, Callie whispers, "Pizza after rehearsal? All together?"

I frown. We haven't all gotten together since our section dinner back in August. There's no way everyone has the time or motivation for that. But, to my shock, each of the members nods in agreement. The tightness in my chest loosens a bit.

I'm the last to arrive at the restaurant because Mom texts to ask if I'll drop Kelsey off at dance since she's overbooked. When I arrive, a chorus of laughter and voices catches my attention. I follow the sound to the back corner where the entire guard is gathered around a big round table.

"There she is!" Li calls.

I wave and sit down. "Thanks for doing this. It means a lot."

"We needed to have a celebration dinner!" Callie says. "And also to vent about the percussion section proving once again that they're the worst!"

The others nod vehemently, but I can't drum up much

anger for the other percussion players. I can't even find the energy to be mad at Brody. All I feel is apathy and an aching sadness.

When I'm quiet, an awkward silence falls over the table.

"Sorry to bum everyone out," I mumble. "I'm not really in a self-righteous, enraged mood right now. I'm just blah."

"So . . . um, you and Max?" Deja says. "That seems so out of the blue. I thought you hated him?"

"I thought I did too," I reply with a little laugh. "At least at one point. But we go back a long time, and eventually I realized that all that hate was maybe turning into . . ." A particular four-letter word floats into my mind, but I quickly push it away. I can't say that out loud now. "Into something else. But it's too hard. I don't know how to trust him."

"You shouldn't trust him," Addison says. "He's percussion."

There are a few snickers around the table.

"Don't kill me, any of you," Li interjects, "but I think Max is a pretty good guy. We've been playing D&D together and he's been cool to me."

"I was the one secretly dating him, so it's not like I can judge you for liking him," I reply.

"So . . . like, is it *over* over?" Keira asks. "Or is there a chance you'd get back together with him?"

I meticulously fold the paper covering from my straw rather than look her in the eye. My mind says that we'll never get back together. He's burned bridges that he can't rebuild. But my heart . . . I miss Max so much. It's hard to do anything but think of him. I don't want him to be a stranger again, or my enemy, or my ex.

"I'm not sure," I say slowly. "I don't know how we can get back to where we were after everything that's happened."

They exchange glances.

"But you miss him?" Devin asks.

I nod because I don't trust myself to speak.

"Well then, maybe—"

"You've got to be kidding me," Madisyn interrupts. "Did they follow us or something?"

I turn around to find Felix and Niko walking in the door, deep in conversation. My first thought is that I'm glad Felix is making more band friends. And my second thought is that this dinner just got really awkward.

"Do you want to go somewhere else so we won't be overheard?" Addison whispers.

"No, it's okay," I say. "I'm actually friends with Felix. We play D&D with him too."

"Traitors," Callie mutters, but she only looks a little bit mad.

Felix freezes when he sees all of us staring at him. His eyes immediately find Li.

"Uh, hey?" Li says and waves. Felix and Niko slow next to our table, while the host waits to take them to another section of the restaurant.

"This is a weird coincidence. Is everyone craving pizza today?" Felix asks.

"I guess so," I reply.

"Huh. Well . . ." He glances around the table and over to Niko. "I hope you guys have a good time. Glad you're celebrating."

He moves to walk away, and I make a snap decision.

Maybe things are messed up with Max, but I don't want this animosity to continue next year after I've graduated. If there's a way to make things less awkward for Li and Felix, I want to do it.

"Actually, do you want to sit with us? We can make room." I nod to the guard, who all stare at me with overly large eyes like I casually mentioned having a serial killer sit down with us.

Niko also looks alarmed. "I don't . . ."

Felix blinks, then recovers. "I think it's a great idea. Marching band is almost over, and you guys already won the bet, so we might as well get to know each other." Felix grabs a chair from another table and pulls it over to Li. "Can I squeeze in here?"

She grins and scoots over.

There's a fair amount of maneuvering to make space, and a bit of quiet grumbling, but we make it work. Once we're settled and the guys have given their drink orders, we all sit in silence. What in the world do we talk about now?

"It doesn't seem like you're celebrating," Felix tells me. "So, I assume that means you're moping too?"

I cover my face with my hands. Welp, I guess we have *that* as a discussion topic.

A few guard members chuckle and Li nudges him.

"What?" he asks. "You and Max weren't nearly as secretive as you thought you were."

"Thanks for ruining the milkshakes Saturday, by the way," Niko replies.

"And thanks to Max for ruining their relationship," Madisyn snaps.

"Oh, don't get me started on him. He's such a mess it's not even funny." Niko rolls his eyes. "I don't know how we're going to get through practices with him acting like that."

Felix sighs. "Brody's going to smell blood in the water if Max isn't careful."

"I thought I saw Max talking to Sire when I was leaving today," Addison says, leaning in. I should have known Madisyn, Addison, and Devin would become completely invested once they recognized the drama happening. Those three love their gossip. "Sire looked angry. Do you know what that was about?"

Niko and Felix shake their heads. "No idea."

"I don't want to know," Niko says. "All I want is to get through state next Saturday."

"Us too," Callie says. "Though we'll be the ones earning Superiors again."

Felix shrugs. "Whatever. At this point, I don't care anymore."

"I'm over it," Niko replies.

"I'm over it too," Deja says. Her cheeks grow red when everyone looks at her. "I hate competition."

"Why does everything have to be about marching band all the time?" Keira asks. "Sometimes I just want to eat pizza and talk about *Dancing with the Stars.*"

"I love that show," Devin says immediately.

"My mom always has it on," Niko replies. "She complains about the judges every week."

"As she should!"

Several other people jump in with their thoughts and I

sit back, both surprised and happy. This isn't exactly a celebration dinner, or a moping fest, but it might be something even more rare: a normal conversation between color guard and percussion members. Someone needs to call the Catholic Church, because I think I might be a miracle worker.

Chapter Thirty-Three

The next week and a half is weird. I guess I shouldn't have expected things to change drastically with the color guard just because we got pizza together one time after school, but I was hoping that might be the beginning of us spending more time together. Instead, everyone gets increasingly standoffish as the days pass. When I suggest hanging out together, they already have plans, even Li who always seemed excited to spend time together. They were probably more upset about me secretly dating Max than they let on at the dinner. We don't even have D&D on Sunday because Nova and Felix both text that they had other stuff come up. Part of me is grateful to be able to avoid Max for another week, but every day I also get a little lonelier.

There's no denying that I still miss him. I want to talk about our upcoming state competition, and get back to painting those miniatures, and maybe play another Settlers of Catan game so we can finally answer the question of who the best player is. But I don't know how to move forward with Max. Finding out he'd kept things from me brought back every insecurity and trust issue I'd ever had with him. And hearing the way he casually dismissed me in front of the percussion didn't help. Even if I could get past everything else, I don't think I'm strong enough to be his secret anymore, or the girlfriend all his friends despise. I want to be with someone who's proud to be with me.

"Feeling okay?" Nova asks, her expression concerned. We're standing together in the band room Thursday afternoon, and I may or may not have zoned out in the middle of our conversation.

The band awards are today and I'm a nervous wreck. Everyone is anxiously waiting for Sire to begin. Even Faith is standing at the front of the room with the other assistant directors. For how much we all care about these awards, it's not a very fancy ceremony. At the end of the school year, close to graduation, there's a more formal award ceremony for everyone in the music department, but these awards are handed out with little fanfare.

I shake myself and turn to her. "Yeah, I'm fine. Mildly nauseous, want to fast-forward time until tomorrow, you know, the usual."

It doesn't matter, I repeat to myself for the two hundredth time today. The award doesn't come with any prizes or money or fame, except the fact that your name gets added in tiny font to a huge plaque at the back of the room and you get your own plaque to take home. I let my eyes linger on the list of names as we file in from the outdoor rehearsal. Two days from now, no one will care about that

Most Valuable Senior plaque . . . but if I went up to it right now and looked back enough years, I'd find my mom's name. I know she'll care.

Nova chuckles and nods sympathetically. "It'll be over soon."

"*Everything* is going to be over soon."

Our last big rehearsal is tomorrow—along with a celebration to hype us up for state—then the competition is Saturday and then . . . that's it. Our football team didn't make it to the playoffs, so football games are done for the year. There will be a few local parades to march in, usually a holiday parade in early December and then a Memorial Day parade next May, but our band isn't taking any big trips this year like some do. No Macy's Thanksgiving Day Parade or Disney World for us. Suddenly it hits me, how fast the last few months have gone by and how one of my favorite things in the world is about to be done forever. I'm finally understanding what Mom's been repeating to me for so long.

I'm embarrassed that tears well up in my eyes. I blink them away and hope Nova doesn't notice, but she's my closest friend, so she knows immediately. She reaches out and squeezes my hand.

"No matter what, everything will be okay. We're going to kill it at state."

More people come into the band room. I recognize a few parents, but since this isn't a formal ceremony, and it's in the middle of the workday, hardly any adults are here. Usually it's just a handful of extremely involved ones—the people who chaperone the band buses and oversee the concessions and run the band boosters group to raise money for our programs.

In other words, people like my mom and dad.

"My parents weren't able to get off work," Nova says, but she doesn't seem upset. They're rarely able to come to things like this. "I assume yours will be here, though?"

I give her a small knowing nod. Honestly, it would be a relief to have Mom and Dad skip today. That way I could focus on myself instead of having to process their emotions about the award alongside my own in real time. But that won't be happening. I can't think of a single band event they've ever missed.

I'm surprised and happy to see Max's mom, Melanie, walk in and stand on the far side of the room with two other adults. I didn't think she'd be able to make it. I take a risk and glance in Max's direction. His whole face brightens when he sees her. I'm really glad she was able to come, although I'm reminded of what Addison said last week about Max speaking tersely with Sire. Did that get resolved? I want to know, but I'm not sure how to ask him without having a very awkward conversation.

After another minute, Dad walks in, scans the room, and gives me a huge wave. He's so goofy. Nova and I separate so we can go sit with our sections. The room is unusually quiet. Li smiles at me when I sit down, but she doesn't say anything. She looks almost as nervous as I'm feeling. Maybe all that talk during our last D&D game about us voting for her backfired. I hope today doesn't ruin her feelings about band if she doesn't win.

The minutes tick by so slowly that I could swear someone has messed with the analog clock in the front of the room. A few more people drift in, but Mom hasn't shown up yet. She's probably out buying an enormous bouquet to present me with if I actually win this thing. Or she's going to walk in wearing that horrible shirt with my face plastered on it. I should have made her swear she wouldn't wear it today.

Sire chats with the parents, then makes his way to the front of the room. The whole band grows quiet without him needing to say anything.

"Good afternoon!" he says even though he's already been with us for rehearsals earlier today. "First, I'd like to welcome everyone who was able to make it today. Without your support, we wouldn't be able to continue the amazing work we do, so thank you very much."

My eyes skim the small cluster of parents in case I missed Mom's arrival, but no. She's definitely not here.

"As you all know, before we travel for our state competition, we want to take some time to celebrate all of you, especially those who have put in the work to get us to where we are right now. So, if I could have all the section leaders stand so we can celebrate you?"

Feeling self-conscious, I stand and look around the room at the others. My heart swells seeing us all. Many of us have been in band together since fifth grade, and I almost want to run around and give everyone hugs. Well, almost everyone. I catch Nova's eye, feeling especially lucky to be here with her.

"And now, without further ado, I'll announce the awards.

Thank you to everyone who voted. Please know that it is always an extremely hard decision and each of you is to be commended for your hard work this season." He clears his throat, and I glance again at the door. Surely, Mom will walk in any second now. "I am very excited to announce that the Most Valuable Freshman award is going to Li Xiang."

I'm so caught up thinking about Mom that it takes me a second to understand what's happening. Li stands and screams, and then I do the same.

"You did it, you did it!"

Around me, the rest of the color guard is out of their chairs, clapping and cheering. Nova, Max, and Felix are standing as well, and even a few percussion players, including Niko. Li heads up to the front to receive her plaque and take photos with Sire.

I give her a hug as she walks back to her seat and we all get settled for the next award, which goes to a sophomore trumpet player. I try to listen and smile and clap like a sane person, but inside, my nerves are twisting more tightly. The senior award is almost here, but my mom isn't. Did something happen to her?

The junior award goes to a tuba player who starts crying when his name is announced. I look over at Dad. Could Mom have gotten into a car accident? Is Kelsey sick and she had to run to her school instead? Dad isn't paying attention to the awards. His head is bowed, and he's typing rapidly into his phone. I watch him, trying to decipher what's going on. After a moment, his shoulders sag.

He looks up at me, his face drawn. He gives me the

smallest shake of the head, and I understand what he's telling me. She's not in an emergency situation. She's not in danger. But she's also not coming.

I sit back against the chair. There's a roaring in my ears that makes it hard to hear the rest of the band. She's not here for the awards ceremony. She's not going to see me win or lose. I . . . should be happy. This is what I wanted, right? One of the things I was most worried about was the look on her face when she realized I'd lost, and now I don't have to see that. But instead of feeling relieved, I'm surprised to feel heat pricking behind my eyes.

"And last, but certainly not least, I have the pleasure of announcing the Most Valuable Senior award," Sire says. He sounds like he's underwater. "This year, we had a truly tremendous group of seniors, and this was an extremely hard decision. I wish I could give out at least five awards, but there's only space for one name."

I scan the band members. Every single person is staring at Sire with rapt attention.

Except Max.

He's looking straight at me and the worry on his face is enough to puncture a hole in my neutral facade. I swipe at my left eye before a tear can fall, and he moves to stand.

"Nova Walsh!"

We both freeze and our heads whip to Nova. She sits stock-still with perfect posture, her mouth open, while the entire clarinet section screams and encircles her. Max and I both rush to Nova's section. Out of the corner of my eye, I see Brody standing as well, but his expression is full of anger and disappointment. A fleeting moment of gratification hits me that he didn't win, but then it's gone. He doesn't deserve a second of my thoughts. I push everything from my mind and throw my arms around Nova as soon as I'm able to get close enough.

"Nova! I'm so happy for you!"

She's shaking. I let go of her so Max can hug her as well.

"How did I get it?" she asks.

"Because you deserve it!" I say.

Her brows furrow as she takes in my expression. "Are you upset? You wanted it so much."

"Oh . . . no, it's not . . ." I try my hardest to rearrange my features and push Mom further from my thoughts. "I'm not upset that you won. I'm so, *so* happy for you, truly." I lean in and whisper, "I voted for you."

She makes a little sobbing sound in the back of her throat, which brings tears to my eyes.

"I voted for *you*," she says.

"We canceled out each other's votes!" Now we're laughing *and* crying.

"Nova, if you wouldn't mind coming down to collect your award?" Sire calls, his voice bemused.

We all step back to let her get away. Sire says some other things I don't listen to, the winners head back up to the front of the room for group photos, and the rest of the band disperses for the day. I'd like to escape with them, but Max comes up to me before I can bolt.

"I'm sorry your mom didn't make it," he whispers.

I bite my bottom lip. "Thanks."

He hesitates for a moment and then turns away.

"Max?"

He spins back around immediately.

"Are things all right with you? I heard that maybe something happened with Sire? Not that you have to tell me . . ."

He sighs and runs his hand through his hair. Ugh, his stupid, beautiful hair. "Yeah, it's okay. I, uh, told him that I was the one who stole your key, and I gave it back to him. With the awards coming up, I didn't want him to think it'd been your fault."

I blink a few times. "Oh . . . well . . . thank you. What did he say?"

"He was pretty mad. I think he was close to banning me from performing at state, but then he said he wouldn't hurt our section by pulling me out." He chuckles humorlessly. "It was pretty clear from our conversation that I wasn't winning the senior award, though."

I open my mouth and close it again. Max *had* to have known he was sacrificing his possibility of winning MVM when he told Sire. I swallow tightly.

Just then, Dad walks up. "How's everyone doing?"

I glance between them. I don't want to stop talking to Max yet, but I can't tell my dad to leave when he came to school just to see me.

"Actually, I should really go see my mom," Max says apologetically. He takes a few steps away from us. "It was good to see you both, though." He turns and weaves through the crowd.

Dad stares after him, then turns back to me. "Well, it was great that one of your guard members won the freshman award. Just like you! And Nova looked absolutely thunderstruck when she won."

"Where is she, Dad?"

His face falls. "She . . . well, she got the times mixed up. She thought it was an hour later so she scheduled a meeting and couldn't get out in time."

I blink rapidly. She missed the award ceremony . . . for the award that she's been obsessed with since day one of the season . . . because she got the *time* wrong? My worry and sadness recede, and anger fills me.

"I know, I know," Dad says quietly, "but try not to be too upset with her. She's devastated. You know how much this meant to her."

"Oh yeah, I'm *very* aware of how much she cared about this award. She never let me forget it."

He frowns. "It was an honest mistake. She's been here for everything else." He looks down at his phone. "She just texted that she's leaving work now. Do you want her to come here?"

"Tell her to go home. There's no reason to come here now."

"All right." He studies me for a second and then texts Mom back.

I cross my arms over my chest and stare stonily at the cinder block wall on the other side of the room.

"Are you going to be okay?" Dad sounds nervous. He's not used to dealing with real emotions when it comes to me.

"Sure. At least Mom didn't have to see me be a loser in real time. You can break the news over text."

"I haven't said anything to her about the results." He puts a hand on my upper arm. "And you are *not* a loser. Do you hear me, Hazel? We are incredibly proud of you."

I shrug again.

He pockets his phone so he can put both his hands on my shoulders. "Don't forget, I didn't win most valuable member as a senior either." He lifts an eyebrow. "My best friend beat me too."

I almost smile, hearing him speak about Mom like that. But I'm not ready for smiling.

"And honestly, as much as your mom cared about winning that award, it's not that big of a deal. Losing it didn't affect my future at all." He gives me the tiniest shake. "You've got so much great stuff coming up—try to focus on that. And take it easy on your mom when you get home."

He gives me a hug, and my annoyance dampens slightly. It's nice to have a moment alone with Dad. Sometimes Mom's overbearing presence drowns out our relationship.

"Why don't you head to the house now," he continues. "I need to go pick up Kelsey from school and run a few errands."

I know what he's doing. He's going to kill time so Mom and I can talk alone. There's nothing I'd rather do less, but I don't think this is something I can avoid anymore.

Chapter Thirty-Four

Mom is sitting at the kitchen table when I walk into the house. She gives me a weak smile.

"Hey."

I take my time dropping my book bag on the ground and toeing off my shoes. I wish I could walk straight past her and up the stairs to my room, but she'll only follow me. Or maybe she won't and then Dad will come home and make us sit down together.

I sigh and sit across the table from her. I will admit, she doesn't look good. Her eyes are rimmed in red, her face is blotchy, and her hair is a mess the way mine gets when I'm frazzled and can't give it the time it requires. I avoided reflective surfaces on my way home, but I'm sure I'm not looking much better.

"Hazel." Her voice is soft and low. I don't look at her. "I'm so sorry about missing today. You know how much I was looking forward to being there to support you and the rest of the band. I promise it wasn't intentional."

"I know it wasn't."

If it was intentional, we'd be having a whole different conversation. My thoughts drift to Max and how upset he was when he heard his dad was choosing to skip state. There's something almost cruel about that. Mom only made a mistake, and I know I've made plenty as well. Resentment still bubbles up inside me, though. How could she put so much pressure on me and then not take it seriously herself? She could make elaborate meals for her D&D games, and advise Kelsey's 4-H club, and volunteer for every position known to man, but she couldn't prioritize today?

When I stay silent, she asks, "So . . . do you want to tell me how it went?"

My stomach twists and my throat grows tight. I don't want to tell her and watch her try to hold back her disappointment. I don't want to hear her patronizing words. At least if she'd been at school, there would've been a possibility of missing her initial reaction since I'd be too busy cheering for Nova. But now . . . in this silent kitchen? I don't know that I can get the words out.

"Uh, Li won the freshman award," I reply, chickening out.

"Oh, that's wonderful!"

"She was really shocked." I smile for a moment. "But she was a shoo-in. There was no question."

"Like you freshman year."

I meet her eye, and the tears I've been fighting against finally spill down my cheeks. "I didn't win, Mom. Okay? I know you really wanted me to, but I didn't win." I swallow down a sob. "I'm sorry."

I push back my chair to leave, but she leans forward and grabs my hand. "Wait, Hazel, please." She stands and pulls me up to my feet and then into her arms. "It's okay," she whispers.

I cry harder and I think maybe she's crying too, but I'm not certain. After a few minutes she pulls away and studies my face.

"I didn't know you wanted it this much."

I shake my head. "I didn't. I'm not crying about that. I mean, sure, it feels good to win things and I worked really hard with color guard this season, but it's okay. Nova won and she totally deserved it—she's never won anything like that before and I have. I'm happy for her."

"I am too. She's a great kid."

"But I know how much *you* wanted it for me. You wanted me to continue your legacy, and I didn't." I swallow to stop my voice from breaking. "I let you down. It's probably good you weren't there to see it."

"No!" She lifts her hands to cup my cheeks. "I don't care about the award. I don't care if you get Superiors at state. I don't care if you decide to drop out of band tonight. I just want you to be *happy*. That's all I've ever wanted."

I shake my head at the words.

"It's true. Listen to me when I say this." She lowers her hands from my face and instead squeezes both my hands. "I don't care about anything but your happiness. Yes, maybe I've been a little intense this season—"

I snort-laugh, which is a very weird feeling because I'm also still crying. She smiles ruefully.

"My intensity wasn't about the awards and the rankings and all that. I just remember how happy I was in band and the joy I felt when we performed well at state and how special it felt to get that award. Those were some of the best times of my life. And so I thought, if you had similar experiences, then you'd feel the same way as me. But clearly I was very wrong."

"I was already happy, even without all that stuff. And it's not that I don't want the band to do well, but it's exhausting having this pressure on me all the time. Like today, I wanted to focus on Nova and Li, but all I could think about was the fact that you weren't there and how you were going to react when you eventually found out the results."

She slowly drops down into her chair, wiping at her tears, and I do the same.

"I never meant for any of this to happen." She crumples in on herself. "I'm sorry if you didn't have the experience you were hoping for this year because of me. That's the opposite of what I wanted."

She looks so crushed. Since the moment I realized she wasn't coming today, I've been upset and resentful, but more than anything I've been scared. I was worried her reaction would break me, but instead I'm the one doing the breaking.

I lean forward. "Mom, I had an awesome year of marching band. I was with my best friend, I had an amazing group of guard members, and we actually won against Oak Grove. No one has done that in years. Maybe our senior years weren't identical, but they were both really great. You don't have to worry about that."

"Yeah?" She lifts her eyes hopefully.

"Yeah." I squeeze her hand. "And I also had parents who came to every single show, and cheered so loudly I could hear them across a football field, and wore embarrassing T-shirts and buttons—"

She laugh-sobs and I do the same.

"And not everyone has parents like that. Senior year wouldn't have been as good without you there for every step of it."

"Oh, Hazel," she whispers and pulls me into another hug. "I'm so sorry I wasn't there today."

"It's okay." I squeeze her back. "But there's something you can do to make it up to me."

She sits back expectantly. "Name it, I'll do whatever you want."

"Don't wear those shirts to state with that horrible picture of me on them?"

She bursts out laughing. "Hey, I tried my best on those!"

"You chose a picture where you can clearly see my zit!"

"Did I? I didn't notice. You always look beautiful to me."

"Mom! It's a very bad picture." I sigh. "Fine, I guess you can wear them—but *only* for the performance. Bring sweaters or something to put over them for the drive home."

She chuckles. "Absolutely."

I'm shaky and my heart is still racing from our conversation, but I also feel weightless, like I could float away into the sky if there wasn't a ceiling above me. Mom, on the other hand, looks absolutely exhausted. If she laid her head on the table, I bet she could fall asleep in an instant.

"Is everything okay with you?" I ask. "Not to rub it in, but you never miss band stuff."

She laughs sadly. "Do you ever have a day—or a week—when it feels like you've taken on way too much and there's no way you can handle it all?"

"That sounds like a lot of my weeks."

She leans back in her chair. "Really? But you always have your life together."

My mouth drops open. "*I* have everything together? It's the opposite. Between being captain and DMing for the first time, plus school, I felt like I was constantly dropping balls and letting people down. You're the superhero around here."

"Not lately, I'm not. If you ever looked at my Notes app on my phone, you'd find about five billion half-completed notes to keep me on schedule. But even then, the wheels fly off the bus sometimes. Like today."

"Maybe today was a good thing? In a very weird way."

"Maybe. I'm glad we talked, though I wish the circumstances were different. Thank you for not shutting me out."

"Thank you for taking time to create shockingly embarrassing T-shirts of me."

She laughs and stands up. "You're very welcome."

"Do you need help with dinner?" Usually Mom has a Crock-Pot or Instant Pot or some kind of pot going by early evening.

"Definitely not. I'm texting your dad—we're all going out to eat tonight. I think we could both use the break."

Chapter Thirty-Five

Today is the day before state, which means it's Balloon Day—a celebratory day where the whole band spends rehearsal time eating cupcakes, sharing memories, and—shockingly—receiving balloons from the band boosters. We also march through the halls of the high school at the very end of the school day. Most of the year, people couldn't care less about marching band, but on the Friday before state, everyone lines up to watch us parade down the halls . . . even if some people spend the whole time on their phones.

Color guard marches in the very back, right behind percussion, and I can't keep my eyes off Max. I've been thinking more about his conversation with Sire and how he prioritized me over his own hopes of winning the MVM award. It took a lot for him to do that. And I'm not sure he was ever going to tell me. It means more knowing he chose to do the right thing rather than only doing it to get the brownie points.

He counts off and the percussion section begins a cadence

that gives me goose bumps. I know I'm biased, but there aren't many things in the world more electrifying than listening to a well-executed drum cadence.

I hold my head high and enjoy the smiles and waves as we march around the school. If we tried to twirl our flags, there's a good chance we'd smack someone in the head, so we just lift our flags straight up and down and keep time with the band.

When we're finished, we march directly into the band room and break into screams and cheers. High-strung energy fills the room . . . along with hundreds of green and white Mylar balloons tied to chairs. Each year, the band boosters come into the room while we're away and decorate each of our seats with balloons, flowers, and cards. People around me squeal with delight and run to their chairs to see what's waiting for them. It's one of my very favorite moments in the season.

Li comes up beside me. She's clearly awestruck. "What is all this?"

"*This* is how we celebrate going to state."

"It's amazing."

I elbow her. "Well, band *is* pretty great. Let's go check out our chairs." I point to the back of the room where an extra row of chairs has been set up for guard.

In addition to the balloon that everyone gets, I splurged (with my parents' help) and got each of the guard members an additional congratulations balloon, a thank-you card, and a small photobook of us during the season. I'd been worried I wouldn't have enough happy pictures to fill it, but in actuality I had a hard time choosing.

Li holds up her card to me. "You made it out to Ellywich!"

Callie wraps her arms around my neck from behind. "And Puff! You're awesome. Thank you!"

I grin. At the last minute, I decided it'd be fun to use the D&D character names they made at the beginning of the season rather than their actual names. The rest of the guard silently reads their cards. I personalized each one, not just with their D&D name, but with details of how they grew during the season and helped our group to succeed. I may have had to take a grade penalty for turning in my history essay late, but the lower grade is absolutely worth it when I see their smiles.

"Hazel, this is so sweet!" Madisyn cries and pulls me into a hug. Addison and Devin pile on and we all hug each other tightly.

My chair is piled high with things—flowers from my parents, balloons, cards from Faith and Sire, and a tiny stuffed opossum from Nova, which makes me laugh. I don't have anything special from the guard, which is a little disappointing, but I push the emotion away. I don't need objects to know how much we've grown together as a group.

When Faith walks in, late as usual, I gather the rest of the guard from where they're hovering around the snack table. We all chipped in to buy her a big bouquet of flowers and a card. It's not enough, knowing that we wouldn't be here if it wasn't for her, but it's something.

"Faith, thank you so much for everything this season." I hand over the flowers to her with a huge smile.

"You guys, thank you! I'm so incredibly proud of how far you've come." She gives Addison a subtle nod and puts her flowers down on the closest chair. "Hazel, we also wanted to give you something." The rest of the guard circles tighter around me. They're practically quivering with excitement.

"I put in the order, but otherwise I won't take any of the credit," Faith continues as Devin pulls a small gift bag from behind a chair. "It was completely their idea. But I think it's very well deserved and I'm happy I could help."

I gingerly remove the tissue paper, my hands shaking, and pull out a small black plaque. Crossed flags are engraved along the top, and below are the words:

BEST COLOR GUARD CAPTAIN
IN THE HISTORY OF THE UNIVERSE
HAZEL BUCHANAN

I can't help it. I burst into tears.

They all rush in and wrap me in an enormous ten-person hug.

"You didn't have to do this!" I blubber.

"Of course we did!" Li argues. "We all voted for you and think you totally deserved to win the senior award. You really are the best color guard captain we could've ever had."

"Thanks for doing those dance break warm-ups," Devin says.

Keira nods. "And for helping me with my tosses."

"And for making sure I hit my marks on time," Deja says.

Faith touches my shoulder. "And thank you for being here when I couldn't be. They're right, the season wouldn't have been possible without you."

I hug each one of them individually, squeezing just a little bit harder for Li and Faith. My heart is so full, and

I couldn't have asked for anything better than this. Having their support means everything.

We spend some time chatting and eating too many cupcakes. As the time winds down, Sire calls the room to attention.

"We have one final surprise for the end of our day," Sire announces. "A special performance from some of our very own band members, led by none other than Max Coleman. An extra special performance, as I understand it." Sire's eyes flick to me and I freeze. "They'll be performing on the practice field in a few minutes, and they're requesting that we all come outside and watch."

At that, Max heads for the door . . . along with the *entire* guard, plus Nova, Felix, and a few other miscellaneous band members. Even the majority of the percussion players follow. I grab Li's arm as she passes.

"Li, what's happening?"

She laughs. "As if I'd tell you. Just come on."

Sire and Mrs. Lewis usher the rest of the band toward the exit. My heart pounds as I follow them. When I step out into the cool October afternoon, Max is waiting for me.

"You're doing a performance for the band?" I ask.

"No." He steps closer, his gaze roving over my face. "I'm doing a performance for *you*. But the band is allowed to be here too. In fact, that's kind of the point."

"The point of what?"

"I've been trying to think of a way to show you how much you mean to me, and this is the best thing I could figure out. If you're up for it? It'll be very public. There are going to be a lot of people in those stands."

There's a humming in my ears and my whole body is trembling. I don't know exactly what he's planning, but I also know there isn't a single thing in the universe that could pull me away from those rickety metal bleachers right now. I nod.

"Good." He takes a deep breath. "Well . . . I hope you like it."

He leaves me and I walk slowly up into the stands, unable to process anything but the practice field. There are at least twenty-five people out there. Nova is messing with the microphone she uses when she plays her solo for the competition. Are they about to perform part of our show? But they aren't in the usual formations. In fact, they aren't really in a formation at all. They're standing in straight lines across the field, with all the color guard and percussion members intermixed. And . . . are the percussion players holding flags?

Max jogs over to Sire and takes the megaphone from him. "Hey, everyone. Thanks for coming out for this. So, I've had an awesome time being part of the Glen Vale band this year." He scans the crowd until he finds me. "But the best part of being here has been getting to know Hazel again."

Giggles fill my ears. People turn to stare at me, but I don't pull my gaze from Max.

"As you're probably aware, the percussion and color guard have had their ups and downs with each other. And Hazel and I have also had some ups and downs, mostly because I can never get out of my own way. I've done some really stupid stuff, and I know I don't deserve her, but Hazel is my very favorite person in the whole world. And to illustrate that, I've put together something, with the help of some very hardworking people."

My throat is tight, and I feel lightheaded.

Max runs back to the field, grabs his quad drums, and stands in front of the others. He smiles at me for a moment, and then begins to play. It only takes me a few counts to recognize the rhythm. I squeal before I can stop myself. He's playing "I Want You to Want Me," the song we danced to in the car when we were driving to the game store last month.

A few counts later, the rest of the group jumps in. Nova and some of her other clarinet players play the melody, and I laugh with delight. There are a few trumpets out there as well, and Socks is playing tuba. How did Nova learn this song? How did *any* of them learn this? They're missing a few notes, and the song wouldn't win any Superior ratings, but it's still remarkable that they're doing this at all.

And that's *nothing* compared to what's happening behind them. Not only has the color guard seemingly choreographed their own routine to match the song . . . but the majority of the percussion section is performing it alongside them. My eyes bulge at the sight. With everything going on, I hadn't cared enough to insist that the percussion follow through with the terms of our bet. But here they are, using mismatching flags, as they sneak glances at the guard and try to keep up with a series of windmills and figure eights. And the craziest thing is that they're laughing while they do it. They actually look happy to be making fools of themselves up there. In a thousand years, I never thought I'd witness this.

I press my fingers to my mouth, trying to soak in the performance. Was this the reason that none of the guard members had time to hang out? I glance from Nova to Felix and Li, who can't stop laughing as they perform drop spins next to each other. Did the group cancel D&D last Sunday so they could work on this performance?

Max steps forward as they move into the last part of the song, which seems to trigger them to march into a new formation. I take a few steps down the bleachers so I can see his face more clearly. He doesn't look cocky or proud like he often does when he's playing. Instead, his eyes are locked onto me with the most hopeful, heartbreaking expression I've ever seen. My stomach lurches and I take another step closer to the field.

Everyone in the stands breaks into cheers and *awws*. I blink and force myself to take in the entire group again, instead of just Max, and yelp in surprise. They've left their straight lines behind to form a heart. I barely have time to clap in appreciation before they transition again to form . . . a triangle? That's a weird choice. And then moments later, they march into another formation: the number twenty.

I blink in confusion and then laugh as understanding dawns on me. The heart is obvious, but the twenty must refer to a Natural 20—the highest number you can roll on a d20. And what goes with our D&D games? Nachos, of course, made with triangular-shaped tortilla chips. I shake my head, completely dumbfounded. The performance might very well be the cheesiest thing I've ever seen in my life . . . except my vision is too blurred from happy tears to know for sure. Everyone around me is laughing and clapping along. They're having a great time, even though I doubt they fully grasp what's going on here.

But I understand.

There's absolutely nothing secret about me and Max now. Every single person in the band knows. Max literally announced how he feels about me into a freaking megaphone. I can barely breathe from the realization.

The group hits their final note, and the whole crowd cheers for them. There are exaggerated bows and high fives, while Max quickly lifts off the shoulder straps from his drums and runs toward me. I race down the rest of the steps to the field. We almost smack into each other because we're moving so fast.

"Max. That was . . ." I shake my head in disbelief. "The song from the car ride? And all those formations? Are you kidding me?"

"Yeah?" I can feel some of the tension fall away from him. "I couldn't decide if that was way too much or not enough."

"It was the perfect amount of everything, and also completely outrageous and over the top." I stare at him in awe. "How did you *do* this?"

"I told Nova about my idea first. She's been pretty pissed at me, as I'm sure you know, but eventually she got on board when she heard what I was planning. Felix and Li agreed immediately. They're loyal party members until the end. Then Li suggested I approach the rest of the color guard, which I wasn't too sure about because, well, you know, but they were surprisingly open to it. They grilled me too, for sure, but I guess they liked all my answers because they dropped everything and came up with that choreography on their own." He smiles softly. "And the others out there are friends. The percussion players thought it'd be a nice gesture to perform with the guard, even though it's not exactly the performance we agreed on. But they're on better terms now. Obviously not all of percussion were willing to join, but . . ."

"You can't win them all."

Vaguely, I'm aware that no one else has left the field or stands. They're all staring at us and murmuring.

"That's a lot of eyes on us," I whisper.

He cringes. "I know, I was worried about this part. Do you want to go somewhere? Maybe we could talk and—"

"Max!" one of the guard members—I can't tell who, but I'm thinking Addison—screams at the top of her lungs. "Tell her you love her!"

I freeze in horror. My eyes lock onto his.

"Omigod," I say. "That's so embarrassing, you don't—"

"Hazel." His hands tentatively lift to either side of my face. I expect him to look twitchy from the huge crowd around us, but he's unruffled. His fingers are warm on my jaw, and I'm absolute putty in his hands. "*Of course* I love you. I've been borderline obsessed with winning you over ever since we played that stupid Glare game in band and you wouldn't look at me."

My legs feel so weak that he might be holding me up at this point. "But . . . you said that was your strategy for winning?"

"I didn't have a strategy—I just couldn't look away." His thumb grazes the tender bit of skin right beneath my ear and shivers roll down my spine. "I needed you to look back at me. Just once. And then you did."

"There's no way that's true. You'd never voluntarily lose a game against me."

Max's hands slide down my neck. "That *was* me winning."

I swallow down the threat of tears.

"You're my best friend. There's no one else who gets me like you do," he whispers. "There's no one I'd rather spend time with, or fight with, or lose a bet to. I'll go up to every person here and tell them the same thing if that's what you want. I've been a huge idiot and I'm so sorry for hurting you. I know I don't deserve your trust." He leans his forehead against mine. "But I'm so in love with you. I'll do anything to get you back."

"Max," I breathe. "I love you too. So much. I've been absolutely miserable without you."

"You have?"

"Yes," I whisper. "Nothing in my life is as good without you in it. But you need to do something for me."

He pulls away from me, his forehead furrowed in concern. "Anything."

"Will you *please* kiss me now?" I give him a pleading look. "I'm dying here."

He laughs, the sound sharp and bright. "I've never been happier to do anything in my life."

Then he dips me backward with a flourish. I can feel the smile on his lips when they press against my own. Shouts and hoots of delight reverberate around us.

For the first time ever, we're both winning at the end of a band performance.

Chapter Thirty-Six

When Max and I step off the band bus together at the state competition, I'm relieved to find we have perfect weather. It's the kind of fall day that everyone wishes for and hardly ever gets—crisp without being cold, blue skies and sunny without sweating through our costumes, and no wind. I'm taking it as a sign from the universe that today is going to be a good day.

"We're finally here, huh?" Max says and takes my hand in his.

We basically haven't stopped touching since we kissed on the football field yesterday afternoon. Everyone was surprisingly cool with us blowing them off and going out by ourselves Friday night. We went out for nachos, because of course we did, and I got to eat more than my share because I kept peppering Max with questions about how that performance came together. But we also never stopped holding hands across the booth. We were *those people* and I was totally fine with it. Luckily, eating nachos with one hand isn't too difficult.

I lean into his side. "We're almost done with marching band. Forever."

"Not forever. Maybe high school marching band, but tons of colleges have marching bands too. And they'll need incredibly talented color guard specialists and percussion players just like you and me. Next year could be just like this . . . except no parents."

I warm at the casual way he talks about us being together next year at college. I hope that happens. And I'm not completely done with high school guard either. I got the idea last night to try bringing back winter guard, which could be even more fun than color guard. Winter guards perform a routine to prerecorded music and compete by themselves indoors, rather than with the larger band. We'd have the freedom to choose our own show theme, flags, everything. Back at band camp I wouldn't have thought it possible, but we have enough dedicated people now that I think we should try. Of course, we'll also need Sire and Faith to buy into the idea, and our parents, but I'm feeling optimistic.

Max and I are forced to separate after that so we can warm up with our sections.

"You look so happy," Callie says. "I was kinda worried you'd be mad about yesterday."

"Mad? Yesterday was the best thing that's ever happened to me."

Li nods smugly. "See, I told you," she says to the others. "I could tell from our dinner that you weren't over him."

"I still can't believe you all voluntarily chose to do more

color guard rehearsals," I say. "*And* hung out with percussion?"

"They're not that bad once you get them away from Brody," Deja says.

"So . . . are we going to count that as their performance for our bet, then?" I ask. I'm fine with that, but it needs to be a group decision.

The others exchange glances.

"We could," Addison says. "They definitely put a lot of time into it."

"But we never forced Brody to perform," Callie argues.

"True. Although he looks miserable enough to make me satisfied," Madisyn says and nods subtly to the left.

Brody and Kyle are huddled together, muttering and throwing angry looks at the rest of the percussion, who are chatting together a few yards away. It looks like Brody's popularity has finally taken a nosedive. Max had mentioned last night how annoyed the others were that Brody wouldn't learn the guard routine with them. He always was a sore loser.

"There's one other thing to consider," I say. "If we force Brody to go through with the stakes, we'll have to spend more time with him."

The others laugh and throw their hands up in the air like they're surrendering.

"Very good point. I don't want any more guard memories tainted by him," Rosa says. "Especially now that our season is over."

"Almost over," I correct. "We have this last performance to nail. And I have another idea for spring that I want to run past—"

But I'm interrupted by Sire calling the entire band to come together. It's almost time for our performance.

We're the quietest we've ever been as we wait to march onto the field. I've never known nerves like the ones I'm feeling right now. I can't talk and I can barely move. Everything comes down to these next few minutes. No more rehearsals or time to prepare.

We're given the signal to come onto the field. I head to my first mark and place my lightning bolt flag on the ground. An announcer booms, "Glen Vale Marching Knights, you may begin your preplacement and/or warm-up."

This short reprieve gives me enough time to take a calming breath, nod reassuringly to Li, and glance up at the stands. Even from this distance, I can see Mom, Dad, and my extended family. I know Max's mom is with them as well. They're standing in their matching shirts, waving pom-poms and signs. The people seated around them are probably annoyed, but I'm grateful. The sight of them gives me courage. We've worked long and hard for this, and we're coming for that Superior rating.

As soon as we hit our first pose, I let the choreography and training take over, just like Mom told me to. Adrenaline keeps me smiling and moving and it feels like we're performing at warp speed. It's almost like an out-of-body experience, and soon we're off the field again. There are hugs and tears, excitement for things that went well and lamenting over any mistakes.

I care about the ratings, there's no denying that, but whatever the rating is, it won't take away from how much I love all these people.

Because we're the last to perform in our section, the judges' ratings will be ready soon. Nova finds me as we wait.

"Did you and Max have fun last night?" she asks with a knowing smile.

I beam at her. "We had the *best* time. Thank you again for what you did. I wasn't sure if you really approved of us together."

"I approve of anyone who can make you smile like you are right now. He definitely needed to redeem himself to me, but it's obvious how he feels about you. He was a bigger perfectionist during those secret rehearsals than Sire ever was."

I laugh, imagining it.

The announcer begins to read off the ratings for the earlier bands. Nova and I join Felix, Li, and Max, who are sitting a few rows above us. We link arms to form a human chain of support and anxiety.

"Next up are the ratings for Glen Vale High School. Ranking for musicality: Superior. For percussion: Superior."

The five of us fly out of our seats.

"For auxiliary: Superior."

Now we're a jumping, shrieking mass of hysteria.

"Overall ranking: Superior!"

There's definitely going to be permanent hearing loss in my future given the cacophony of screams around me.

The next thirty minutes are filled with hugs, more screaming, and lots of picture-taking because Mom and Melanie want to document every second. Dad hugs me for a long time when he gets his turn, and Mom hugs me even longer. She and I are both teary-eyed, and we don't say much since we've already said it all, but I'm never going to forget how tightly she squeezes me or how I squeeze her back just as hard. Even Kelsey hugs both Max and me and tells us congratulations. She's definitely more enthusiastic about Max's hug than mine, but honestly, I can't argue with her logic.

Finally we're calm enough to talk in complete sentences again.

"It sounds like a lot of color guard families are going to celebrate at a new Italian restaurant close to here," I tell my family.

"Then we'll go there too," Mom says immediately. "I'd love to catch up with their parents."

I turn to Max. "Do you think you can convince your section to go?"

"I'm not sure I could stop them."

"So guard and percussion are going to celebrate together?"

"It's kind of fitting, actually," he says. "I don't think percussion would be half as good if we weren't competing with you this season."

"But what are you and I going to compete over now?" I ask.

"Settlers of Catan, finally?"

"Absolutely, but we already know who'll win that one." I tap my chin. "Maybe who gets to play most with Zoinks during D&D?"

"I've got the perfect one. Which of us gets the first kiss of the day."

"Nope. It's who gets the last kiss." I kiss his cheek and dash away toward my parents' car.

I hear footsteps, and then Max's arms wrap around my waist from behind and pull me into his chest. "You'll have a fight on your hands for that title." His voice is low, and it sends a cascade of goose bumps down my arms.

I twist around and kiss him again. I'm happy to lose this particular competition to him every time.

Acknowledgments

The last few years have been wild in the best possible way, and that's because I have the most wonderful readers in the world. Thank you so much for supporting my books, for reaching out to me, and for telling me all your D&D stories. (Shout-out to all the players who have married their Dungeon Masters!)

Wendy Loggia and Hannah Hill, thank you for seeing the potential in Hazel and Max from the beginning and for helping me to make their story shine. I appreciate all of your hard work. Thank you to the Random House team for everything you do: Makena Cioni, Katie Dutton, Rebecca Gudelis, Kortney Hartz, Jacqueline Izzo, Jamie Johnson, Rachel Knapton, Kimberly Langus, Sarah Lawrenson, Gillian Levinson, Sarah Reck, Tamar Schwartz, Megan Shortt, Liz Sutton, and Stephania Villar. Thank you to Hannah Babcock, Helen Boomer, and Claire Rivkin on the subsidiary rights team for absolutely killing it. And speaking of dream teams, Liz Parkes and Casey Moses, you are both brilliant and it's an honor to work with you!

Kristy Hunter, I'm so happy to be with you on this journey. Thank you for keeping me calm and collected and for being a huge support!

I'm very grateful to the foreign publishers who have taken a chance on my books. Thank you to the editors, translators, and readers around the world for your excitement.

Some of my very best high school memories come from my days as a color guard member in the River View High School marching band. I want to send a huge thank-you to Tom (aka Sir) and Kathy McLeish for all the time, effort, and care you put into our marching band and color guard. I know I speak for *many* former students when I say how grateful I am to have been in band with you both. The same is true of Jim Bundy, who was my music teacher in elementary school and my assistant band director in high school. Thank you for taking the time to speak with me about the details of Ohio marching band competitions! I also want to thank Mary Beth Camillus, one of my closest friends as well as a former color and winter guard member, for sharing her memories with me so I could bring the guard scenes to life as much as possible.

Writing books about friendship is a lot easier because of the awesome people in my life. Thank you Keely, Carrie, Sabrina, Stacie, Pam, Cheryl, Holly, Brieanna, Laurence, Anna, Kristin, Melissa, Kristy, Rosalee, Courtney, and David for cheering me on! Annette, Diane, Becky, and Kathryn, thank you for the dinners, ice cream, and encouraging texts! Debbi, thank you for always being there for me (and listening to me whine without complaint)!

Thank you to my family, especially my dad, mom, mother-in-law, aunts, uncle, and cousins. Maggie and Emmett, marching band wouldn't have been *nearly* as fun without you! Thanks for convincing me to join and for all the years since.

Liam, thank you for being my biggest cheerleader whenever I get good news. "New York Best Times Seller" will always be my favorite! And Mike, my fellow bass clarinet player, thanks for inspiring a D&D romance *and* a marching band romance, as well.

LIVESTREAMING LOVE . . .

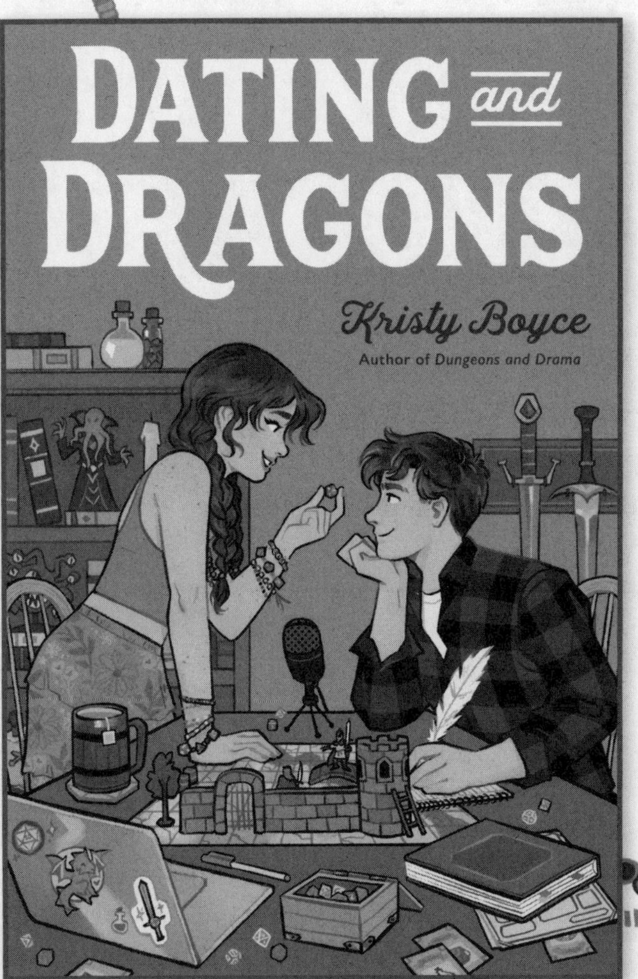

Excerpt copyright © 2024 by Kristy Boyce. Cover art copyright © 2024 by Liz Parkes.
Published by Delacorte Romance, an imprint of Random House Children's Books, a division of Penguin Random House LLC, New York.

Chapter One

I thought I'd already experienced every "new girl at school" nightmare imaginable in the run-up to today, but I guess my brain wasn't creative enough to come up with this scenario. I'm not arriving at school naked or late for a final exam I haven't prepared for . . . but I am being dropped off at my new high school for my first day of junior year by my overly excited grandma, who is insisting we take first-day-of-school photos together in the parking lot.

"But it's not the first day of school," I argue for a third time.

"It's your first day at *this* school, Quinn," Grandma replies. She grips the steering wheel with both hands and leans close so her face is only a few inches away from the windshield. "It doesn't matter if it's February. Can I park here?" she asks, pointing to an open spot.

I look out the window. "No, the sign says it's for the seniors."

"Well, I'm a senior!"

I turn to the back seat. "Andrew, care to help me out at all?"

My fifteen-year-old brother lifts one shoulder without looking up from his phone.

Great, he's as engaged and useful as ever. I face Grandma more fully. "The parking lot is filling up. It's really okay—we can just get out. We can get pictures another time or we can take a selfie in the car." Or I can do everything in my power to make sure Grandma never drives us again. I grab my book bag to show her I'm ready.

"Nonsense. My only grandchildren are finally living close enough for me to see them every day, and I'm making up for lost time. I want a first-day-of-school photo."

She frowns and adjusts her orange silk scarf. You'd think it was *Grandma's* first day of school the way she dressed up for this ten-minute drive, but then she's always prided herself on being the most elegant woman in any room. She doesn't wear stereotypical "grandma clothes"—she's always in colorful blousy tops, linen pants, and her ever-present floral scarfs. She'd fit in better on a yacht than she would in rural Ohio.

My brain flails and I glance feverishly around the parking lot for onlookers. A ton of students are still meandering into the building, so there's no way we can do this without witnesses. I begged Mom and Dad to let me drive this morning, but they needed both cars to get to their new jobs. We just moved two hours west to Laurelburg, Ohio, a week ago to be closer to Grandma. "She'll get such a kick out of it!" Mom had argued with pleading eyes. "You know how happy she is to see you two!"

Oh, she's happy, all right. To my horror, she's rolled up

to a group of guys circled around a fancy red car. And if their varsity jackets are to be believed, they're athletes. I scoot down in the seat like a snake slithering into a hole.

Grandma lowers her window and waves at them. "Hey, boys, hope you aren't getting into trouble over here. What a good-looking group you are!"

A small moan comes out of me, and I squeeze my eyes shut. There's no one in the world Grandma won't talk to. Behind me a door opens and slams closed. I glance over my shoulder to see Andrew dashing through the cars toward the school building before Grandma can notice. The *traitor*! I can't believe my younger brother is smarter than me.

"Can I get you to take our picture?" Grandma says, and I slither down farther.

I hear muttering and a hoot of laughter and then Grandma drives away. "Well, *they* were very rude. Don't waste your time on them."

"I'm sure that won't be a problem," I say.

Grandma is making sure I have absolutely no chance of making new friends here. I don't need help being awkward. I've never been popular, but at least—for a while—I had close friends at my old school. Everything had been so comfortable and easy with them . . . until our group imploded. I take a deep breath and remind myself that this move is for the best. It's what I wanted. I don't miss the old school or the anxiety I felt there, always worrying about running into one of them in the halls.

Grandma continues to slowly drive down the parking lot row and my gaze catches on a group of five students chatting together. I can't exactly explain it, but they look like my kind of people. Like under the right circumstances, I might have enough courage to walk up and say hi. And is the South Asian girl wearing sparkly green d20 earrings? My hopes lift even more.

Unfortunately, Grandma notices them as well.

"They look nice. I bet one of them will take it." This time she powers down my passenger-side window and leans across me. "Hiya! Can I get one of you to take a photo?"

Unlike the other group, who just laughed and ignored her, these kids stop and turn toward the car. They exchange confused glances and then one of the guys steps forward. My stomach flips over. Why does he have to be cute? Like, *annoyingly* cute. His light brown hair is swept over his forehead, his blue eyes match his winter coat, and his cheeks are pink from the cold. His gaze catches mine for a second before he flashes a grin at Grandma. "Sure. In the car?"

"Not in the car, of course! We need it with the school in the background!" She puts the car in park right there and turns on the hazard lights, blocking anyone else from driving through this aisle. Then she beckons me out of my seat, and I force myself to follow, sweating profusely under my coat despite the frigid February air.

"Wait, where did Andrew go?" she exclaims.

"He ran for the building a minute ago," I say quietly.

"That boy," she mutters. "Well, at least I'll have a photo with my *favorite* grandchild."

Picture Boy chuckles and my cheeks heat. The rest of the group has shuffled a little closer so they can witness the scene. To my delight, the South Asian girl *does* have on dice earrings. I imagine someone wouldn't wear those unless they were a gamer. I'll have to look for her in my classes . . . assuming this weird situation doesn't ruin my chances of being friends with her. Next to her stands a South Asian boy her same height, his hands in his pockets and a delighted look on his face, along with another person I can barely see beneath their puffy coat and rainbow crocheted hat. And then there's *that* guy—you know, the one who always seems perfectly fine in sandals and cargo shorts in twenty-degree weather. His long hair is pulled back in a low ponytail and his face is tipped up to the sky.

Grandma hands her phone to Picture Boy. The phone is attached to a large fabric strap so she doesn't lose it. "I'm so glad to find a well-behaved young man here. Some of these kids are twerps." She tilts her head back toward the other group.

"Oh yeah, anyone could tell you that." He glances at me. "Do you go here?"

"Um, yeah," I mumble.

He studies me, as if he either doesn't believe me or is trying to figure out if he's seen me before. "Huh, okay. I'm ready when you two are." Then he holds up the phone and gestures for us to stand closer. I glance down at myself, feeling self-conscious. Most of my clothes are a bohemian style—lots of long, patterned skirts and cropped sweaters and beaded necklaces, which I think look cool together, but not so much when my top half is wrapped in a quilted purple coat. Grandma slips her hand around my waist, and I stand up straight.

"Say 'fuzzy pickles'!" he calls.

I smile at the odd phrase despite my current misery. He

takes a few, going so far as to take pictures both vertically and horizontally.

Grandma nods approvingly as she swipes through the photos. "Oh, that's cute! Thanks so much." She pushes me closer to him. "My granddaughter is new here. Will you look out for her? She's nervous."

Can I *please* wake up from this nightmare now? But before I can respond or pull an Andrew and sprint toward freedom, Grandma has already turned her attention on the rest of the group hovering close by.

"Aren't you freezing?" she says. "Where are your *shoes*?"

Picture Boy's mouth tugs up into a smile and he shifts slightly so his back is to the rest of the group. "First-day pictures, huh?"

"I tried to talk her out of it."

"They're better than some of mine, at least. I'm straight up glaring in my fourth-grade photo—Mom keeps it on the fridge to make her laugh."

I chuckle lightly. "If I tried that, Grandma would haul me back here tomorrow morning for a reshoot."

"From my view, the photos were too good to need reshoots."

His gaze catches on mine and nerves swirl in my stomach. Is that his roundabout way of flirting with me? Or am I being egotistical and he's only complimenting his own photography abilities?

"We should get inside," someone from the group announces, clearly eager to escape Grandma's clutches.

Picture Boy rocks back on his heels. "Any chance I'll see you in French first period?"

I shake my head. “Pre-calc.”

“Oof, good luck with that first thing in the morning. I’ll look for you. I wouldn’t want to let your grandma down.” He flashes me a grin and my pulse leaps. Maybe I’m not so grumpy about Grandma stopping the car here anymore.

I grab my book bag and kiss Grandma quickly on the cheek, her skin papery and cool. Today might be a good first day after all.

ROLL THE DICE ON LOVE!

IT'S A LOVE STORY.